I0578269

DOC T

SKYE MCNEIL

HOT TREE PUBLISHING

ALSO BY SKYE MCNEIL

The Mobster Files

Appointed by Fate

Exonerated with Love

Credence

Atlas Series

Hearts Abroad

Oceans Away

Macha MC Series

Doc T

Doc T © 2020 by Skye McNeil

All rights reserved. No part of this book may be used or reproduced in any written, electronic, recorded, or photocopied format without the express permission from the author or publisher as allowed under the terms and conditions with which it was purchased or as strictly permitted by applicable copyright law. Any unauthorized distribution, circulation or use of this text may be a direct infringement of the author's rights, and those responsible may be liable in law accordingly. Thank you for respecting the work of this author.

Doc T is a work of fiction. All names, characters, events and places found therein are either from the author's imagination or used fictitiously. Any similarity to persons alive or dead, actual events, locations, or organizations is entirely coincidental and not intended by the author.

For information, contact the publisher, Hot Tree Publishing.

WWW.HOTTREEPUBLISHING.COM

EDITING: HOT TREE EDITING

COVER DESIGNER: BOOKSMITH DESIGN

EBOOK: ISBN: 978-1-922359-15-5

PAPERBACK: ISBN: 978-1-922359-16-2

For my Uncle Greg who showed me the world of Harley Davidson.

P.S. There are more Twinkies in the shop

PROLOGUE

"This isn't what I wanted for her."

Lorcan O'Brien—Reaper to his club—heard the blood pumping in his ears. It was only drowned out by the angry shouts on the other end of the international phone call. Gaelic words flowed easily in the background, and gunshots rang true. His fists ached to join in on the action on the other side of the world, but he couldn't. His duty was in Colorado.

"Phantom, send her to the Swiss Alps instead. Her mother has family there."

"Don't you think I considered that first?" Malcom Kerry sighed, the weary sound unusual for the lively Irishman. Though it had been nearly two years since they last crossed paths, Reaper knew Phantom to be upbeat. "I need you to keep her safe. Please, Reaper. I wouldn't ask if I wasn't at my wits end. I can't lose another woman I love to the MC."

Even without seeing the other man, Reaper knew the desperation on his brother's face. They'd been through hell and back for the women in their lives. The only difference was Reaper's old lady stayed. Phantom's didn't.

"All right." He glanced out the window, the Rocky Mountains in the distance. "Does she know who you are?"

Phantom let out a strangled laugh. "Not yet. But her mother is dying, so I suspect she'll tell her soon."

Reaper inhaled sharply. Losing any woman was tragic, but the mother to his child was another story. "I'm sorry. I didn't know."

Phantom coughed and cleared his throat. "My daughter will soon be on her way here. I can't put her in the crosshairs. The Twelve Brothers want blood because I won't let them into our territory. Now that I'm president, they'll try for my blood first. She's an easy target in Ireland."

"We won't let that happen. When she shows up on your doorstep, send her to me immediately."

"Thank you, brother. You have a new life debt owed."

He chuckled. "Be sure to use the old passes through the mountains. The Twelve won't look there for an escape."

The two presidents signed off without another word. It was still odd to him to call Phantom the president of their founding Macha location in Northern Ireland. But everyone had to retire someday, and his older brother, Grady O'Brien—aka Grenade—decided to step down before his retirement was caused by a bullet.

Walking across the dimly lit bridge between the two

sets of stairs in the lodge, Reaper held in a chuckle at the carnage below. His men earned an alcohol-fueled night after raking in an obscene amount from their business ventures in Snowshoe over the last week.

He leaned his forearms on the railing, his smile fading. They'd soon be hiding a woman until the danger passed. Any one of his men could handle the job, but he couldn't choose one just then. He spotted Brewer and Rubble. Either would do the assignment without question.

He shook his head. He needed new men in the MC. The prospects wouldn't do. This was Phantom's daughter, after all. Reaper needed a man he trusted. He needed to live up to his name and draw in fresh blood for Macha.

A new sunrise slowly spread rays of orange across the valley, an idea formulating simultaneously.

"Since when do you rise before the sun?" a voice groggy with sleep asked.

Glancing to his right, Reaper couldn't stop the smile from spreading over his sun-kissed face.

"Since Phantom needs our help." He looped an arm around her shoulders. "I'll tell you all about it, but first, I need to call my nephew. It's time he officially joined the family business."

1

———

TAD

"O'Brien, you finish those reports yet?"

Looking up from his computer screen, Tad O'Brien met the chief's face in the doorway. After coming off a double shift where blood wasn't the only body fluid he battled to save lives, he wasn't in the mood to chat with his micromanaging boss. Plus, losing a motorist on the last call made him edgy. He hated losing, especially when he did every damn thing right. But he was no match for a head-on collision. No one was.

"On the last one, boss." He saw a slight nod, then lowered his eyes to the screen again. Another ten minutes and he'd be out of this place for three whole days. It sounded like nirvana after the last month. A break in winter was in the air in Iowa, and that meant more people being dumbasses on the roads. Iowa was finicky no matter what season, but the melting snow combined with early storms caused more accidents than he cared to keep track of. That was what the DOT was for anyhow. He just cleaned up the messes. It was what he did best.

He saved the reports and sent them to his boss before shutting down his computer. After being a paramedic for five years, he was ready for more. *Should've finished that doctorate.* He waved at the next crew on shift, then walked out the back door.

Taking care of his family came first. When he found out his mother had breast cancer, he'd quit his last year of medical school to return to Iowa. His mom needed him, and even though she died after a year of his constant nursing, he couldn't face Stanford again.

Walking through the parking lot, he picked up his pace when he saw the motorcycle waiting for him. Everyone joked about motorcycles being donor-cycles—even him—but he'd grown up around bikes and couldn't get them out of his blood. *And the chicks around here dig them.* He buckled his helmet and grinned at the engine's deep rumble. No, he'd never give up his motorcycle. His dad would turn over in his grave if he did.

Gliding toward the street, he waved at the fire truck turning into the drive. He'd see them soon enough. They all liked to hang out at a bar down the street after shift. He couldn't think of a better start to his time off.

Inhaling the scent of fresh snow and asphalt, Tad opened up the engine. His pulse thrummed in his neck, the adrenaline never losing its hold over him. Life in Iowa wasn't perfect, but it'd do.

IT WAS ON HIS SECOND SHOT OF WHISKEY THAT TAD'S phone buzzed on the pool table. Eyeing it, he shrugged and took aim. The cue ball bounced off the side and hit the eight ball before it sank into the pocket. "That's game, boys."

The two other men grumbled and handed over their cash. He stuffed his earnings in his back pocket and noticed his phone still alight with a call. Narrowing his eyes, Tad recognized the Colorado area code. *This can't be good.*

Taking a swig of beer, he grimaced at the lukewarm liquid. Dropping a tip in the jar on the bar, he nodded. "I'm out. See you next week." He waved at his coworkers from the fire station and grabbed his leather jacket before stepping outside.

A chill left over from winter snuck across his black T-shirt, sending goose bumps up his tattooed arms. His mom never liked his ink, so he usually kept it hidden. Since her death, he showed off the fully inked sleeves as much as possible and had even added a few to his canvas.

His phone vibrated in his back pocket, and this time he answered. "This is O'Brien."

"You sound just like your old man."

Tad assumed who the caller was based on the area code, but the gravelly voice with a hint of an Irish accent confirmed it. "Lorcan."

He swallowed as memories flooded him. His uncle

Lorcan hadn't gone by that name in more years than Tad was alive. "Or should I call you Reaper?"

"Until you're in Macha, Lorcan is fine."

Tad leaned against his bike. Over the years, he'd sent his uncle tidbits of information about the gangs and MCs in the Midwest. It wasn't much, but his father would be proud of him for staying part of the family business. "I don't have anything new for you, sorry."

"No worries. I'm actually calling to bring you back to Macha."

Straddling his black motorcycle, Tad watched the traffic light change. "Is that so?"

His father warned him this would happen. "You're Irish and the son of the MC. They'll call you one day," his old man said a week before succumbing to a gunshot wound. Plus, his uncle's MC name, Reaper, wasn't given because of the souls he took from this world but the ones he brought into the Macha fold. Reaper was famous among other MCs for how easily he could convince a man to join.

"You heard right, boyo. Your blood is as Irish as Macha. You can't deny your upbringing anymore. You've been as much of a prospect from Iowa as the boys here. It's time. I think you've known this."

Tilting his head, Tad stared at the starry sky. His father perished wearing the Macha cut, and now he was being summoned to the same club. As a kid, it'd been his dream: ride bikes and flirt with pretty ladies. As he grew, it didn't sound like the better side of life. He always suspected his interactions with Macha would come to fruition.

"I'm not my old man, Uncle. I have nothing to offer the club."

"Sure you do. Saving dumbasses. That's what I want you for here. The brothers need you. Macha needs you."

He'd heard the same thing said to his father. Every time, the old man went, too. A part of Tad wanted to tell his uncle off, but another part craved to be a patch member of the organization his father loved more than his own son. His unofficial prospect status would become official the moment he stepped foot on Colorado soil.

"Why now?"

His uncle sighed heavily. "We recently lost our doctor and need a new one. You're the best, or so you brag whenever given the chance."

He shook his head. "You have plenty of men who could learn. Get one of them—"

"They're not my blood. You are, Tad." The biker cursed under his breath. "You provided the information about Del Rossi, which gave us time to protect Colorado from mafia infiltration. We need you."

His uncle wasn't wrong. He'd gladly given over intel about the Italy-born mob. Along the way, he'd made a few friends, but playing a double role gave him something to look forward to each new day. That lone thought tipped the scales.

"You have nothing holding you to Iowa anymore. Your mum is gone. Your family is Macha. It always has been."

Thinking back to his childhood, Tad couldn't deny his uncle's words. Before his parents split, he'd spent nearly every day at the clubhouse in Snowshoe, Colorado. He'd learned more about women and bikes in those thirteen years than any other kid his age. The rules of the club formed him into the man he was today. He followed the MC laws even though he wasn't a member. Macha was in his blood.

"I can't end up like my old man. The club destroyed my family. I won't let it destroy me too."

"You've much to learn, nephew, but if you wash out before you patch, I'll let you out, no questions, no threats."

Tad wasn't sure if he could trust him but had no other choice. The day had finally come. *When Macha calls, you answer.*

"Check your email. Your flight leaves in the morning."

Ending the call, Tad clenched his jaw. In the back of his mind, he knew it'd happen one day. He always had that tingling feeling that he would become a Macha member. His mother begged him to stay away while his father urged him to patch. Both were dead, so it didn't matter what he did now.

After feeding Macha intel over the last five years, it was time to return to his roots. He'd make better decisions compared to his father's. He was sure of it.

Turning on his motorcycle, he stuffed his phone in a pocket and headed the two blocks home. Lorcan was right. He didn't have a life here. At least not one he would miss. *But I won't end up like my old man. When I find the woman I love, I'll protect her instead of sending her away.*

2

———

DOC

SIX MONTHS LATER

THE BRIGHT JUNE SUN PIERCED DOC O'BRIEN'S eyelids. He winced, cursing the unshaded window. Rolling over, his arm landed on a warm body. Popping open his eyes, he smirked. *Two bodies, to be exact.* He withdrew his arm and the blondes cuddled close to each other. His cock tempted him to stay put and wake up the club nymphs for another round, but his parched throat won out.

He slowly sat up and swung his legs over the side of the bed. His black leather cut sat on the dresser, the freshly added patch summoning pride from the depths of his belly. They'd celebrated his patching into Macha the night before, and he couldn't wait to start in on the day.

Doc yanked on a pair of jeans and a blue T-shirt before donning the cut and slipping from the room. He pushed back his blond hair to the left side of his head and walked into the communal bathroom. No one greeted him, and when he caught sight of the time on the clock above the sinks, he realized why. It wasn't yet nine, and after partying all night, it'd be miraculous if anyone woke before noon.

He relieved his bladder, difficult with a hard-on but not impossible. He'd find release with a nymph or two later. Now he had to find a cure for the drumming in his skull and dry throat.

He staggered to the kitchen. Beer bottles were strewn everywhere, a few prospects passed out on the cool floor. He stepped over them and grabbed a bottle of water from the fridge. Only after chugging the whole thing did he feel remotely better. He snagged three more bottles and moved toward the back room. It was dark, quiet, and empty. Just what his hungover ass needed.

Slouching onto the couch, Doc flipped on the television and rolled his eyes at the porn from the last user. *Dumbass prospects.* He found a history channel and let the commentary fill the space.

Life in Macha wasn't what he expected. *It's better.*

The first few months sucked being a prospect, but he'd earned his place. The late winter storm helped secure his role as Doc in Macha MC. The horrific motorcycle accident on the mountain path was caused by black ice. He'd been at the tail end of the pileup and remained unscathed. Using his paramedic background, he managed to save Boulder from losing an arm and patch the members up before the ambulance arrived. Then and there, he knew his prospect days were numbered.

"Basking in the glory of brotherhood?" a voice teased behind him.

Doc turned his head and spotted Hawk. The shirtless man looked as sober as him, which wasn't saying much. "More like trying not to barf on the couch."

Hawk lit a cigarette and inhaled. "I know the feeling."

He sat next to Doc and rested his head on the back of the couch. Cigarette smoke swirled around them. Despite knowing the effects of smoking, Doc didn't condemn his new brother. They all had vices. Hawk's was cigs. Doc's was women—nymphs more specifically.

"How's it feel to wear the patch, Doc?"

"Better than being a prospect."

Hawk chuckled and flicked his ash in an empty coffee can on the table beside the couch. "Anything's better than that."

They sat in the cool room, the AC rumbling out low temperatures. Out of all the Macha members, Hawk was the one Doc got along with best. They both enjoyed whiskey and fast women. *Hell, everyone here does.* But Hawk was the first to show Doc any form of friendship. He'd never forget it either. He'd do anything for Macha.

Doc smirked. *Something I never thought I'd say.*

"That was some party." Hawk inhaled deeply, the orange glow from the cigarette showing his face.

Doc thought back over the endless drinking, laughing, and initiation. "It was very fun. I think I'll like being Macha full time."

"Aw, poor baby can't spend all your free time at the clinics anymore," Hawk teased.

Instead of replying, he just shrugged. He'd find time to

volunteer at the free clinics in Snowshoe. It felt good to give back when he could. His uncle—and club president—didn't mind and in fact encouraged community work from the MC. Most merely gave money, but Doc preferred time.

"You smell like perfume."

Doc lifted his arm and sniffed. Sure enough, it reeked of nymph. "Yeah, I need to shower. Just waiting for the room to stop spinning."

"How many this time?"

"Two."

Hawk crushed the butt and laughed. "Yeah, you're Macha all right."

"Hey, I can't help if the nymphs love me."

"Whatever, bro. Just don't knock one up." Hawk patted Doc's shoulder and stood. "C'mon, move your ass before all the showers are full. Nobody wants to use a stall after Shovelhead."

Joining him, Doc grabbed the last bottle and followed him to the residential hallway. From each room, gradual sounds echoed. Hawk left to grab fresh clothes, but Doc hopped under the shower after stripping. Clothes could wait.

After a quick rinse, he wrapped a towel around his hips and emerged just as Brewer, Rubble, and Cueball reached the bathroom. Each one reeked of booze, cigarette smoke, and nymph.

"How the fuck you up already?" Cueball asked, cradling his bald head.

"Thirsty," he replied, leaning against the wall. Brewer

eyed him, then stepped into the bathroom. It felt like a fraternity house the longer he was in Macha. But the better version. The Irish version instead of Greek.

Rubble yawned and nodded toward Doc's room. "How many you avoiding today?"

"Yeah, should've given you a different club name," Cueball added. "Doc? Hell no, more like Co—"

Doc's door opened and the two platinum blonde nymphs scurried off to their hole. When two more hurried out, Rubble slapped Doc's back, then laughed all the way to the showers.

"Shit, I lost count." He shook his head and peeked into the room. It was empty. *Thank God.*

"Sober up, Doc. You have a job." Reaper's accented voice turned Doc's head.

"This early?"

"Yep. Her flight arrives within the hour."

"Who is she?" he asked, pulling on fresh clothes.

"Isadora Walsh."

The name jumbled in his mind but didn't ring any bells. He buttoned his jeans. "Why does that name sound familiar?"

Reaper grinned. "She's the reason you're here, Doc." He patted the wall. "We weren't sure when she'd arrive, but the time's come. Until I say, you're her bodyguard. Do not let her out of your sight unless I approve. I trust my men, but you're blood."

"Oh yeah." Doc pulled on his cut. "She's Phantom's daughter, right?"

"Yep, so handle with care. She's one of us. Better even because she's Macha royalty."

He snorted. "Great, I get to babysit a Macha princess. I guess it won't be too bad."

A peculiar smile crossed Reaper's face. "Sure, Doc, whatever you say."

3

___

ISA

GRAY EYES FLICKED TO THE FRONT OF THE PLANE, then back to the seat in front of her. She never liked flying. Being a homebody, she never had a reason. The airplane dipped, and her stomach mirrored the act. Her left hand gripped the empty paper bag, her breakfast somehow staying put. They were making the final descent into Colorado Springs. That was what the pilot said over the speakers.

Isadora Walsh pushed back her light brown hair, reminding herself to add highlights once she landed. She'd never let herself go this much. Her mum, Colleen, wouldn't hear of destroying her long locks with dye. Isa, on the other hand, tended to live on the artsy side of life. She managed a small smile, tears welling in her eyes. Now she was on her own and didn't have an Irish mum to scorn her for tattooing her ribs or piercing her nose.

The wheels hit solid ground, jolting Isa's gaze up from

her hands to the window. Specks of snow were visible on the distant peaks, reminding her of Ireland. *Will I ever go back?* She clenched her hands into fists. She had to. Her entire business hinged on her return.

Other passengers started readying for their arrival, but Isa was still in Ireland. Or her mind was, at least. She'd shown up at the Macha clubhouse only to be shipped off shortly thereafter. The family reunion she'd hoped for was dashed equally as fast as their first meeting in twenty years. She barely remembered her father. When she saw him yesterday, Malcolm Kerry wasn't the same man she knew as a child. He was rough around the edges and looked much older. *Probably because he's the MC president now.*

Her mother—*God rest her soul*—told her the truth of her father's occupation on her deathbed. Somewhere deep, she'd known her father wasn't merely a motorcycle repairman as she'd been told growing up, but hearing the club involvement put the pieces together for her. It started to make sense why Colleen Walsh left the club life to raise her daughter. They'd never gone by her father's name. Isa was a Walsh for as long as she could recall. *Although, technically, I'm a Kerry.*

She let out a steadying breath. The little research she'd done on Macha MC was unrewarding. The club stayed out of the limelight until a rivaling MC, the Twelve Brothers, decided they wanted Macha's territory. That'd been six months ago. She'd read the articles but never made the connection to her father.

After her mum's death, she went to see Malcom Kerry

—Phantom, as she'd heard his fellow bikers call him. Her father, while excited to see her, was more worried for her safety, she could only assume because he was the president and she was his child. *Why couldn't he have hidden me in Ireland?* That was the root of contention, but she eventually obeyed his request to stay with the Colorado chapter of Macha. But only after her best friends encouraged her to have an adventure. She'd been scared out of her mind to leave, but the decision was simple: she needed to see a bit of the world, even if it was only Colorado.

The pilot came over the intercom and the seat belt sign flicked off, summoning Isa to shaky legs. Her head hit the lowered ceiling above the seat, and she grunted. Having her father's height never pained her more than this moment. Normally, she adored her five-foot-eleven stature. Today, she loathed it. Being stuffed in an airplane with hardly any room to stretch out made flying drop lower on her preferred methods of transportation.

Phantom—*not "Da" like he'd prefer*—promised to retrieve her once the MC fight was put to bed. He couldn't give a time frame, which pissed her off. She didn't like to wait. Especially when it had nothing to do with her.

Retrieving her carry-on, she slung it over her shoulder and followed the crowd off the airplane. Phantom said to expect an MC man to be waiting. *Just what I need. Another man giving me orders.* She'd gotten used to being alone. Well, as alone as she could get living five minutes away from her protective Catholic mother.

The Colorado Springs airport wasn't overly busy. Isa

took her time weaving through the hallways, watching planes depart through the large windows. She was in no hurry to begin a mandatory exile from the land she loved. Her father's Macha man could wait. *He's probably just some ratty old guy anyways.*

After stopping at a Cinnabon and filling her belly with her favorite treat, Isa continued slowly toward the baggage claim. She stopped by a cute tourist shop and perused the trinkets. A tie-dye T-shirt boasting the Rocky Mountains caught her eye, and she had to purchase it. Wherever she went, she bought a T-shirt. She hadn't been many places, so her collection was in dire need of a facelift.

When her phone started ringing, she pulled it out of her carry-on. "Orla, I miss Ireland."

Her best friend laughed. "You've been gone a whole day. Give it some time."

Isa plopped into an empty seat near a departing terminal. "My da—er, Phantom said he'd come for me when it was done. Why don't I believe that?"

"Probably because he's been a no-show your entire life." Orla sighed. "We miss you at the shop. Niall is already driving me mad. He's trying to recreate that dress you made last week. I'll send you pictures. It'll help your mood."

"My mood is fine," she snapped.

"Oh, aye, I can hear that."

Knowing her best friend was right, Isa tried to steady her nerves. Leaving home without her blonde-haired twin was difficult. Most people assumed they were sisters, their height and eye color the only differences. Orla and Niall were her best friends since childhood, and the only time they'd been apart was on holiday. It'd taken longer than expected for Niall to admit he was in love with Orla, but now they'd been married two years, and their love antics only made Isa envious.

"I miss Mum."

"That never goes away, love. But Niall and I are here for you when you return. Don't you worry your pretty little head about it."

She chewed on her bottom lip, eyes darting across the travelers passing by. "Are you sure you can't come over?"

"Who'd run the shop—our shop?"

They'd opened the small candle and soap shop that also provided Isa the opportunity to try her fashion designs on the locals. Thus far, they loved her shirts, dresses, and skirts. Her plan was to become famous. *As famous as a Northern Irishwoman* can *be in fashion.*

"I know. Wishful thinking is all." She glanced at the clock on the other end of the terminal. Almost two hours had passed since she landed. Time was never something she managed well. "I better find my chauffeur. I'll call once settled."

Setting her laced-up boots on the floor once more, Isa hurried to the baggage claim and scoured the signs for her flight. Panic lined her gut when none of the signs showed her flight number. She ran a hand through her thick hair. "Eejit, I shouldn't have dallied."

"No, you shouldn't have."

The deep voice sent a tingle down Isa's back. Slowly, she turned around and was pleasantly surprised as she looked straight into a man's piercing eyes the color of a tumultuous sea. The look on his face said his attitude was equally stormy.

"Isadora Walsh?"

"Last I checked."

The man wearing a leather cut and dark blue jeans nodded. "I grabbed your bags when you didn't show up. They kept going around the belt, squeaking annoyingly. I don't like to be kept waiting."

"That's too bad, because I like to dawdle."

Isa slowly ran her eyes up and down the man she guessed was a few years her senior. He was definitely not what she expected when *biker* came to mind. A greasy-haired scoundrel, sure, but a man who could double as a model? No. This man had lean muscle and a wide chest. Tattoos curled around his biceps all the way down to his wrists. She'd bet her sketchbook there were more hidden beneath his black T-shirt and jeans. His blond hair was a bit too long and completely wind tousled, giving him a vibe she could only describe as smoking hot. His dark blue eyes were cautious, searching her curiously. For a moment, she saw a flicker of a smile, but he hid it just as fast.

Heat flushed her face when she noticed he was equally scrutinizing her appearance. Normally she'd mind, but with this biker, her pulse skyrocketed.

"Doc." He held out his hand. That too held tattoos. Her mind went wild at the intricate designs and how fun it'd be to trace every last one. Her small village didn't have many tattooed men. She'd Internet surfed, of course, but seeing a man like him decked out in tattoos of all colors made her pulse quicken.

Get it together. She pasted on a smile. "You can call me Isa."

Doc shook her hand, then grabbed both bags under his arms. "All right, Isa, let's go. We're already late."

Isa struggled to keep up with his long strides. Normally it wasn't such an issue, but he evidently wasn't in a good mood and wanted to punish her for being tardy. "Late for what?"

Pausing in front of a black pickup truck, he tossed her luggage in the back. "For church."

She wrinkled her brow. "Church?"

He smirked and unlocked the truck. "Not the hymn type of church. The MC meeting church."

"Oh." She climbed into the jacked-up truck and barely got the door shut before the vehicle squealed out of the parking lot. "Are you trying to kill me?"

He pushed his hair out of his eyes, then slipped on a pair of sunglasses. "Just what I was going to ask."

Isa's gaze whipped to him, no longer concerned with the seat belt. "What?"

"Nothing." He nodded to her skirt. "You may want to change before you meet the club. We're respectful of women, but the way you wear that miniskirt will make more than one brother toe that line."

Her hands immediately went to her thighs. In retrospect, wearing the gray tweed skirt wasn't her idea but Orla's. She'd loved the skirt matched with a flowing, long-sleeved white shirt paired with old-fashioned lace-up boots. She adored the outfit. "You're saying men in America can't keep it in their pants?"

He chuckled. "Oh, we can." He glanced over to her, a crooked smile showing perfectly straight teeth. "I'm just saying I won't particularly like my Macha brothers ogling you."

Isa crossed her arms over her chest. "Why would you care if they ogled me?"

Instead of answering, he fixed his gaze on the highway. His jaw tightened, as if his words were meant to be silent. Despite the blond scruff, she saw the grin.

A hint of a thought echoed in her mind. She shivered at the notion that he might want her all to himself. She'd never been anyone's before. Not in the real sense.

Sneaking a peek over to the solemn Doc, Isa's stomach flipped unexpectedly.

Maybe this trip won't be so bad after all.

4

———

DOC

FUCK ME, SHE'S GORGEOUS. Doc PULLED INTO THE CLUB parking lot and threw it into Park. The entire ride from the airport had been hell for him. Isa's lavender scent filled the truck cab, and her tiny skirt made it impossible to concentrate on anything she said. Her Irish lilt tempted him to pull over and kiss her luscious lips.

Fuck, I don't get bent up about women.

When the Macha princess didn't show up on time, he'd been pissed. He called Reaper to bitch, but of course the man didn't answer. He'd arrived six months ago to help his uncle on the medical side of the club. He'd never guessed an ulterior motive. Reaper failed to explain why Doc was chosen for this particular protection detail, but he always enjoyed the role when it rotated to him. Most of the time, the jobs were simple and done by dinner. *Until today.*

He climbed out of the cab and grabbed her bags from

the bed. Isa's sandy blonde hair swept over her shoulders, enticing him to run his fingers through the lengths that almost reached her delectable ass. Walking around the truck, he held his breath. Her long and slender legs did him in. The instant he saw her, he imagined her willowy body wrapped around his.

Fuck. Stop it! He didn't get cockeyed over a woman. Then again, he'd never met this woman before.

Isa turned enough to grace him with a smile he didn't deserve. He'd acted like an ass since meeting her. He barely spoke during the drive to town despite her best efforts. Her soft words sent him over the edge, and he had to stay quiet lest he fuck up his job already. It was bound to happen if he didn't stop thinking of Isa like she was a goddamn goddess.

"Where am I staying?" Her gray eyes swept over the main clubhouse in Snowshoe. It was next to the garage, where he spotted a few members working on cars. The place could use a fresh coat of paint but overall fit the biker motif.

"For now, you'll stay here." He nodded toward the front door. Already, three patch members had caught sight of Isa in her skimpy clothes. If she were his woman, he'd swat her ass until she swore to never show that much leg around the brothers again.

"Hello," she greeted Cueball, Klink, and Snoopy. The three were always around each other. That was what he'd learned since arriving. That and they tended to share their women. They were the three amigos, if the legendary three had tattoos and smoked nonstop.

Snoopy tilted up his ball cap and whistled low. "*Mamacita*, don't tempt me."

"Shut up, Snoop," Doc growled.

The Hispanic man and his two buddies roared with laughter. "Oh look, our newest patch got himself whipped already."

Doc refrained from completely wailing on the trio. He was no match. Being the newest Macha member meant he was lowest on the pecking order, and they'd use it to their advantage given the chance. Cigarette smoke wafted in the air, and he picked up his pace.

Opening the door to the clubhouse, he was pleasantly surprised when Isa lifted her head defiantly and ignored the catcalls from Snoopy's groupies. While Macha held women in high regard, the patches didn't always color in the lines when it came to club nymphs.

But she's no nymph.

"Who're they?" she asked, pausing in the doorway. Her eyes sought out his, and when they collided, Doc forced his body to stay stoic.

"Patch members of the club. They like giving people a hard time."

"I don't like them."

He smothered a grin and followed her inside. "Not all members of the MC are as awesome as me."

"And as humble too."

He walked deeper into the room dotted with pool tables. On the back wall sat a long bar, beer tapped at all times. Most of the club members had rooms here instead of living in town. A select few lived in Snowshoe, but most members preferred being close to the MC action on the edge of town.

Hawk and Rubble were playing a game nearby. Both paused and looked their direction. Rubble's expression remained unreadable, but Hawk might as well have drooled all over the floor.

"She a new nymph?" Hawk called, grinning at Isa.

"You wish," she said sassily.

Doc exchanged a humored look with his brothers and followed the tall woman. She didn't even know what a nymph was, but already she'd made her status known among the members.

"You know where you're going?" he asked when she scrunched her nose at the three hallways. The little diamond piercing in her nostril was perfect for her cute little nose.

"No."

"I'll set you up in the spare room." He held in a smile when he added, "It's connected to mine through a door. The place used to be a hotel. Macha bought it and refurbished it years ago to fit the club."

Isa's light brows lifted, but she didn't reply. The sooner she realized he was going to be glued to her until the danger passed, the better. Isadora Walsh was the Belfast chapter president's daughter. To the club, she was royalty and would be treated as such.

He plopped her two bags on the floor. "It's not much, but until Reaper says otherwise, you're here."

Isa sat on the bed and laughed when it creaked. "Any chance the bedding has been recently washed?"

"Of course. What do you think we run, a hostel?" a woman's voice said behind him. Both turned in time to see Queenie step into the doorway. Her rich brown hair was lined with auburn highlights, and her cut-off shirt showed tatted arms. "I'm Queenie, Reaper's old lady."

Standing, Isa held out her hand. "Nice to meet you." She rubbed her lips together. "How long do I have to stay here?" A moan sliced through the air from down the hall, and her face turned bright red. "I, um... I'm not used to roommates."

Doc snorted, and Queenie shushed him. From where he stood, the little princess wasn't very worldly. The realization bolted his feet to the floor. If she was as innocent as she seemed, he couldn't let any of the brothers near her. He'd protect her no matter the cost. No one would lay a finger on his princess. He'd make sure of it.

"We'll get you set up at the lodge next week. The guys are finishing up the renos." Queenie laughed. "Damn men like to take one too many smoke breaks."

Isa nodded, but her face didn't match her compliance. "Sure. Any chance I can speak with Lorcan—I mean Reaper? My... er, Phantom didn't explain much before he shipped me out. I have a few questions."

Glancing at the clock on the wall, Queenie nodded. "Supper will be ready at seven. You can meet the rest of the club now or after we eat. You and Reaper can chat tomorrow." She eyed Doc. "Aren't you late for church?"

The time registered, and he stepped into the hall. "Yeah, I'll catch the tail end. You'll make sure she's okay?"

Queenie nodded and promptly shut the door in his face.

He stood there for a good twenty seconds before his feet followed his command. He didn't want to go anywhere without Isa beside him. No woman ever had this effect on him, and he'd only met her an hour ago.

I'm in deep shit.

"THE LAST TOPIC TODAY IS OUR LATEST PROTECTION detail, Isadora Walsh." Reaper looked over his small reading glasses. It was only a matter of time before he'd hand the reins to someone else. According to Hawk, Prez didn't ride his chopper as much these days either.

Doc leaned forward, watching his uncle. He was moving slower since his arrival. If a member couldn't ride, he had to step down and retire. No one wanted to lose Reaper. He was the best president they'd had. But at the same time, each member was eager to know the successor for the Snowshoe chapter.

"Isa is Phantom's daughter. She was sent to us while Belfast takes care of an issue with the Twelve Brothers MC." A rumble of grunts echoed around the table. They all knew the bad blood there. It wasn't merely territory the Twelve Brothers wanted. They desired Ireland to be held only by them.

Reaper's gaze swung to him. "Doc is assigned to her, but I expect each one of you to watch out for her as well. Macha's never lost anyone under our protection, and I'm not about to start now." He shuffled to his feet and grabbed the small gavel. "May the goddess ride with you."

With church officially adjourned, the members stood and started chatting. The unique ending unnerved Doc at first. Once he learned the complete history of the club patron—not the dumbed-down version his dad used to tell him—he'd wanted the badass goddess protecting him too, no matter how odd the closing prayer sounded.

"You helping at the bar later?" Brewer asked, clapping a hand on Doc's shoulder.

"Nah, but I may stop by later with the princess." He grinned. "I'm sure after meeting all you assholes, she'll need a drink."

Snoopy flipped him off, and a couple other patches laughed. They left the room as a group and headed to the main living area. Dinner was still a ways off, and with Queenie watching Isa, he figured he'd better take advantage of the free time. *Not that I mind her all that much.*

Cueball let out a loud catcall, and Doc looked up in time to see a group of nymphs headed their way with beer in hand. Their role was twofold tonight: serving drinks and serving their bodies to the Macha men. They were paid handsomely and treated equally well.

Since he arrived, only two nymphs had left and were replaced with new ones. According to Boulder, they left to pursue alternative careers with club backing. That among other reasons cemented Macha in Doc's veins. They didn't use and then discard anyone. They supported the people under their care until they left.

"Care for a cold one?" a busty blonde with short denim shorts and a low-cut paisley shirt asked, sitting on his knee. She looked familiar, but he couldn't place her.

Doc took the offered beer just as Hawk grabbed a cue stick and headed to the nearby pool table.

"I had fun with you last night," the nymph said, wrapping an arm around his neck.

He sipped the beer and kept his gaze on the felt tables. "Yeah."

"Jules and I are ready for another round if you are." She nodded to the other blonde nearby.

For a moment, he glanced between the two nymphs. Both were gorgeous. The problem was he could hardly recall them. "Maybe another time." He took a long gulp and tried not to give the nymph a reason to stay. His body wasn't reacting like usual. He doubted any amount of sucking his dick would get him there mentally. *Not tonight, for some reason.*

"Aw, come on, Doc. We had a good time." She kissed his neck. "We can have even more. You know we'll do anything for you... to you, if you want."

He finished his beer and shook his head. "Not tonight, nymph."

The blonde sat up and pouted. "But—"

He glared at her, and she immediately got to her feet.

Once she stalked away in a huff of blonde hair and perfume, he let out a breath.

"Damn, Doc, you done pissed off that nymph."

He eyed Hawk. "She'll get over it."

Cueball took a shot, and a striped ball sank into a pocket. "Since when do you turn down pussy?"

"Yeah, I've never seen you do that," Brewer added, joining the group.

"Just not in the mood." He shrugged and grabbed another beer from a passing nymph.

"The fuck you talking about?" Hawk scoffed. "You're always in the mood for a quickie. Hell, last week you had a line of nymphs out your room, just fucking them and then sending them on their way. It was epic."

Brewer nodded. "And the week before that, you sent a prospect out to Costco to get condoms because you already went through the megapack."

Doc gripped the bottle tighter. They were right. Turning away nymphs was seldom for any of them, but especially him. He'd earned a reputation among the nymphs for being fast and rough but equally satisfying, and they kept coming back for more.

"Had her last night," he improvised since he didn't have a good excuse. "I like to keep them on rotation."

The other men seemed to accept his statement and continued on with their pool game.

Standing, Doc watched for a while, mind unable to focus. It was too busy wondering how Isa was settling into the club.

He didn't do relationships. He didn't get wrecked over women.

So why is this one consuming me?

5

―

ISA

THE SCENT OF LEATHER CLUNG TO THE AIR DESPITE Doc's absence. After telling her about the club members, Queenie left to check on dinner preparations. Doc was the newest member, and Queenie was the proudest aunt she'd seen.

She'd learned a few things about the MC from the president's old lady. More than her own father cared to mention.

Firstly, Macha, the Celtic goddess of war, life, and death, was their patron. Each patch member had the same ghost raven tattoo in honor of their goddess. The members revered women, no matter their place in the club. Queenie let it slip that the club nymphs—or club whores, as Isa discovered—were simply that. The members could sleep with them but must never make them their old ladies. Macha took care of them, and in return they earned money from working for the club's businesses.

Secondly, no Macha member could ever lay hands on a woman, nymph, or old lady. If he did, his patch would be stripped, burned, and force-fed to the member. That was before a brutal beating and banishment.

Queenie made it brazenly clear that they weren't a church by any means, but they were strict in their treatment of women. That being said, the president's old lady also mentioned that sexual innuendos were more common than cigarette butts.

The rest of the Macha rules would make themselves known, Queenie implied. Isa wasn't too concerned with it. If she had her way, Colorado would be a short vacation, and then she'd return to Ireland to run the shop and live in the flat above it.

Digging through her first suitcase, she found a pair of jeans with a couple fashionable rips. *Surely Doc won't complain about these.* She rolled her eyes. They'd known each other a whole two hours and he acted like he was her savior. *Cheeky bastard.*

She glanced around the room. It lacked a homey feel, but it was a room. A bed sat in the middle, a dresser to the side with a mirror above it and a small closet. True to his word, a door on the right wall was locked but when she opened it, she saw it led to Doc's room. It'd do until they moved her to the lodge. *Wherever that is.* She fluffed her hair and opened the door right as Doc's hand lifted to knock.

His blue eyes dipped over her outfit, then back to her face. "Supper's on," he said gruffly.

Taking a breath, Isa hurried to keep up despite her own long legs. When they reached the dining area, he abruptly stopped, and she barreled into his back. The scent of leather and musk drowned her nostrils.

"Blimey, can't you warn a girl?" she grumbled, pushing at him. When she noticed he wasn't meeting her gaze, she turned. A table full of food sat waiting, as did about twenty men and women. "Oh, bugger."

A balding man with a white beard at the head of the long table chuckled. "You're Phantom's girl all right. Have a seat, lass. I'm sure you're starved."

Noticing Queenie next to the man, Isa identified him as Reaper, the president of Macha's Colorado chapter. Seeing two open seats, she pulled out one and heard Doc take the other. The members dug into the food, chatter lively from all sides. It sounded and felt like one big happy family.

Surveying the room, Isa admired the handcrafted wood table and chairs. No doubt one of the members' handiwork. The food spread along the table looked scrumptious. From pot roast and potatoes to lasagna and garlic bread, not one plate was empty.

She pushed around the boiled carrots and slice of beef, gut queasy from the long flight. As delicious as it all smelled, her senses were on overload. If not from the food, then from the varying scents each man and woman possessed. Car oil, suntan lotion, and cigarette smoke assaulted her until her stomach refused to let her eat.

"You all right?" Doc asked, leaning over.

She shook her head. "I think I'm going to be sick."

His eyes widened and he set down his slice of bread. Standing quickly, he pulled her out of the room and to a toilet before she spewed her measly stomach contents everywhere. Isa held on to the porcelain bowl as if her life depended on it. "Feck."

Doc knelt beside her, brushing her hair out of her face. He used a rubber band from his wrist to keep the lengths at bay when another round of nausea ripped through her. His big hand tenderly rubbed her back.

Groaning, Isa felt tears creep into her eyes. Most men wouldn't be caught dead within five feet of a puking woman, but Doc wasn't going anywhere, it seemed. Being so far from home with no one hit her hard. Fat tears fell down her cheeks, and he sighed.

"Come here, princess." He held her against his chest, and she hated herself for sobbing into his shirt.

"I'm not a princess," she mumbled, eyes heavy.

"You are to me."

Isa stirred more than fifteen hours later, her eyes swollen from crying but not nearly as stiff as her body. Yawning, she fluttered her eyelids and held in a gasp when she saw Doc lying next to her. She double-checked beneath her sheets and sighed in relief that she was in her pajamas.

Wait, how'd I get in these?

He shifted beside her, and she looked up in time to see

his eyes pop open. "Shit, I must've dozed off." He got to his feet and checked his phone.

It was then she noticed he was still fully dressed in the same clothes. "How am I wearing pajamas?"

"Queenie."

"Oh. Why didn't you go to your own room?"

Running his hands through his hair, he shrugged. "You weren't feeling well. Being sick in a new place... I figured you could use a familiar face."

Isa bit back a snarky reply. He *was* a familiar face, even if only barely. "Thanks. You didn't have to."

"I did. It's my job." He shoved his hands in his back pockets. "But you're awake. I'll let you get up, and I'll grab some food since we missed breakfast."

Watching his hasty retreat, she smiled. Her appetite was back, and after last night, she was in dire need of sustenance.

Sitting up, she glanced around the room. Doc's cut was on the chair next to the bed. A shimmer of black metal beneath the leather cut made her do a double take. Even without seeing the entire thing, she knew it was a handgun.

Gathering her toiletries, she went in search of a shower. Thankfully, she found one, and fifteen minutes later, she felt like a new woman. Running a comb through her straight hair, Isa almost missed the slight intake of breath when Doc entered the room. She glanced in the mirror and saw him behind her and to the left. His gaze was glued to her, his blue eyes darker than before. Looking at her reflection, she saw the reason. All she wore was underwear. It wasn't uncommon for her at home. On warm days, she'd spend all day in them with a robe overtop.

"Sorry, I should've knocked." He averted his eyes and held out a sandwich. "This should hold you over."

She took the offered food and waited for him to meet her gaze again. He wouldn't. He kept his eyes glued to his black boots. According to him, this was all a job, and his failure to look at her meant he wanted to keep it as such.

"When you're, uh, done, Reaper wants to talk with us," he said, turning on his heels and closing the door behind him.

Isa took a big bite out of the sandwich, disappointed he didn't let his eyes wander over her.

Her skin flushed at the thought. She'd never been with a man, but suddenly she wanted all Doc could offer.

6

———

DOC

STANDING NEAR THE DOOR, DOC TRIED HIS DAMNEDEST to keep as far away from Isa as possible. With her lavender-scented body wash, his actions were for naught. She filled the room, and he was trapped in her confines.

"How do you like Colorado?" Reaper asked, leaning back in his chair. After lunch, the MC president called them into his office, most likely to discuss the situation.

Isa shrugged. "I haven't seen much of it. Jet lag has kept me sleeping for most of my stay." She shifted her weight to her left leg, which looked longer thanks to the tiny shorts she wore.

Reaper's eyes flashed to him. "My nephew will take you on a tour once we're through. There's much to see in Snowshoe."

"Such as?"

"Our businesses, for one." Reaper stood and pulled

open the shade. The bustling city of Snowshoe lay in the distance. "I hear you design clothes."

"Aye. I designed all the clothes I brought."

This got Doc's attention. A drop-dead gorgeous woman who was good with her hands and made his mouth water? *Yep, this is very bad.*

Isa nodded, her dirty-blonde hair falling over her chest. "My best friends and I own a shop. We mostly sell candles and soaps, but I try out my clothes designs too." She grinned. "The locals like them."

Reaper's bushy gray eyebrows lifted. "As they should. If you get a chance, chat with Queenie about designing something for the club. I'm sure the boys would appreciate some new Macha shirts."

A slight blush crossed her features. "I'm not sure they'd like my style."

"I guarantee they will." He moved closer and gave her a fatherly hug. "You're under our protection, Isa. If you need anything, let Doc know. He's your bodyguard of sorts. He'll do anything for you."

Isa's gray eyes lifted to his. "Anything?"

The mischievous gleam in her gaze made Doc's jeans tighten. Behind her innocent facade was a woman craving to be turned into a goddess... if she let him.

He nodded curtly, careful to keep his demeanor professional. He'd just patched. The last thing he needed was to be labeled a pushover.

Reaper's phone rang, and Doc chose that moment to

escort his charge from the office. "What would you like to see first?"

Isa ran her hand along the wall. "You're new, aren't you?"

"Yep."

"Why'd you get chosen for this job, then?"

"We rotate through the club. It was my turn."

"Bollocks. Tell me the real reason."

Doc stopped and crossed his arms over his chest. Looking as fierce as possible, he lowered his gaze to hers. Instead of fear, he saw defiance. "Because I'm Reaper's nephew, that's why. My father was VP before he died. Macha is in my blood just like it's in yours."

Isa narrowed her eyes. "Bullshit. You don't want to be here on protection detail."

"I didn't until I met you."

Her sudden gasp tempted him to show her how true his words were, but Cueball stepped into the hallway. The pool shark slowly pulled off his sunglasses and let his brown eyes slide over Isa.

"Hello, hot stuff. The name's Cueball. I heard there was a new girl around the club." He licked his lips, eyes lingering over her perky body. "Sorry I missed you at dinner last night."

Doc stepped forward, but Isa interrupted his act. "Do you like breathing?"

Cueball smirked. "Last I checked."

"Then I suggest you back off before the Belfast president finds out you're drooling over his daughter."

Doc bit back a laugh at the expression on Cueball's face. The other man stepped away, hands up in surrender. "No harm intended." He glanced to Doc. "They grow them feisty in Ireland."

He jerked his chin up. "Wouldn't have it any other way, brother."

Cueball chuckled and maintained his path toward the bedrooms.

When Doc turned back around, he met Isa's glowering face. The more time he spent with her only intensified his longing to put her over his knee. She was sassy when needed, and that stirred up the most primitive sensations in his mind. Suddenly, being uprooted from his familiar role as the club doctor wasn't so bad.

"Are all MC members horndogs?"

Doc took a step closer and tugged on the bottom of her shirt. It barely covered her navel, leaving plenty of skin available to tempt any man. "Have you seen yourself, Isa? You're the prettiest girl in the clubhouse." His eyes fixed to her lips, where she was rubbing them together. "And that fire of yours only makes it hotter." He reached over and ran his knuckles down the side of her neck, goose bumps spreading at his touch. "Because we all like to play with fire."

"What if I burn you?" she whispered, the sound airy and uncertain.

He chuckled and stepped away. "You're worth the scars, princess."

7

ISA

Holy hell, he's hot. Isa swallowed her sip of water and tried to concentrate on Doc's words. It was difficult because she kept getting caught on his lips instead. They were subtly hidden beneath his scruff but looked perfect in every way.

They were halfway through the clubhouse tour, though she'd need a refresher course if there was to be a quiz. So far, she gleaned that she needed to stay away from the patch members and prospects. Evidently, they weren't her *cuppa,* as Doc implied. *Cheeky bastard doesn't know my cuppa.*

They toured the garage where Rubble, Reaper, and a few prospects worked. She decided Doc was right about Rubble being the toughest man in the club. The hulking man looked like he could break a tree trunk with his bare hands. Plus, his mismatched eyes, one blue and one green, gave her eerie chills. After chatting—or rather Doc chatting

—with the garage guys, Isa decided Rubble wasn't too bad but needed to smooth out the edges of his personality. *Probably why they call him Rubble.*

Next, Doc showed her the tattoo parlor and bar named Booze and Tattoos. It was catchy, even if she wondered if people regretted their decision to drink and ink. Brewer ran the bar while Snoopy and his girl, Lily—or, more affectionately, Legs—handled the tattoo parlor along with Hawk.

Someday, Isa promised herself to ask if these MC names had stories behind them. Lily's was obvious. Her legs were covered in intricate tattoos and extremely shapely. Brewer, well, she assumed it was because of his occupation at the bar. The ones Isa wasn't sure of were Hawk, Klink, Boulder, and Shovelhead. She honestly didn't care about any of them. *Well, except Doc's.* His seemed self-explanatory. She'd yet to ask how he'd earned his club name but hoped he'd volunteer the information.

"Are you ready to take a ride?"

Isa shook her mind away from the last hour of visual overload. Walking in on Hawk and a club nymph a few minutes earlier nearly sent her straight for the mountains. She'd seen plenty of romance movies and a few pornos, but the actual act frightened her.

"Um, yeah?"

Doc handed her a helmet. "You don't sound very enthused."

She eyed the large Harley in front of her. It was decked out in chrome and gleamed in the sunlight. "I've never ridden one before."

"I don't think you've ridden anything, much less a Harley." She inhaled sharply, and he didn't even bother to look ashamed.

"Bloody bastard." She scowled at his implication. "That's none of your business."

He folded his arms across his chest, eyes intently scanning hers. "You sure? Because I think it is."

Heat simmered in Isa's veins. She didn't want to discuss her experience or lack thereof. Even if he sent a bolt of lightning straight between her legs. "On to the bike."

"All right, all right, but you should get used to being open about shit like that, Isa."

"Why? I don't plan on being here long."

"Just long enough, I hope."

Her eyebrows shot up. "Excuse me?" She stomped to him and waved her finger in his smug face. "If you think I'll sleep with some low-life biker covered in tattoos with floppy hair, you have another thing coming."

Doc's usually teasing eyes softened. "Princess, I promise to keep you coming long into the night."

Shaking her head, she laughed at the sheer insanity. In one conversation, the man made her blood boil yet somehow turned her on at the same time. "You think you're hot shit, don't you?"

"Usually." He carefully clipped her helmet in place before securing his own. "Hop on, babe. You're in for an experience you won't forget." She opened her mouth to protest, but he kept talking. "This lady was my dad's. She's the best bike in two hundred miles. I recently refurbished all the parts, so she runs like a kitten."

"A kitten?" She timidly straddled the bike behind him. "More like a cougar," she said when he turned on the engine.

Doc patted her thigh. "Hang on."

Isa wrapped her arms around his waist in time for the bike to roll onto the street. She closed her eyes and buried her face in Doc's wide back, pounding heart drowned out by the motorcycle's roar. Despite his cheeky behavior, he was the only person at the clubhouse she could minutely trust. *Even if he wants to get in my knickers.*

Only after they made the first turn did she peek out from behind him. The open road sprawled out in front of them, mountains on either side. The warm summer air knocked her breath away for an instant. Squeezing him tighter, she inhaled and grinned. *This isn't so bad.* She watched trees whiz by on either side, the town of Snowshoe quickly approaching. She figured the MC was in city limits, but their location outside the town center made sense. They were the first line of defense, or so Doc told her earlier. Why, she wasn't sure. It gave her a good feeling, though, that the town appreciated the MC instead of fearing it.

Clinging closer to the unruly biker, she scanned the horizon. It was an endless road. From where she sat, it didn't look scary or intimidating but exhilarating instead.

Doc's smile caught her attention, and she held back from kissing his scruffy cheek. *Bugger, why do I want to do that?* They were both new to the MC, and somehow that rationalized her mind.

Isa rested her chin on his shoulder. The scent of oil and musk overpowered the fresh rainfall. It was completely Doc, and her stomach jumped when he reached down and rubbed her thigh comfortingly.

I could get used to this. Riding behind a sexy, muscular man, the whole world ahead of us.

Her train of thought stopped there. She couldn't let herself wonder what could happen between them. She wasn't worldly. Not like the club nymphs. Doc sure as hell was worldly. She'd recognized the lustful gleam in his blue eyes on more than one occasion. She couldn't imagine anything with him. It'd only end in disappointment.

The motorcycle slowed, and they took a left turn up toward the mountains. She glanced over her shoulder and watched the buildings fade from view. Only trees and mountains were in their path now.

"I thought we were going to town," she said against his ear.

He shook his head. "Nah, maybe next time. I'm showing you the good stuff."

Shivering when a patch of cold air hit them, she snuggled closer. His body heat did more than succeed in warming her. She could stay in her spot and never get sick of it. *Maybe Macha really is in my blood.*

After thirty minutes, the motorcycle stopped outside a large fenced area. Leaning over, Doc punched in a code, and the gate swung open.

"Where are we?"

"Macha's mountain lodge." He didn't give her the chance to ask more, simply drove up the long and winding driveway. The dense trees broke apart at the top of the incline, an enormous lodge sitting atop. Trees lined the driveway, two sizeable garages on both sides of the main cabin.

Doc parked and helped her off the back. The change in temperature sent her teeth chattering, and she rubbed her hands up and down her arms. A surge of heat surrounded her, and she smelled Doc before his leather jacket rested on her shoulders.

"Should've warned you. It gets pretty cold up here sometimes." He tucked her under his arm and led them to the front door. A wooden awning held up by stone pillars kept visitors out of the elements until entry. After punching in another code, the door clicked open and warmth greeted her.

"Whoa." Her mouth gaped at the interior. While it looked like any other expensive lodge from the outside, the inside surprised her. It looked nothing like a cabin in the woods but more of a compound. A catwalk across two sets of stairs grabbed her attention first. The entire space was warm and welcoming. The cherry hardwood floors throughout disappeared through several doors and hallways. Televisions were mounted on the walls, comfortable-looking couches filling the space. A large fireplace sat farther in a den off the living room.

"That's what I thought too." Doc smirked and plopped

onto one of the couches, turning on the TV across from him.

Ignoring him, Isa kept exploring the space. She could make out the doors leading to a back patio and swore under her breath at the floor-to-ceiling windows back there. A blue glow beckoned her further, and she gasped at the sight of the pool just through the doors.

"It's a hot spring," he said, somehow beside her. "It stays warm all year round." He grinned down at her. "Skinny-dipping is more than acceptable if you forgot to pack a swimsuit."

Rolling her eyes, she shoved him away from the door and opened it. Sure enough, the large deck boasted a full-sized pool with plenty of outdoor chairs. Another smaller, crescent-shaped pool sat to the side.

"The moon pool is cold water," Doc informed. "When it gets really warm in the summer, it's nice to soak in that one."

Craning her neck, she could make out an open garage to the far right. It was empty now but hinted at the perfect spot for UTVs or motorcycle parking. Another deck sat on top of the garage, tables and chairs ready for use as well as a fire pit. Instantly, she wanted to roast marshmallows and stargaze on that upper deck.

Behind the fenced-in pool area sat untamed wilderness. If she looked hard enough, she swore she could see wildlife back there. It was an ideal location to lie low and enjoy the serenity of nature.

Turning on her toes, she took in the backside of the

lodge. It looked bigger from here. The front kept the true size of the compound well hidden. Windows dotted the back of the oversized cabin. *Bedrooms.* She'd bet her sketchbook on it. From here, the lodge looked like at least two stories of solid defense. Positioned on the side of a mountain, overlooking the valley, it was the ideal spot for a fortress.

"This place is incredible."

"Wait until you see upstairs." Doc waved her inside, locking the door behind them.

They made their way up the stairs, the scent of pine lingering in the air. Doors lined the wide hallway, and Isa stayed close to him until he paused at a room. "This is where you'll stay." He walked inside. "The boys need to add the finishing touches, and then you'll be set."

Isa glanced around the room that boasted a vaulted ceiling. It was empty save for a ladder. Blue-gray walls gave the space a homey feel. As did the walk-in closet and large bay window overlooking the pool. The mountains and trees in the background made her think of Ireland. No other buildings could be seen from this spot. "It's perfect."

"Once they get a bed and dresser, yeah." Doc rested his arms above the doorway. "My room is across the hall. Macha uses this place for weekend fun and when there's trouble."

Her eyes snapped to him. "Am I in trouble?"

He searched her face. "No, but they're taking extra precautions. If the Twelve Brothers finds out your identity and location, we'll be ready."

Suddenly the leather jacket felt paper thin. Retreating to the door, she wrapped her arms around Doc and buried her nose in his shirt. Instead of reacting, he stayed perfectly still. It should've encouraged her that she was safe with him, but it only made Isa feel alone in a world full of bikers who may or may not want to hurt her.

As if sensing her mood, he gently enclosed her in a hug. "You're safe with me, Isa." He kissed the top of her head. The simple act overshadowed his earlier innuendos. He wasn't as tough as he acted in front of everyone else. "I won't let anything bad happen to you. I swear."

"Doc?"

"Yeah?"

She tilted her head up, their lips inches apart. "I'm scared."

His blue eyes dipped to her lips and back again. "I'd be worried if you weren't."

A loud thud from the first floor broke them apart. "We should go. The guys are back from break. We'll be in their way." He disappeared down the hall before Isa could utter another word.

By the time they arrived back at the Macha clubhouse, Isa realized three things. One: she loved the feel of a motorcycle between her legs. Two: she liked matching wits with Doc. Three: she equally loved the feeling of being in Doc's arms.

8

———

DOC

"How's Isa settling in?" Reaper asked the next afternoon.

Doc sipped his favorite beer. He'd managed to get five hours of sleep last night, though only after taking a shower to get Isa's smell off him. It lingered more than any woman's perfume. The lack of sleep got to him earlier when he helped Brewer and Rubble clean up the bar. Evidently, the crowd from the night before had been rowdier than usual. He wouldn't have minded the work except the club nymphs kept pawing at him. While he was in dire need of release, he didn't want to hook up with one of the women who threw themselves at him.

"It's taking a bit of time, but that's normal." He watched Klink hunker down by his motorcycle to check the oil. "The guys sure like her."

Reaper chuckled and took a drag from his cigarette.

"I'm not surprised. Hell, her mama was a beauty back in the day." He coughed. "But nothing like Queenie."

Doc rolled his eyes. He'd never accuse his uncle of being unfaithful. The man worshipped the ground Queenie walked on. It didn't happen like that for every couple, but it was more common for Macha old ladies. Hell, the few patch members who had old ladies wouldn't be caught dead with one of the club nymphs. Despite the few who had open relationships, a member didn't give a woman his patch unless he meant to make their patron proud.

"They're treating her right, though, aren't they?" Reaper's face was tanned from years of sun damage, and the wrinkles on his forehead deepened when he frowned. "Because I'll shove my foot straight up their arses—"

"I'm taking care of it." Doc finished off his beer, eyes fixed on the parking lot. It was nigh on opening time for the bar, and stragglers from Snowshoe were already filling the open spaces.

His mind turned to Isa. She was safe in the clubhouse, but he still felt the need to check on her. After sparring with her the other day, all he'd wanted to do was fuck her up against his bike. She was a virgin like he thought. She'd all but admitted it. Knowing that fact, he was even more determined to keep her safe. Keeping things professional with Isa was becoming increasingly difficult, though. He couldn't stop wanting her.

"You like her." It wasn't a question. They both knew the answer.

He nodded slightly.

Reaper patted Doc's back once. "Don't get attached unless you're willing to make her your old lady. Isadora isn't a club nymph."

"I know that," he snapped, eyes flashing to his uncle.

"Good. Then you'll also know she's returning to Ireland once the tiff is over." He dropped the cigarette and snuffed it with the toe of his boot. "Just like you'll go back to hopping from nymph to nymph after this is done."

Doc crushed the beer can and tossed it in the nearby recycling bin. "Maybe."

"Maybe? Why the change of heart?"

"Didn't say that, but it makes me wonder about the future." The sun had completely set now, the overhead lights flickering on in the dusk. He shrugged and shoved off the porch. "Don't get me wrong. I like the feeling of just me, the road, my bike and a couple guys I trust."

Reaper gave him a wicked side-eye. "You've made friends, then?"

"Somewhat." He laughed. "I think they all tolerate me."

"Well, you earned a patch last winter saving their sorry arses, so I guarantee they more than tolerate you, Doc." Reaper started toward the clubhouse. "Once you earn your place in Macha, the members respect you. We don't hand it out like candy at Halloween, but once it's earned, only death or treachery can relinquish it."

His uncle was right, of course. Doc used to hang out at the clubhouse in his youth. He'd seen many members heckled. The comradery between the men was what he yearned for and what he had with a few. Sure, he'd had friends at the fire station in Iowa, but none he wanted to hang with off shift more than a few hours. The MC offered lifelong friends. At thirty-two years old, he needed something permanent in his life. He'd gained Rubble, Brewer, and Hawk, and couldn't fault the brotherhood he felt with them.

Rubbing his left shoulder, he watched the patch members filter into the bar. With Isa safely in Queenie's care, he was off shift for the night. *A game of pool and a few beers will help.* He set off toward the building, slipping inside the dark bar. Country music blared from the radio, the bartenders and waitresses outfitted in cowboy hats and fringe shirts. The interior was a mixture of western and motorcycle. Snowshoe was big into the western motif, so Macha took that and ran with it in their design. The bar was connected to the tattoo parlor by swinging saloon doors in the back.

Grabbing a shot of whiskey from Brewer, he downed it before the Jason Aldean song ended. A frosty mug of beer made it to his hand before he walked over to the pool table where Cueball, Boulder, and Rubble played.

"I've got next winner," he said, tossing some cash into the growing pot.

Cueball leered. "Shove off, Doc. This game's for established members only."

"Aw, come on, Cue," Brewer said, delivering a round of shots to the table. "The guy's Reaper's nephew. In a year, he'll probably be president."

Boulder and Cueball mumbled under their breaths and returned to the game.

"Don't worry. They'll warm up to you," Brewer said before making his way back to the bar.

Doc nursed his beer, watching the trio play. Cueball lived up to his name. The guy was a pool shark if he ever saw one. Boulder wasn't bad but got sloppy the more he drank. It was Rubble who shocked him. The guy was built like an ox and had more muscles than a bodybuilder, but on the sergeant at arms, it fit. He was always ready for action. In fact, Doc didn't see more than one beer pass the big man's lips.

"You're up," Rubble said, handing him a cue stick. "You break."

Cueball moved to a seat with a club nymph in tow, and Hawk stood nearby, watching as closely as his name demanded. He didn't miss anything.

"You're Tank's son, right?" Rubble said after Doc sank two solids in the pockets.

Doc lined up for another shot but missed. "Yeah. Did you know him?"

The bald man with tattoos on his skull lifted his cue stick. "No, but I heard he was a legend." Rubble hit three stripes into pockets. His gravelly voice bespoke years of chain smoking. "You plan on staying here or going to Ireland?"

"Not sure yet." Doc finished off his drink. "I guess it depends how this goes."

Rubble's mismatched eyes met Doc's. Looking into one

green eye and one blue had an eerie effect . He didn't know which one to focus on while they talked.

"Let me give you some advice."

Doc leaned closer.

"Don't fuck up."

Cueball chortled from his spot. "Yeah, don't fuck up."

"Shut up, Cue. Should've named you motherfucking Parrot," Rubble barked.

Cueball immediately got to his feet and dragged the nymph with him. Only after Cueball left did Rubble nudge Doc with his elbow.

"That guy gets on my nerves fast." He smirked. "Just takes a little to scare him."

Swallowing the initial panic from Rubble's reaction, Doc laughed. "You're not too bad."

The other man sank the eight ball into the pocket and stashed the cash in his jean pocket. "Yeah, yeah. Don't let the other guys know. They'll think I'm a softie."

Doc zipped his lips, causing Rubble to chuckle.

"Come on, you look like you could use a stress reliever." He wrapped an arm around Doc's shoulders and led him toward the back of the bar. A group of patch members sat in a large booth in the corner. Smoke wafted above them, empty beer glasses on the table.

"Have a seat," Snoopy said, motioning to the open spot.

Only after Rubble sat did Doc. Snoopy's old lady, Legs, sat on his lap, affectionately kissing his neck. Klink was beside him, a club nymph only visible by her bobbing head under the tabletop. Boulder was sandwiched between Klink and Rubble, his lap filled with a busty brunette.

"That Irish girl is so fucking hot. I'd like to sink inside that ass. Too bad she's off-limits," Boulder said, pinching the brunette's breast. She squealed in delight and started kissing down the older man's body. Doc didn't have to guess where she'd end up—under the table just like the other nymph.

"What do you think, Doc?" Snoopy asked, his dark eyes alight.

"She's very hot." He glanced to Rubble and saw him smile into his drink. This was some kind of test. If he reacted, they'd know how he truly felt about Isa. Hell, he didn't even know how he felt about the quiet woman yet.

"You been with plenty of nymphs, yeah?" Boulder asked. "I heard you've been celibate since Phantom's daughter arrived."

Keeping his face complacent, Doc nodded. "What of it?"

"I doubt she'd like it if you were trouncing around with the nymphs."

He shrugged, not liking the conversation's direction. *How does not fucking nymphs give me away?*

Boulder took a shot of vodka. "We all figure you and the Irish cutie will get together."

"Why's that?"

"Cuz she's your type," Klink said.

"Oh yeah? What's my type?"

A waitress dropped off another round of beers, and Doc

slowly sipped his. He needed to stay sharp. Macha members weren't known for their stupidity but keen awareness and ability to thrive in any situation.

"Anything with a hot body," Snoopy finally said, pointing to the other side of the bar. "And that Irish lass is smokin'."

Following his finger, Doc kept in a groan at the woman in a short red dress, dirty-blonde hair flowing around her shapely breasts. Even without seeing her face, he knew her identity. *Isa.* His pulse skyrocketed at the mere sight of her. He couldn't even think about what she did to his cock.

He glanced back to the table and chuckled. "She's allowed to have a good time, Snoop."

Snoopy laughed. "Yeah, but this isn't a members-only bar. You better keep a close eye on her, or one of the locals will try to slide between those long milky legs of hers and fuck her raw."

Doc looked over to Isa again. Sure enough, several Snowshoe residents were sizing up the delicacy from Ireland.

Nobody's tasting her except me.

Legs giggled, and Snoopy kissed her hard. The nymphs beneath the table paused their ministrations long enough to see what he would do.

Rubble rubbed his long beard, eyes dancing with merriment. They were all getting off on his pain.

"If you'd rather Rubble protect her, just say so," Legs taunted. "We won't hold it over your head."

The hell you won't. Doc finished his beer in one long

chug and slammed the empty glass on the table. He stood and saluted the group. "See you fuckers tomorrow."

"I told you he liked her," Legs whispered before he was out of earshot.

Doc straightened his shoulders and made a beeline for Isa. The damn woman was shaking her ass to Luke Bryan, and more men were drooling over her than before. Naturally, she had no clue what was happening or how seductive she looked swinging her little hips to the rhythm.

Taking a breath, he leaned down and whispered, "Keep shaking that ass and I'll put you over my knee."

Her hips paused and she twirled around, eyes wide. When she recognized him, a shy smile crossed her kissable lips. He balled his hands into fists, the urge to hike up her skirt and fuck her then and there irresistible.

"You wouldn't dare. I'm a MC princess." She took a shot of what looked like vodka and wiped her mouth with the back of her hand.

"Oh, now you like the nickname?" He narrowed his eyes. Ever since he'd called her by it, she'd seemed disgusted by the term.

"Maybe I like when you say it," she slurred.

Damn, how'd she get wasted already? He hadn't seen her when he arrived, which meant Isa got tipsy fast. He glanced around the room but didn't spot Queenie. Surely she didn't think letting Isa loose without an escort was a good idea.

"Hmm, not sure you'd agree when you're sober."

Isa shrugged and started gyrating her hips to the beat of

the music. It would've been fine if a drunken asshole hadn't rubbed up against her ass. Acting quickly, Doc shoved the other guy, who didn't even seem bothered by the act and went to grind on another single dancer.

"Come on, Doc, I wanna dance." Her Irish accent sounded heavier with the alcohol running in her veins.

Gripping her waist, Doc pulled her flush to him. Her eyes shot gray daggers at him, but there was a softness to the glare. "Isa, you need to come with me. You're not safe here." He looked over and saw two sturdy-looking men ogling her backside. He could handle one drunken asshole, but a whole bar full of them? Not even close. "Now, princess."

For a split second, he thought she'd argue, and he'd have to haul her out over his shoulder. Finally, she nodded and draped his arm around her shoulders. Doc managed to flip the bird to the table in the back. What they didn't know wouldn't hurt them.

They made it out of the bar before she started giggling. Her little nose scrunched up in the cutest way, her diamond stud glittering in the moonlight. She staggered out of his grip.

"Isa—" he started.

"I'm fine, Doc," she shot back, moving the wrong direction. "Why'd you have to go mess up my fun? I was having a good time."

Catching up to her, he guided her toward the clubhouse. She'd need a bottle of water and some aspirin before bed, and he wasn't about to leave anyone else to the task.

"Yeah, and a few minutes later you would've been strip-ping on the bar top." He kicked open the door and steered her down the hall. "Not that I'd mind all that much." She tripped on the rug outside the bedroom, laughing loudly when he caught her and put her upright again.

Doc closed the bedroom door, and before he could speak, Isa was there, arms wrapped around his neck. She leaned into him, her breasts perky and lacking any sort of bra. How he missed that before was beyond him. *No wonder everyone was staring. Damn woman.*

"Kiss me," she demanded, pouty lips ready for action.

The temptation nearly outweighed his better sense, but he shook his head and kept his mouth out of reach. "Not like this, Isa."

She frowned and shoved at him. "Eejit."

He caught her hand on his chest and fought the urge that felt so natural. "Believe me, there's nothing I'd rather do."

"Then do it."

For a split second, he almost did. The glassy look in her eyes unearthed a speck of honor. "I can't." He helped her to the bed, but she merely stood next to it. "You won't remember any of this tomorrow."

Isa crossed her arms over her chest, pushing up her breasts. Fuck, he'd have one hell of a time with her if she were a mere nymph instead of a protected princess. The longer she stood there looking like heaven on earth, the more his groin protested.

"Why can't you kiss me?" She finally relented and

crawled under the covers, yawning as her head hit the fluffy pillow.

Doc stared down into her gray eyes, darker in the dim lighting. "Because when I kiss you, I want you to remember it."

"I'd never forget a kiss from you." She giggled, then hugged the pillow beside her, sleep overtaking her instantly.

Sitting on the bed, he watched the slow rise and fall of her chest. Her breaths gently moved her long hair, and he couldn't resist. Sliding a tendril through his calloused fingers, he sighed. Every fiber of his being raged when the patch members goaded him about fucking this princess. They wanted her for a quick screw because she was gorgeous. He wanted her for much more than that. *Longer too. Much longer.* Kissing Isa would set off a domino effect. If he had her once, he wouldn't stop until she was his permanently. He wasn't certain if he was ready for the kind of commitment a princess like her deserved.

He carefully lay next to her, her slight wheezing making him chuckle. Isa deserved better than a washed-out doctor turned paramedic turned motorcycle club member.

He leaned over and kissed the tip of her slightly upturned nose.

Isa deserved a prince. He was a mere servant.

IT WAS SOMETIME IN THE MIDDLE OF THE NIGHT WHEN

Doc woke to Isa's long hair sprawled over his face. He looked over long enough to see her draped over him like a blanket. He tried to move her back to the other side of the bed, but she only wrapped her body tighter to his.

Being the good guy never felt worse. He lay there in complete agony until she loosened her grip enough for him to slip off the bed. Checking his phone, he guessed he had another two hours before the bar closed.

Standing, he adjusted his hard cock through his jeans and stalked to the door. None of the nymphs would be up, so a shower would have to do.

Isa reached out to the spot beside her and grunted when he wasn't there. "Doc?"

She sat up, and he held his breath. The room was pitch dark, a dim light from the hallway the only glow. Isa slumped back over and cuddled his pillow to her chest. When she moaned his name again, it was erotic, and he bit his tongue. If that little minx was having a sex dream about him, he'd spill his load then and there.

He waited quietly until her breathing mellowed out, and he rubbed a hand over his face.

Yeah, a very long shower.

THE WOMAN WAS DRIVING HIM MAD, AND SHE'D ONLY just arrived.

Doc hurried out of the clubhouse and went in search of Hawk. He found him outside the tattoo parlor. The familiar buzz of the tattoo machines comforted him for the first time that night. It was familiar and a constant in the club.

Hawk grabbed a cigarette from his pack and lit it. "She a sleeping beauty yet?"

"Something like that." He leaned against the shop's exterior. Queenie would have their hide if they damaged the recently painted shop, but he didn't give a shit at the moment. He needed a release of some kind. *But not a nymph.* For some reason, he couldn't force himself to call for one.

"You seem tense." Hawk exhaled a puff of smoke. "She more of a handful than expected?"

Doc reached over and took a cigarette from the carton. "Shut up."

Hawk's brows lifted. "Wow, she must really be bad if you're smoking. I haven't seen one pass your lips since you arrived."

Lighting the cigarette, he drew in a deep breath. He'd never smoked more than a pack in his life, but every now and then, the nicotine eased his nerves. Tonight, though, it barely scraped the surface.

"She's stubborn, gorgeous, and off-limits." He shook his head. "Feels like a test."

Hawk chuckled. "You think Prez wants to see if you can keep it in your pants around Phantom's daughter?"

"Dunno, maybe. Reaper *is* my uncle."

"Yeah, but he's not cruel." Hawk took another draw. "All right, not premeditative cruel."

Doc studied the curling smoke above them. "The smallest things she does set me off. I mean, hell, she was having a sex dream about me just now. Not to mention how she asked me to kiss her." He shook his head. "And I want to. So badly."

"Then do it." Hawk flicked ash on the cement.

"Are you kidding? That's asking to get my ass handed to me. I just patched. And I can't fuck Phantom's daughter like I want. She needs somebody gentle. I'm far from that."

Hawk waved at two women entering the tattoo shop. "Then resist the temptation to slip between her legs, brother. Get a nymph. They'll ease your urges." He grinned. "Maybe. You do have a knack for being insatiable."

"Fuck you."

Hawk laughed and turned toward the door. "Gotta get back to it. Those ladies are my last appointment." He opened the door. "You gonna be okay, or do I need to put a chastity belt on you?"

Doc tossed the cigarette to the ground and crushed it with his boot. "I'm good, thanks."

Hawk nodded, then slipped inside.

Pacing the parking lot, Doc couldn't get Isa out of his mind. He watched the bar fill with more Snowshoe residents, the music louder by the minute. Grinding up against a nymph wouldn't suffice. *Nothing will.*

9
___

ISA

RAINSTORMS MOVED IN DURING THE NIGHT, AND BY the time Isa woke, the entire valley was covered in a dense fog. She pulled on a pair of pants, a sweatshirt, and shoes. A chill lingered in the clubhouse hallway. The dark sky peeked through the windows, reminding her of Ireland. Tears welled in her eyes. The thought of home always did that. Even when she was miles from her little shop apartment.

Doc was nowhere to be found when she woke. The vivid dreams she'd had made her grateful for his scarcity. She didn't feel like explaining why he was the main character in her adult-rated imagination.

Drinking last night was a mistake. She winced at the bright kitchen light and frowned at the lack of bodies. The clock above the stove said it was early morning, and distant snores echoed down the halls.

After gulping down a bottle of water, Isa made her way

through the clubhouse. The décor wasn't anything special. No doubt the old ladies didn't even bother with the place. This was the patch members' haven. From pool tables to dartboards, the place reeked of masculinity.

She found a smaller room with a television and two couches and sank into the one nearest the door. It was odd to be in a place like this. Her mother never went into great detail about Malcolm Kerry's occupation. Seeing a sliver of what her father lived with over the last two decades, Isa pitied him. While the MC life had perks, all she could see were the pitfalls.

She stared at the Macha emblem on the wall. The ornate goddess with long red hair wore all black and stared at Isa with dark eyes, her faithful raven and horse by her side. The folklore of the Irish heroine was one she'd heard throughout childhood. Isa frowned. Now that she thought of it, the stories were from books sent from a distant relative. Her mother never explained who sent them. *It was Phantom.* Part of her wanted to be furious with her mum for keeping her father from her. The other part of her appreciated the safety. She'd had the chance to grow up without the fear of warring MCs coming for her.

Snatching the remote, she flipped on the television and rolled her eyes at the adult station. The cheesy lines and music made her mute it immediately. *I'm just going to forget I saw that.* Finding a history channel, she watched a show on King Henry VIII until her eyelids drooped once more.

An hour later, she woke with a start and sat up. Scanning the room, she sighed. The clouds hadn't lifted yet, but she heard rustling throughout the clubhouse. Stretching, she stood and yawned. A myriad of framed photos caught her eye on the wall, and she walked over, tracing the snapshots. Some were black and white, others Polaroid, but they all had one thing in common: each one held patch Macha members.

Lifting her eyes, she searched for a familiar face. None came to her. Her heart dropped slightly when no women appeared in the pictures.

"Is the Macha brotherhood really enough?"

"Don't let Reaper hear you ask that. He'll skin your hide," a feminine voice teased.

Looking over, Isa noticed a short woman outfitted in tight leather standing in the doorway. With cascading black hair, pierced brows, and a pair of dazzling eyes, it was hard to miss her. "Who're you?"

"The boys call me Dolly, but my real name is Dorthea." Her dark blue eyes scanned Isa. "But don't you dare call me that." She walked over and tapped one of the frames. "My old man loved this MC. Hell, it's where he met my mom." She straightened her leather jacket over her white tank top. A hint of tattoos covered her chest, the green and blue tempting Isa to ask their origins. "Once MC, always MC."

"You're a member?"

Dolly chortled. "Fuck no. I work behind the scenes." She plopped onto the couch and propped her booted feet on the back. "I take care of the nymphs."

"You're a...." She couldn't finish the thought. Suddenly

her sheltered life in Ireland seemed a whole lot better than this one.

"Madam? Yeah." Dolly swept her black hair into a high ponytail, a raven tattoo behind her ear coming into view. "Why? You interested in joining? The girls are very happy with Macha." She looked over Isa approvingly. "I guarantee those boys would want you."

Isa self-consciously crossed her arms over her breasts. "I'm not, um, interested. I'm actually here because—"

Dolly snapped her fingers and sat up. "You're Phantom's girl, aren't you?" She whistled low when Isa nodded. "Sorry. I've been gone the last few days. My aunt needed somebody to help her with some shitheads on the block."

"And you did that?"

Dolly smiled, a pair of dimples popping into view. "Honey, just because I'm a woman doesn't mean I can't take care of myself and the people I love." She hopped to her feet. "It's a must in my line of work. I can teach you a few things if you'd like."

"Thanks, I would." Even though their lives were completely opposite, Isa liked this woman. She was gutsy and not afraid to flaunt it.

"Great, come on."

"Wait, right this minute?" She barely got the words out before Dolly grabbed her hand and hauled her down the hallway. For a woman five inches shorter than her, Dolly could move.

"Better than later."

They reached the doors to the parking lot behind the

bar. Remnants of last night's party that had trickled outside sent Isa's stomach lurching. The fog seemed to have thickened in the last hour, clouds tickling her exposed skin.

Dolly shed her leather jacket, revealing tattoos covering her arms and most of her chest beneath the tank. "Come at me." She motioned at her.

"I can't fight you."

"Somebody chicken?" Dolly taunted. "Come on, girl. Show me what your Irish daddy taught you."

"He didn't teach me a bloody thing." Gritting her teeth, Isa moved for Dolly, fists ready. She swung a punch, but it was easily blocked. Jabbing fast, she caught the side of Dolly's shoulder, but her victory was short lived. In one swift move, the shorter woman kicked Isa's ankles and slammed her to the asphalt.

Isa groaned in pain once she caught her breath. "Shite!"

Straddling her, Dolly kept her hands pinned to the ground. "You're feisty. That'll work well in Macha, but you need to hone your anger. Don't let it control you."

"What're you talking about?" She struggled to move but found it pointless. Dolly was stronger than she looked.

"The boys talk, Isa. I know why you're here. Hell, my girls are trained to get info from them." Dolly released her wrists. "You can't blame your dad for this. He can't control the Twelve Brothers. No one can. They're the scum MC of Ireland."

"I can and I will." She shoved at Dolly, the act meaningless when she all but lay on top of Isa.

"You've already lost your mom. Don't throw away a

relationship with your dad too." Dolly's eyes clouded. "You'll miss them once they're gone. Believe me."

Isa stopped fighting. "Your parents?"

"Yeah. Motorcycle accident two years ago." Her eyes shadowed. "They were Macha until they died. I'll be the same." Dolly pounced to her feet and pulled Isa with her. "And so will you. After a bit of training." She grinned. "There's a reason why a woman is the club's patron. Men are lost without us."

"You *would* say that," a new voice called from the bar entrance.

The women glanced over and saw Brewer with a shit-eating grin on his face. His button-up shirt fluttered open in the breeze, hints of tattoos beneath. "You spewing bullshit again, sis?"

Dolly flipped him the bird. "And so what if I am? What're you gonna do about it, big brother?"

Brewer ran his fingers through his red hair, the color a bright contrast to the fog around them.

Isa glanced between the two. She didn't see the similarities right away, but then again, Brewer did have a bushy red beard to match his hair. He walked closer, and it was then that Isa noticed they had the same baby blue eyes that saw straight to the soul.

"I didn't realize you were related."

Dolly draped her arm around Isa and kissed her cheek. "Macha is full of surprises. Come on, I'll introduce you to the nymphs. They'll love you, especially since you're not competition."

Looking over her shoulder, she saw Brewer grin before following them. She wasn't sure what to expect, but with Dolly and Brewer, it was bound to be fun.

Meeting the club nymphs took over the next two hours. The initial meeting was short, but once the nymphs started talking, Isa couldn't shut them up. In a way, they reminded her of Orla. She discovered most of the patch members were respectful when it came to sex. The few times things got out of control, either Dolly or one of the other members would protect the nymphs.

In a weird way, she was proud of the MC for their dedication to the women they used solely for bodily pleasure. From the little she knew about club life, that wasn't the norm. Every Macha nymph had a tattoo like the patch members. The one difference was they also had a small nymph beside the black raven. It was surreal to Isa that these women were part of something so big, even if in just a small way.

The nymphs offered makeup and hair advice—not that she took much of it. She'd never been huge on the makeup front, and her hair was always kept different shades of blonde. If people didn't like her the way she was, they were no friend of hers.

Lunch rolled by, and three nymphs were called to help prepare the meal, then promptly disappeared afterward. Dolly didn't seem concerned by it. Apparently it was normal to catch a member's eye during meal prep. Dessert, as Dolly called it, didn't always happen behind closed doors either.

Yeah, I noticed that last night. Isa pushed back her long hair. The bar boasted plenty of dark places for people to hide—or not hide—their sexual acts. The worst part was that she wasn't repulsed by it. *I'm becoming callous already.*

"Weren't you with Doc last week?" she overheard one of the nymphs say. Moving closer, Isa held her breath.

"Yep. He was a freaking god. Hasn't come around in a while, though. I'm blaming the Irish bitch. I'll bet she's getting fucked every night instead of us."

Isa held a hand over her mouth, grateful for the curtain between them.

"Well, she's one lucky girl," the first nymph cooed. "Doc sure knows what he's doing."

"True, but he's a little rough sometimes," the other said.

"Oh, stop, you pussy. There's nothing wrong with a man knowing exactly what he wants."

Isa stopped listening after that. She didn't want to hear any more about Doc's exploits or even his praise. He was a cocky son of a bitch, albeit a cute one. But she hadn't come to Colorado to get laid.

She walked down the short flight of stairs and caught a glimpse of Doc and Hawk along with two prospects. Hawk was ordering the prospects to wash the cycles after the rain, and each one appeared annoyed by the request. They didn't baulk, though, merely followed the patch member outside and got to work.

"This is such a weird place," she muttered, entering the kitchen. During her chatting with the nymphs, she had missed lunch.

"I'm sure I'd say the same about Ireland." Reaper came into view. "You seem to be making friends." He grinned and took a seat at one of the barstools. "I don't think Dolly's warmed up to another woman like that in years."

She opened the refrigerator and pulled out a bowl of fruit. "Really? She seems really cool. I mean, for a biker chick."

He chuckled. "Dolly is one of a kind. Just like you."

"How does it all work?"

"What?"

Isa grabbed a fork and sat across from him. "The club, the nymphs, the businesses."

For a moment, Reaper merely stared at her and scratched his bearded chin. "The nymphs are under Macha protection. They all work around the club businesses and offer the members reprieve in between." He gave her a weak smile. "Your mum would kick my arse if she knew I was telling you this."

"I want to know everything." She took a bite of a slice of pineapple. "It helps me understand."

"Well, in that case, Macha and the mayor of Snowshoe work hand in hand to keep hard drugs out of the city. Yeah, we've got marijuana here, and they even sell it at the lodge, but the citizens are more worried about heroin and cocaine.

One of my groups patrols the city to make sure any drugs moved are done with permission. If not, well, the sheriff is also on our side."

"That's fascinating. How did—"

"Don't ask questions, just listen."

Isa clamped her lips together. She needed answers, and if sitting silently was how she'd get them, then she'd do it.

"Our day-to-day expenses are mostly covered by the proceeds from the garage, tattoo parlor, bar, ski shop, and ski lodge. During the colder months, we host several big snow events. It helps the community and our club, so the town is good with it."

"What about illegal things?" She bit her bottom lip. "I mean, other than regulating the drugs."

"The only illegal thing we do is protect people." He smirked at her scrunched face. "Sounds weird, I know, but Macha is sometimes hired to protect people hiding from other clubs. It's not illegal to the law, but to the MC code, we've made many enemies."

She put down the fork. "So, you're telling me Macha protects people who need help, and that's why you have enemies."

Reaper took a deep breath and nodded. "Mostly. We're mouthy from time to time too." He grinned. "Can't help the fights that causes, lass."

"I always thought motorcycle clubs were a bunch of hell-raising assholes who moved drugs for the cartel."

"Some do, but not ours." He patted her shoulder. "Never ours."

"That's oddly comforting." Everything her mother said hadn't been true. Malcolm Kerry wasn't a soulless bastard. *He's actually pretty badass.*

"I'm off to the garage. I have a few errands I need Doc to run." He stood. "You should tag along. The two of you make quite the pair."

She snorted. "Yeah right."

Reaper clucked his tongue, a twinkle in his brown eyes. "I know when opposites attract."

"You're mad," she called before he walked out of the room. In reality, he wasn't. He was dead-on. She felt the surge of desire whenever Doc was in the room. It didn't happen with any other club member. It'd never happened ever in her life, for that matter. There was something between them, but she wasn't sure she wanted to find out what. Not unless he wanted to kiss her as badly as she wanted to kiss him.

10

DOC

"I need to help Brewer at the bar tonight. You want to come?" Doc waited in the doorway. He'd barged right into Isa's room and caught her mid-change of clothes.

Not your best move, O'Brien.

"What's my alternative?"

"Hang out with Queenie, probably." He sniffed, her lavender scent invading him.

Her face scrunched and she stood. Her long legs looked even more tempting in the skinny jeans. *How the fuck did she get in those?* While his Irish princess was slender, her ass was more than two handfuls.

"I'll go with you. Maybe if it's not busy I can work the bar."

"You bartend?"

Her gray eyes dropped to her stylish black boots. She didn't need the damn heel, but it did make looking right into her eyes even more attainable. He'd never in his life met a woman her height, and he instantly adored it.

"No, but I'd like to learn."

He opened the door. "Tell ya what. If it's not too busy, I'll show you how to make a few drinks."

"Really?"

He laughed and met her excited eyes. "Really."

An hour later, Doc was immensely regretting his offer to bring Isa along. The bar was chock-full of patrons. The normal Snowshoe residents didn't bother him. The group of Greenback Cutthroats in the corner did. The men with red cuts on weren't causing trouble, but he doubted that'd last long.

"Why don't they go to their own bar?" Brewer bitched, garnishing a drink for the woman on the other end of the bar. They'd split the bar, Brewer's usual prospect ill that evening. Even with three extra nymphs, neither had a moment to even take a piss.

"'Cause they're assholes and like to stir the pot." Doc wiped off his station, eyes focused on their rival MC. They surrounded the jukebox, loudly trying to decide what song to select.

"All right, I think I got this one right." Isa presented him with a small tumbler. Since arriving, she'd tried and failed to make a correct whiskey sour. Heaven help him, but he admired her persistence.

Using a small straw, Doc dipped it in the drink, then brought it to his mouth. "You're sure?"

She nodded confidently, so he tasted it. Keeping her

gaze, he let her wallow in uncertainty. The way she pouted her lips made it too tempting to pass up.

"Well?"

He tossed the straw in the garbage bin. "It's perfect, Isa. Good job."

She beamed and hugged him before he could stop her.

"All right, all right. Why don't you check on Snoop and Rubble? They're probably getting low on drinks."

Isa didn't need to be told twice. She walked out from behind the bar, and Doc watched her sweet ass sway out of sight.

"Got a little drool there, brother," Brewer said, flicking his chin.

Doc cleared his throat and eyed the other man. A knowing grin lined Brewer's face, and he wanted to wipe it right off. "A man can look."

"Mmhmm, but you don't want to merely look."

Brewer went to help a customer, stealing Doc's opportunity to chew him out. His brother wasn't wrong, though. He did want to do more than look at Isa's jeaned ass.

Focusing back on the three drink orders, Doc didn't think about Isa again until he heard a ruckus toward the Greenback crew. He glanced their direction and had to do a double take.

"Is that...?"

He tossed the ice out of the glass he was prepping. "Yep, it is."

Brewer chuckled. "Well, damn. She fits in real well."

Doc shot him a glare and hurried from behind the bar.

He fought through the crowd, never taking his eyes from Isa's long hair. Reaching her, he steeled himself for the inevitable backlash. She was dangerously close to the Cutthroats, and the bikers had no issue with telling her exactly what each one wanted to do with her long legs.

"Isa, we need you at the bar," he said, grabbing her wrist.

Isa turned guarded eyes to him, and he swore he noticed a flash of relief. How the hell she'd moved from helping Macha to serving the bar, he needed to know the moment he got her out of there.

"Nah, Macha, I think this little filly will stay here a while with us," the biggest Cutthroats member said, tugging on Isa's other wrist. She toppled onto his lap, and the seven bikers surrounding them laughed.

Doc casually smiled at each one, silently sizing them up. He couldn't handle them all. Not without help.

"Sorry, I really need her."

The Cutthroat trapped Isa on his lap with his arm across her breast. Ice flowed through Doc's veins at the look of sheer horror on her beautiful face.

"Look, man, I don't want any trouble. Just need my girl back." He took a step closer, willing himself to stay cool. An all-out bar brawl wouldn't be good for business.

The highest-ranking Cutthroat chuckled darkly, his eyes equally black. "She your woman?"

Doc glanced around at the bikers slowly closing in on them. "She's one of our girls. You know how we like to keep them close."

"One of your nymphs, then?" The biker smiled. "Perfect, I could use a nice blow job." He yanked on Isa's long hair, and Doc gritted his teeth at the terrified sound that escaped her. "How 'bout it, sweetheart? Suck me good, and then I'll fuck you like no other." He nodded at his men. "Maybe even let my brothers have a taste of your milky skin."

"I'll bet she'd like it in every hole at once," one of the Cutthroats said, and the rest eagerly agreed.

The big man nuzzled Isa's neck. "I'll fuck you raw, then pass you around my brothers before I fuck you again."

The Cutthroats let out a unified "Whoop," and that was it. Doc threw the first punch before his brain registered what he was doing. All hell broke out, but he didn't give a shit. He busted a nose and heard the unsettling crackle of bones in another man's jaw. The tangy taste of blood sent Doc sprawling backward, a Cutthroat jabbing him with his elbow when Doc tried to pry Isa out of his grip.

Before the Cutthroats could react, Snoopy, Brewer, and Rubble were on top of the group, five prospects in tow. Isa's elbow connected with the biggest Cutthroat, and he yelped in pain. Acting fast, Doc snagged Isa's arm and whirled her out of the vortex of punches and blood.

"Hurry up," he yelled, tugging her away from the bar fight that'd drawn nearly every patron in for a swing. They weaved through the crowd, careful to steer clear of misdirected punches. Doc hit the back door with his shoulder and yanked Isa out before slamming it shut.

"Are you all right?" he asked, hands slowly checking her body.

Tears dripped down her cheeks, but she nodded. "I don't know what happened. One of the nymphs asked me to take her tray to the men because she wasn't feeling well. Before I knew it, they were all over me."

Doc gently drew her against his chest. She buried her head in his shirt, and he wrapped his arms around her. Her shoulders shook, though from tears or fear, he wasn't sure. Probably both.

Yells from the bar echoed, and he led her away from the door, lest a Cutthroat decide to make an escape. They made it to the alley behind the bar before she suddenly became deadweight.

"Isa, what's wrong? We need to get to the clubhouse."

She leaned against the brick wall and pushed her hair out of her face. In the moonlight, her skin looked ghostly. "Sorry, I need a minute." She inhaled and exhaled noisily, hands shaking as she paced. "They would've done it, wouldn't they?"

Doc shoved his hands in his jeans pockets. "Yes."

"Why? Do they do that to your nymphs often? I can't believe Macha would let—"

"We don't, Isa." He moved over to where she stood. "The Greenback Cutthroats are exactly that. They're our closest rival and like to rile us up every so often. But they never get our nymphs. Not if we can help it."

He searched her eyes and cursed at the fear he saw there. "I should've left you at the clubhouse. I'm sorry."

"No, it's my fault. I shouldn't have taken the tray." She laughed. "I'm no waitress and definitely not a nymph."

Lifting his hands, Doc tucked her hair behind her ears. "You're better, princess."

"I am?"

"Oh yes. No woman compares to you." He couldn't help himself. She deserved to hear beautiful words every damned day. Lowering his eyes, he stared at her parted pink lips. He leaned in ever so slightly and pressed his lips against hers. She didn't react, too dumbfounded to move. Catching her gaze, he offered her a smile. "And you deserve a man who'll tell you that each day."

Isa opened her mouth only to shut it again. No words formed, and he was fucking glad they couldn't.

"Doc, you out here?"

Stepping away, he called back to Brewer, "Yeah, we're here."

Brewer jogged over to them. "Oh, good. I didn't see you leave." He glanced to Isa. "Everybody okay?"

Isa nodded, still mute, and he hid a smile. *The men in Ireland truly are idiots if they didn't adore this woman.*

"We're good. What about inside?" He nodded toward the bar. "The Cutthroats leave?"

"Yeah." Brewer raked his fingers through his bright hair. "But they'll be back. Said so before they hobbled to their bikes."

"Reaper won't be happy to hear that." He grimaced but didn't regret standing up for their Macha princess. She was his to protect.

11

———

ISA

"Have you ever shot a gun?"

Isa's head turned at the quiet question. "Excuse me?"

Doc sauntered closer. "You heard correctly." He rested his hands on the table. "Do you know how to shoot a gun?"

"No."

A slow smile crossed his face. "Come on, princess. I'll show you."

He hauled her out of the chair before she could sputter a response. He stopped beside a truck and opened the door. "Hop in."

Isa smoothed a hand over her dress. "I don't think I'm wearing proper gun shooting attire."

His blue eyes leisurely looked over her orange-and-white summer dress. It hit two inches above her knees in a bubble complete with pockets. It was one of her more favorite dresses she'd designed and made.

"I think you look just fine." He nodded to the seat. "Get in. I'm hot."

She grumped but did as he said. In retrospect, knowing how to handle a gun may have come in handy after her run-in with the Greenback Cutthroats the other night.

Doc's grazed kiss still haunted her. She couldn't decipher if it was real or merely a figment of her imagination. After the trauma, she could only assume it was her mind playing tricks on her.

Ten minutes later, she shook her head. "No, I'm not shooting that thing." She stared at the handgun on the bar at the shooting range.

"You're a Macha princess. You have to learn." He smirked. "After all, there's only so much Dolly's self-defense classes can teach you."

"How do you...?" She stopped herself there. No doubt Brewer spilled the beans. "I'll smack that bartender good the next time I see him," she muttered, walking closer to Doc. "What do I do?"

"First, make sure you have these handy. Don't want you to lose your hearing." He handed her a pair of large orange earmuffs. "Always treat a gun like it's loaded, and always keep your gun pointed in a safe direction. Next, always keep your trigger finger off the trigger and outside the trigger guard until you're ready." He grabbed the gun.

"Seems idiot-proof."

"You'd think, wouldn't you?" He handed her the gun. "You'll want to grip the gun with two hands at first. Your dominant hand?" He glanced at her.

"Right."

"Right hand should grip the gun high on the back strap. Your left hand supports the other, and you place it over the exposed part of the grip." He watched as she followed the instructions.

Isa easily complied, and he nodded approvingly. "Good, now all four fingers of your supporting hand should be under the trigger guard with the index finger pressed hard underneath."

She folded her left hand over.

"Not quite." Doc moved behind her and covered her hands with his own, showing her precisely how to hold the gun. His overgrown hair tickled the back of her neck, and she felt a shiver down her spine.

"There, good. Now your stance. Feet shoulder width apart with your right leg a little in front of your left. Bend your knees slightly and raise the gun toward the target."

Performing the acts as he spoke, Isa couldn't help the smile crossing her face. She'd always wanted to learn to shoot, but it wasn't a mum-approved activity.

Doc hadn't moved from his spot behind her, and she felt his wide chest against her back. "Good. Now to aim. Always use your dominant—right for you—eye and align the sights." He flicked a small notch on the gun, and she followed suit until it was aligned properly. Doc slid the ear coverings in place on both of them. "Relax, take a breath, and once you're ready, squeeze the trigger."

Isa held the gun up and focused on the bull's-eye at the end of the yard. It wasn't too far away. Fifty yards if she had to guess. The sun beat down on her head, but she didn't feel the warm rays. Birds chirped in the nearby forest, and the chatter of squirrels was unmistakable until the ear protection was in place. Now it was deadly silent. Finally, she took a breath and squeezed. The gun discharged, and she watched in surprise as it hit the target.

Doc let out a whoop. "Way to go, princess! You're a natural." He showed her how to put the safety on, then tugged the orange muffs off.

"Holy shite, that was amazing!" She placed a hand on her chest. "My heart's beating so fast."

He smiled behind his sunglasses. "My heart always beats fast around you."

Isa rolled her eyes and shook her head. "Bloody American flirt."

He laughed but didn't reply.

She spent the next hour learning about ammo, loading, cleaning, and every other little tidbit Doc managed to squeeze into conversation about guns. By the time they made it back to the clubhouse, Isa was confident she could hold her own should the moment arise.

Come for me, I'll be ready.

ROLLING OVER IN BED, ISA STRETCHED OUT HER ARM. Only a pillow met her, and she opened her eyes in the dark. Doc wasn't in his usual spot by the bed. It shouldn't have frustrated her, but it did. Her close call with the Cutthroats still unnerved her.

He's in the next room, Isa. Calm down.

She sat up and turned on the small light beside the bed. Grabbing her phone, she reviewed the missed messages from Orla and Niall. After replying to them, she opened a slew of emails from a blocked address.

Blocked: We know who you are.

Blocked: We'll find you.

Blocked: And take you.

Isa gasped and scrambled out of bed. Pounding on the adjoining door, she called Doc's name.

"What?" he growled, swinging open the door.

Doing her best to ignore his lack of clothes, she stormed into his room and handed him the phone. "I just received these messages."

Rubbing his eyes, Doc stared at the phone, his frown deepening. "Did you reply?"

"No."

"Don't." He turned over the phone and slid off the back. "They're trying to get a rise out of you so they can track you." In one quick move, he disconnected the GPS. "There, now they won't be able to find you."

Isa took the outstretched phone. "How're you so calm? Somebody's sending threatening messages to me."

Doc blinked several times, eyes focused on her. "Princess, I'd be worried if you didn't get messages, but those are emails. If they actually knew where you were, they wouldn't warn you, they'd just snatch you." He crawled back into bed. "I'll have Hawk backtrack the messages in the morning. Honestly, it's probably just some dumbasses."

Mouth gaping, she watched him snuggle up to his pillow. "You bloody wanker! They better not be on their way right now or you'll be sorry."

Doc turned over and propped his head up. "I'm already sorry you woke me up."

Huffing, Isa whirled around and stormed out of the room, sure to slam the door on her way. She jumped back into bed and tried to calm down. *That won't be happening for quite some time.*

She punched the pillow beside her. "The damn eejit better hope somebody doesn't slit my throat during the night." She grabbed the spare blanket and draped it over the one on her bed, pulling both up to her throat and swallowing hard. Even the mere possibility made her uneasy. Suddenly, every sound she heard was dangerous and out to get her. Moans from the room three doors down turned into a bloodcurdling scream in her mind.

"Seriously, princess?"

Isa yelped and tossed her pillow toward the voice.

Doc chuckled and picked up the pillow. "You look like a giant blanket. How many did you grab?"

Placing a hand on her chest, she tried to steady her breathing. Her protector stood feet away, still shirtless and looking as tempting as ever. "Blimey, I didn't even hear the door open."

He plopped onto the spot beside her. "Probably because you were too worried about the boogeyman."

She glared at him, looking so cozy next to her. He closed his eyes, and she immediately wanted to see the blue depths once more.

"Get some sleep, Isa. I'll be here to scare the monsters away."

Patting her pillow, she made sure to smack his gorgeous face before turning over and facing the dresser.

"Arsehole."

"Scaredy-cat."

She closed her eyes and smiled. Having Doc nearby immediately made it easier for her to slip into a dreamland where his lips caressed her every inch.

12

———

DOC

"That girl is a handful," Snoopy said, tossing his knife into the side of a chunk of wood in the empty lot next to the clubhouse. It'd been vacant for a year, so the club purchased it, hoping to build on it. Instead, it turned into a spot where the members drank around a small fire pit, always within earshot of the clubhouse.

"No shit." Cueball shook his head. "I accidentally—"

"On purpose," Brewer added, popping a top off his beer.

"Yeah, whatever. So I walked in on her with Dolly, and that Irish girl nearly bit my head off." Cueball chuckled. "But I kinda like her. She's feisty."

"That can be very useful in the bedroom," Rubble commented.

Doc silently sipped his beer. His brothers could bullshit all day long. Normally it was fine. Today, though, it rubbed him the wrong way. Mostly because they were talking about Isa.

"An Irish lass is trouble," Shovelhead said, spitting his chew into an empty bottle. "Mark my words, she'll destroy us if we're not careful."

The older man stood and walked back into the clubhouse. The remaining Macha members burst out laughing.

"That guy is nuts," Hawk said, tossing his own knife toward the target.

Snoopy nodded and lit a cigarette. "I heard Reaper tell Queenie that Shovelhead would never be president. Something about unsecured loyalties, whatever that means."

Rubble sank into one of the lawn chairs around the fire pit. "It means Prez isn't convinced the issues we had with the Greenback Cutthroats wasn't due to Shovelhead."

Snoopy and Cueball exchanged an uncertain glance. Doc couldn't believe what he was hearing. From the look on Hawk's face, neither could he.

"I heard Prez tell Queenie it'd be better to send him to Belfast." Rubble eyed them all. "But none of that leaves with you."

They all nodded. Being on Rubble's bad side was a death wish, and they all wanted to see the dawn.

A chill from the mountains swept over the area, and Doc pulled his hood up. With Isa safely playing cards with Queenie and Dolly, he'd have a few hours to enjoy solitude with his brothers before returning to sentry duty.

"Think the Twelve Brothers will figure out who she is?"

They all stared into the orange flames.

"Yep," Rubble replied, his voice husky. "Phantom made a lot of enemies when he took over Belfast. Not all the Macha members appreciate how he did it either."

"You think somebody within Macha might be harmful?" Doc asked, the possibility not one he liked.

Rubble glanced to him and nodded. "It's possible. Reaper and I have been meeting to discuss the possibility."

Hawk retrieved his knife and sheathed it. "Anything we can do?"

"Not yet. I'll let you know." Rubble took a sip of beer. "I trust you all more than the rest."

Doc looked to Snoopy and Cueball. He didn't particularly trust them, but if their sergeant at arms did, it was enough for him. They were a brotherhood and would defend it until their last breaths.

Let's hope it doesn't come to that.

One thing he knew for certain, he'd make sure Isa was fully prepared in case the Twelve Brothers came for her. She was the daughter of a legacy member and ought to know every inch of Macha. He was the man for the job.

"How's the Irish gal getting along?" Brewer asked.

Doc pressed the bottle to his lips. "She received a few menacing emails the other night, but we couldn't trace them."

"They're close, then." Rubble sighed. "Dammit."

Brewer took a long draw. "How're the two of you getting on?"

"Good most of the time." Doc watched the embers. "There's just something about her."

"It's between her legs, Doc," Snoopy heckled.

Cueball threw a log onto the fire. "You gonna get some of that?"

Doc shook his head. "She's under Macha protection. Can't touch her."

Hawk snorted and sat next to him. "But you want to."

"Who wouldn't?"

"Especially with that ass."

"That's enough," Rubble stated. His mismatched eyes peered at them. "Must I remind you what I'll do if any harm comes to her?"

Doc swallowed hard. He was painfully aware of the beating the last man received after crossing the line with one of their assets.

"No."

"Good. Now, I'm off to see a nymph." Rubble stood. "Anybody else?"

Cueball and Snoopy stood, and the three made their way across the lot to the clubhouse, where the nymphs held their own little lair beneath the main level.

"Not joining them, Doc?" Brewer poked the fire with a long stick.

"Not tonight."

"Couldn't be because of Isa, could it?"

He met Brewer's teasing eyes. The man was always joking about one thing or another. "I'm on shift after this, that's why."

Hawk patted his thighs. "And on that note, I'm joining our brothers. I've a sudden urge for pussy."

Doc and Brewer remained, though neither spoke for half an hour. It was comforting in a way to Doc. Being able to coexist with so many different personalities was unique and something he never took for granted.

"Don't let Phantom know your feelings on Isa," Brewer warned. "He'll shove his entire leg up your ass."

Chuckling, Doc nodded his understanding. He wasn't about to get tangled up with the Macha princess.

Even if I really want to.

13
———

DOC

THE PAST WEEK HAD BEEN HELL. HE'D KEPT A CLOSE eye on Isa only to find himself growing more attracted to her. It wouldn't have been so bad if she was boring or a bitch. But she was neither. Difficult at times, sure, but nothing he couldn't handle. He smirked and sipped his whiskey. She had her bitch moments, of course, but they were usually earned.

The other men quickly learned that even though she looked harmless, she could shoot daggers from her gorgeous gray eyes. Her friendship with Dolly only secured her more. The MC madam protected her girls and even taught Isa more self-defense tactics. He prayed she never had to use them. He'd watch over her as long as needed. Longer if asked.

The Colorado weather cooperated for the first time after a week of dismal rain. While Isa seemed unperturbed by the precipitation, he was ready for sunshine. They sat at a table behind the clubhouse, a large umbrella shading them. Isa's focus on the sketchbook in her hands made it easier for him to stare. Her long, dark blonde hair was clipped up, a few strands blowing in the breeze. Minimal eyeliner and mascara were the only makeup on her. It suited her ivory skin more anyhow.

Doc finished off his drink, three ice cubes remaining in the glass. He had to pace himself when it came to Isa. His body told him to drink to replace the urge to touch her, but his mind told him to stay alert. Danger lurked nearby; he could sense it.

"It's really hard to concentrate when you stare at me," she said, her Irish accent soft despite her scolding.

Running both hands through his hair, he shrugged. "Just making sure you're safe." He leaned over and caught a glimpse of her sketch. A biker jacket with "Macha" intertwined on the sleeves and back stood out on the page. The ghostlike raven appeared more regal, sitting on the shoulder of the ancient goddess. There was even a place to add a patch on the front that didn't hinder the overall persona of the jacket. He could see many Macha old ladies fawning over such an item. "Wow, that's good."

Isa met his gaze, a hint of pride in her face. "Thanks. Reaper suggested I design a few Macha-inspired items while I'm here." She set the book down. "Not like there's much else to do. Might as well stay productive."

"Can I?" He pointed to the book, and she nodded once. As he turned the pages, his brows rose at the intricate details on the jackets, shirts, and even jeans. A few articles of jewelry displaying the Macha emblem, horse and raven made him whistle. More pages were filled with delicately designed items based off Colorado and Snow-shoe. "Damn, girl, these are amazing. You should sell them."

She sat back and slipped on a pair of pink-tinted sunglasses. "I've thought about it, but my clientele in Ireland wouldn't buy them."

"Then sell them to Macha. The MC will definitely buy your designs, and I'd bet they'd be okay with a form of part-nership." He pulled out his phone and sent a message to Queenie. His aunt had to see the clothes Isa created. He knew without a doubt they'd be top sellers among the crew. A few designs would even sell well at the ski lodge.

"Maybe."

He narrowed his eyes. She'd been distant the last week, and he assumed it was because of how she acted after he refused to kiss her. Hell, most of his time aside from Macha duties was spent outside her room in the clubhouse. At first, he'd tried to make conversation with Isa, but the Irish lass wasn't having any of it. He'd been around enough women to know when they needed space. He'd give it to her even if it meant... longer showers.

The sounds of the MC drifted on the wind as neither of them spoke. Rubble tinkered on a Dodge pickup truck in the garage next door, a prospect power-washed the north side of the clubhouse, and somewhere within the bar, Brewer and his sister were playing a rousing game of pool with Cueball. In all his years as a paramedic, these were the sounds he preferred. He liked the hype of the firehouse, but this felt like a family, sounded like a family.

Snoopy yelled in Spanish from the bar's back door, the angry words directed toward a prospect he was tossing to the curb.

Doc smirked. *Yep, just like a crazy family.* The longer he stayed here, the less he wanted to leave.

Isa's sweet scent tickled his nose, but she wasn't the only reason. Feeling desired came in all forms. Macha's desire ran strong. He wanted Isa's to grip him as well.

He stood, the chair scraping on the concrete. "Let's go, princess."

She scrunched her face. "Where?"

"I'm teaching you how to ride."

"No, thanks."

He grabbed her hand and tugged lightly. "Come on, it'll be fun."

Isa reluctantly let him lead her toward the line of black motorcycles. The sun bounced off the chrome, the scent of wax in the air.

"Hop on." He pointed to his secondary bike. There was no way he'd trust her with his dad's old ride yet. "This is Bob."

She shot him a disgruntled glance. "You named your bike?"

He chuckled. "No, it's a Harley Street Bob." Once she mounted the seat, he turned the key. "You know the basic mechanics?"

"No."

"All right, let's do this, then." He straddled the bike behind her and placed her hands on the controls. "Your right hand is the most important. It gives you throttle and brake." He demonstrated the throttle. "But remember, a little goes a long way. The last thing we need is you popping wheelies."

"You're just saying that because you can't do it."

"Don't tempt me, princess." He grinned and focused on the job and not her flowery scented hair. "Your right hand also controls the front brakes. Just like on a bicycle, if you squeeze too tight, you might go over the handlebars." He placed his fingers over hers and demonstrated the right amount of pressure. Her skin felt so different under his calluses. Different but sinfully perfect. "Nothing to it."

"And the rear brake?"

"Your right foot."

Isa stepped on the foot brake and squeezed the hand brake. "Which one do I use? Both?"

"Nah. It's like riding a bike. Usually I apply the rear first to decrease speed, then squeeze the front brake to stop completely." He rested his chin on her shoulder. "But don't quote me because I don't always do that."

Isa turned her head just enough that her lips were inches from his. The slight intake of breath sent his blood pumping. She was so close. If either moved, their lips would collide. If that happened, he'd never want them to separate.

"What now?"

He eased off the back. The next part she needed to do

for herself anyhow. "Clutch. That's the lever just ahead of the left handgrip."

"I have a manual car at home," she said, practicing. "This should be a cinch."

"Great. Next is shifting. It's a little different than cars, so it may take some time to learn." She shifted through the gears like a pro, and his brows lifted. "Or not."

She beamed at him. "I guess you pick up a few things when you hang around an MC."

"Guess so." He took a step back. "Everything else is pretty easy. Just like a bike. Rev her up. Let's hear the growl."

For a split second, Isa's face blanked, but then she did as commanded. Her right hand twisted, the engine rumbling in response. He nodded approvingly. "All right, show-off. Think you're ready for some real practice?"

By now, several prospects and club members, including Reaper, had gathered around to watch the newbie. They were all eager to see if she'd biff it.

No pressure, princess.

Isa grabbed the helmet off the back and snapped it in place. "Might as well."

"I'll be right here if you need me." He jerked a thumb behind him. "We all will."

A flash of panic spread over her face, but she covered it up fast and slid the kickstand out of the way. Surprisingly, she held the bike up without any help. She was a natural if he'd ever seen one. *Like father like daughter.*

In an instant, she was rolling across the large lot. "Bollocks, I'm actually doing it," he heard her mumble.

He walked alongside, hands hovering over the back in case of emergency. He'd let the damn motorcycle fall on him before he'd let her get hurt.

Isa accelerated, shifting as she did, and he started jogging to stay beside her. She glanced over to him and flashed him a bright smile. "Having trouble keeping up?"

"Nah, this is a cake walk."

Determination filled her face, and he instantly regretted the haughty words.

"In that case, let's pick up the pace."

Doc gulped hard when she shifted again, sprinting now to keep up. He wouldn't last much longer, and neither would the parking lot. She'd be out on the street in fifty yards.

"Isa...." He hoped his voice held the warning his stomach did.

She applied the brake and looked behind her. "Yes, Doc?"

The faux innocence in her voice coupled with the cute expression on her face and the batting of eyelashes behind her rose sunglasses ripped apart his control. He had to have her. She felt the same. He could read between the lines of her body language and words. Their roles in Macha were the only trouble.

Catching up to her, he hopped on the back and kissed her cheek. Before she could respond, he took over the controls and they sped down the street. Hoots from the clubhouse behind him caught his ear, but he wouldn't look back. He needed to focus on the road instead of the spry woman tempting his already hard cock.

"You don't have a clue what you do to me, do you?"

Isa gripped his thighs at the next turn. "No."

He bit down a vulgar response. Instead, he carefully placed her hands over his on the grips. "Take control, princess." She started to argue, so he nuzzled the nape of her neck. "Now."

Her delicate hands gradually took control of the motor-cycle. She slipped on the gears a few times, but he whispered in her ear how to fix it, and they continued down the road without any problems.

Sunlight peeked through the clouds, warming him beneath the leather jacket. They continued through Snowshoe, residents glancing their direction as they passed. He waved to the few people he knew and nodded politely to those he didn't.

"Take the next left," he instructed at the stoplight. "Then stop in the parking lot on the right."

Isa expertly took the turn and cut the engine after she pulled into the lot. Doc kept the bike up until she kicked down the stand. She stood and swung her leg over the bike, but before she could completely step away, he gripped her hips and settled her on his lap, facing him.

Her eyes darted up to him anxiously. "What's wrong?"

He shook his head. "Not a damn thing." He unbuckled her helmet, and her hair spilled out behind her. It was a thing of beauty to watch the golden locks flow in the breeze.

"You sure you've never driven a motorcycle before?"

"A moped, sure, but I tend to pick things up pretty fast." She rubbed her lips together. "Always been this way."

Doc reached up and pulled the sunglasses away, her gray eyes now staring at him intently. "You're good. I'll bet Macha patches you before month's end."

She laughed, the sound infinitely better when it vibrated through to him. Isa slid her hands up his chest and tugged on the shirt beneath it. "And what if they do?"

"I'll gladly ride bitch with you any day."

Her eyes widened in surprise. "Why would you do that?

He cupped her cheeks. "Because then I can smell you, touch you"—his thumbs parted her lips—"and kiss you."

A wispy sigh escaped her before his lips descended on hers. Softly at first, their mouths connected. He tangled his fingers through her hair, pulling her closer to him. Isa responded quickly, opening her mouth and moaning at the connection of their tongues. He deepened the kiss, never getting enough of her. She tasted as sweet as he imagined, her soft lips only outdone by her candy tongue.

Isa scooted up his lap, his cock alive with the thought of having nothing between her bare body and him. She looped her arms around his neck and rubbed against him, teasing him further. For a virgin, she seemed to know her way around a man. He wasn't complaining one bit. Not now that he knew the connection between them wasn't one-sided.

She whimpered when he pulled away. He gently grazed her mouth with his thumb. Her lips were swollen from their recent act, her eyelids still closed. He'd have to go easy with her. She couldn't be taken hard and rough. At least not yet. Isa wasn't ready for him. *But I'll get her ready.*

Doc kissed the side of her neck. "We better get inside before I decide to take you right here on my bike."

She gasped, and he looked up in time to see her worried expression.

"Don't worry, princess. I'll go slow." He lifted her off the seat and couldn't help but notice her shaky knees.

"If a woman doesn't get a little weak in the knees, you aren't kissing her right," his old man told him once.

Well, he was damn sure he'd kissed Isa right.

"Where are we?"

Doc grabbed her hand and led her to the door. "A little project I like to do every once in a while when I don't have Macha duties."

Isa slipped in and stopped at the threshold to glance around the room. "This is a clinic."

"Yep, sure is." He strode past her and greeted the receptionist. "Hey, Laurie. Anything I can help out with today?"

The young receptionist sat up a little straighter and pushed her chest out. Too many women were drawn to the club members, Laurie no exception. "That'd be great." She handed him a stack of files, then looked behind him. "Who's she?"

Doc noticed Isa standing anxiously nearby. She looked completely out of place. "A friend." He saw Laurie scowl but didn't address it. He and the receptionist had shaken desk drawers several times over the past six months. Today, though, he didn't feel anything for her.

Isa's eyes slowly scanned him. *And she's the reason why.*

Turning around, he jerked his head to the hallway. Thankfully, Isa followed without him having to utter a word. Once they were in a small patient room, she opened her pretty little mouth.

"Why are we here? You aren't a doctor. That's just your MC name, right?"

He rifled through the first file, not ready to divulge his entire life story. "Technically, no, I'm not a doctor, but I've worked as a paramedic long enough to help with stitches and such." He grabbed the next folder. "And my MC name has a different story."

"What do you mean *technically*?"

He opened the door and called for the little boy and his mother to come back. "Watch and find out."

14

—

ISA

Isa sat on the rolling stool, eyes intent on watching everything Doc did. He was incredible. Not once did he lose his cool with the patients. He spoke in a soothing voice to the nine-year-old who needed stitches after falling off his skateboard and cracked jokes with an elderly woman when it came time to draw blood. He never flinched when someone commented on his Macha tattoos or his long hair. She hadn't seen the Macha emblem on him before. The dark ink looked new, and she immediately wondered when he'd gotten it.

Over the next two hours, Doc helped fifteen patients who couldn't afford a regular emergency room or walk-in clinic. By the time they were through, Isa could only stare at him in awe. He was much more than a shaggy-haired biker.

"You ready to go?"

She blinked to clear her vision. All she could see was

Doc and the gentle way he treated everyone he came across —his brothers excluded. "Um, yes."

He waved goodbye to the woman at the front desk. Someone she wasn't particularly fond of given the way the woman ogled Doc. Isa hurried to catch up, and the bell above the door rang their exit.

"You're a doctor," she stated instead of asked once they reached his motorcycle.

He straddled the bike and handed her the helmet. "No. I didn't finish medical school."

"Why not?"

"My mom needed me." He glanced to the busy street. "She had cancer and no one to help her."

"You gave up your career for her." Isa's eyes watered. She would've done the same had her mother been given more time. The untimely death barely gave her time to mourn let alone accept it.

"And I'd do it again." He managed a small smile. "Family will always be there for you. A career won't."

She took a step closer and accepted the helmet. "That's why you came to Colorado. To Macha. Because your uncle asked."

He nodded and started the bike. "Yep." She hopped on the back before he added, "And I'm damn glad I did. I don't want to think about what one of the other guys would've done if they were assigned to your protection detail."

She wrapped her arms around his waist and pressed a kiss to the back of his neck. "Me neither."

They reached the clubhouse in record time, Snowshoe

passing in a blur. The fact that she didn't care where they went but only that Doc was with her didn't help her management of time either. The scenery was gorgeous but not as much as what she was imagining. She could see them years from now, Doc running his own clinic while she designed clothes and sold them in the Macha stores.

Isa frowned and unlaced her arms from his waist before they parked. It was all make-believe. None of it would happen. Even if one of them moved, he was a patch member with Macha. Given his parentage, he'd be in the club for life. *Even if he transferred to the Belfast chapter, could I live with that as my life?*

"About time, Doc. We thought you skipped town," Hawk teased from the porch of the clubhouse.

She shielded her eyes and recognized Cueball, Snoopy, and Legs in the shade as well.

Doc rested her helmet on the seat and shrugged. "I wouldn't do that without beating you at pool first," he replied with an easy smile.

"Psh, like you could," Cueball taunted.

"And I'll bet your dick is just as small as your hands," Doc teased, causing their small group to howl with laughter. Evidently, it was more true than false.

"Fuck off," Cueball said, flipping him the bird.

Doc leaned against the porch railing. "That's not what your sister said last night."

Snoopy and Legs added a few less-than-endearing insults to both parties before Brewer and Rubble joined the group, twelve-packs of beer in hand.

Isa walked toward the door, the show of manliness suddenly unappealing. Doc acted sweet and gentle with her, but around the club he was just like them. It annoyed her somewhat. *Which Doc is real?*

Slipping inside, she breathed a sigh of relief when she no longer heard Doc or his MC brothers. "Life was so much easier in Ireland."

She sank onto the mattress in her room in time for her phone to ring with a video chat. Answering, she grinned at the sight of her two best friends on the other end. "Thank God, friendly faces."

Orla's eyebrows shot to her hairline. "What's wrong?"

A tear slid down her cheek. "I miss you. I miss home."

"It'll be all right, lass," Niall attempted to console her. "You'll be home before you know, and then you'll be wishing you were in Colorado instead of Ireland."

"Yeah, plus, the weather here has been so crappy lately," Orla added. "You're lucky to get away for a bit."

"Oh, I forgot to tell you. Mrs. Stapleton actually ate one of the candles in the shop." Niall shook his head. "The old loon thought the cupcake mold was real. She threw one hell of a fit when it tasted like wax instead of cherry fudge."

Isa chuckled and wiped away her tears. Her best friends could always cheer her up. "All right, all right, you convinced me. I'm in the right place for the time being."

Orla took over the frame. "Is there anything else bothering you?" Her brown eyes searched Isa's. "Are they treating you well?"

"If they're not, I'll kick all their arses," Niall called from the shop counter.

Orla rolled her eyes. "Aye, love, you could totally take on Macha bikers and live to tell the tale."

Propping a pillow behind her back, Isa wished she could reach across the phone and give her friends a giant hug. They'd do anything for her and vice versa. "Well, there's this guy, and he—"

"Niall, pack a bag. We've a dumbass to kick in the bollocks."

"No, no, nothing like that," she rushed to say. "He's nice. Sweet even." Isa scratched her head. "Just a little different when he's with the other MC members."

Orla stopped yelling travel plans to her husband. "Hold the phone. Are you saying you like him? As in *like* like him?"

She slowly nodded, warmth flooding her cheeks. In all their years as friends, she'd never had a steady boyfriend. Dates now and then, but no man who ever made her heart leap.

"Ah." Orla put her finger to her lips and walked out of the room. Only once she closed the door behind her did she speak. "Tell me everything."

"It's nothing."

"Psh, poppycock." Orla plopped into the office chair and positioned the phone on the desk so she could type on her laptop. "What's his name?'

"Orla...."

"Isa...."

Nothing would keep her best friend from uncovering her crush, so Isa gave his club name and last name.

Orla's fingers flew across the keyboard, eyes strict on the screen. "He's from Iowa?"

"Yeah but moved here to help his uncle."

More clicking from the other end. "And Reaper's nephew? Oh, I think I found a photo on Macha's website."

Isa parted her lips to answer, but Orla was already ahead of her.

"Holy damn, he's hot." Her brown eyes flicked to Isa. "Girl, he's extremely good-looking. I mean, I don't usually like the tattooed vibe, but dang, this Doc guy makes it look sexy."

"You have no idea."

Orla sat back, a knowing grin on her pale face. "Ooh, do tell. Has he kissed you?"

"Well—"

"Shite, he has!" She sat forward, eyes alight. "Was it good?"

Isa thought back to the kiss on the motorcycle. She'd been kissed before, of course, but the way Doc kissed made it seem like the first time she'd had a *real* one. "Better than any other."

"That's not saying much." She snorted. "So, what're you going to do?"

"I'm not sure." Isa swung her eyes to the ceiling fan slowly oscillating above her. Doc's scent clung in the air, the fan a new form of torture. "You know I've never.... I mean...." She couldn't say the words out loud. She'd never said them. But her friends knew.

"Does he know?"

"I think so. He's protective of me. It's rather charming."

"How so?"

Isa thought back over the past two weeks. "Well, he stood up for me when a few of the MC members were checking me out. Then he stopped me from making a fool out of myself when I got too drunk." She smiled whimsically. "And of course, he's usually never more than a hundred feet away. Even slept in my room a few times."

Orla covered a smile behind her fist, but Isa saw it anyway. "That's really sweet, hon, but isn't his job to protect you?"

"Aye, but—"

"Everything you've said is him doing exactly that."

"What about the kiss, then?"

Sighing, she went back to her keyboard. "You're gorgeous, Isa. Any man would count himself lucky to be in the same postal code as you. But that doesn't mean he feels anything other than animalistic attraction." She bit her bottom lip, face concerned. "Unless you ask him straight out, I wouldn't bank on him being your happily ever after."

"Then you think I'm reading too much into our interactions?"

Orla shrugged. "I'm not there. From what you've told me about the club and from my research online—because I've literally nothing else to do while you're on holiday—if

Doc lets anything happen to you, he's as good as dead to Macha."

Her friend's perception hit Isa hard. She'd concocted a fairy tale when none existed. At least none she could verify. "You're right." She forced a smile. "I'm being silly."

"I'd never say that. Just be careful, all right? I don't want to see your heart broken by some badass biker."

Niall came into the frame. "Love, Mr. Patterson is back, and apparently I'm not feminine enough to help him."

Orla chuckled and blew her a kiss. "Better go help. Love you, sis."

"You too." She sighed as the video call disconnected. She could almost hear ornery Mr. Patterson demanding one of the "pretty ladies" help him with his weekly purchases. He was one of their regular customers, and despite seeing Niall every week, the old man preferred Isa's or Orla's help.

Rolling to her stomach, Isa scanned social media on her phone. Most of her friends were having a dandy summer whereas she was stuck in Colorado with a man who may or may not like her in more than an "animalistic" way, as Orla suggested.

Tearing off her sweatshirt, she snuggled under the covers. For the time being, she'd take a nap and hope that by the time she woke, Doc would be a distant memory.

AN HOUR LATER, SHE WOKE TO THE SOUND OF A LIGHT knock on her door.

"Isa, you in here?"

"No."

Doc opened the door and chuckled. "You have quite the doppelgänger, then." He stepped inside the room and leaned against the door to close it. His tall stature and wide shoulders filled the doorway while his leather-and-musk scent overpowered the vanilla cupcake candle on the bedside table. It was one of the items from her shop she had to bring.

"What do you want, Doc?" She sat up and the sheet fell down her chest. The cool air hit her tank top, and she rushed to cover her braless state. She hadn't expected any visitors.

His eyes dipped to her chest, and he ran his fingers through his overgrown hair, swiping it to the right side of his head. Her fingers itched to replace his, but she'd resist and keep her horny arse on the bed. She couldn't endure rejection if she was off base.

"I, uh, wanted to make sure you were okay before I headed to the bar. You missed dinner, and I was worried about you."

"I'm fine." She yawned and grabbed her phone. New posts from Orla and Niall caught her eye. They were stupidly adorable on their social media accounts.

Boots shuffled to the bed, and she felt his weight sink into the mattress. Flicking her eyes to him, she swallowed hard at his probing stare.

"Are you, Isa?" He placed his right arm on the other side of the bed, trapping her between his body and arm. "If you're freaked out because of the kiss—"

"It's fine. Your job is to protect me." She stared at the green Celtic knot tattoo on his forearm. "Sometimes lines get blurred."

Doc gently gripped her chin, forcing her eyes to return to his baby blues. "That's what you think the kiss was? Blurred lines?"

She didn't answer. She couldn't. Not with him close enough to touch and her traitorous body wanting her to do that and so much more to him.

He stroked her cheek with his knuckles, sending a delightful shiver down her spine. She couldn't look away if she wanted. His perfect eyes paralyzed her.

"I don't kiss women on a whim." His fingers curled in her long hair, bunching it in his muscular hand enough to control her movements. "And I never blur lines, Isa. I take my job seriously, no matter what it is."

She tried to nod, but his hold wouldn't allow it. "Okay."

Leaning down, Doc nuzzled his nose to her neck, inhaling deeply. "At least not until I met you. I don't know what it is about you, but I can't get enough."

His words ignited a spark in the pit of her stomach. The throbbing of her pulse echoed in her ears, and she desperately needed him to explain.

"I wanted you the first moment I saw you, princess." He searched her face. "But not only because you're the most gorgeous woman on the fucking planet."

Her heart jumped. He couldn't be saying what she thought. *Could he?*

"Then why?"

Doc laced his free hand in hers. "You woke me up, and I never want to sleep again unless it's in your arms."

Those final sentiments fanned her fire for him. Even if was merely a line, she didn't give a toss. She closed the minimal distance between their lips and gasped at the force behind their connection. His hands were everywhere at once. His left hand trailed down her body, making small circles on her hip while his right hand cupped the base of her neck, bringing her closer to him.

Doc climbed on the bed and Isa wrapped her legs around his waist, their lips never leaving each other's. His tongue teased the seam of her mouth, and she greedily allowed him entry. She moaned at the entwining of their tongues, threading her fingers through his blond hair. She roughly yanked it and shivered at his growl.

He sat up, taking her with him, and continued kissing her. Isa's eyes fluttered open when he broke free long enough to nip her neck and then return to her mouth. She gasped in surprise, and he grinned. His large hand encompassed her breast and kneaded gently. Sparks of desire shot through her body the more he touched her, and her kisses became frantic when he pinched her nipple.

Using his weight against him, Isa pressed his back into the bed, straddling him. The solid muscle beneath her frightened her for a split second, but when she met his eyes, all anxiety disappeared.

She playfully shoved back his cut and slipped her hands beneath his T-shirt. The defined divots on his stomach tempted her to explore more. Sure enough, he had bundles of muscles up his chest and on his shoulders.

Curious now, she lifted his shirt and noticed the intricate artwork on his body. They were masterpieces. Leaning down, she kissed the Roman numerals. "Six fourteen?"

He touched the tattoo. "Yeah. It's my mom's birthday." His eyes clouded. "Ironically, it's also when she died."

"Oh, Doc." She studied the double meaning. "I'm sorry."

"Me too." His index finger traced her mouth, then down her neck. He stopped at her neckline. "She would've liked you. All fire and sass." He chuckled. "Just enough to keep me in place."

"I doubt that." She rolled her eyes, and he tangled his fingers through her long hair, pulling tightly.

"Whenever you roll your eyes like that, I want to bend you over my knee and punish you."

Her breathing hitched. The idea sounded naughty and exactly what her body craved. "Then do it."

His brows rose and he chuckled, releasing her. "Sweetheart, that'll only turn me on more. I don't think you're ready for that."

Taking the lead, she climbed off the bed and slowly dropped her yoga pants to the floor, then flicked them away with her toes. Undressing even partially in front of a man never came easily for her. She'd done it a time or two, but nothing ever went beyond foreplay.

When she looked up, her nerves jumbled at his gaze. It was a combination of longing and restraint, one she'd never seen in a man before. Standing in only a tank top and panties under his scrutiny caused her nipples to harden to points beneath the cotton.

Doc shifted to sit at the edge of the bed. He kept his hands at his sides, eyes giving away how difficult it was for him to do exactly that.

Summoning her courage, Isa rested her torso over his knees, giving him the ideal view of her backside. She looked up at him. "Is this what you wanted?"

He let out a strangled groan. "Fuck yes, but, Isa—"

"Punish me, Doc."

Her words bolstered his movements. Before she could register his intent, he slid down her panties and his palm connected with her arse. Her eyes widened. The pain singed for a moment but gave way to a new sensation between her legs.

She met his lust-glazed eyes at the same moment he let another whack fly. A giggle bubbled up, and she slapped a hand over her mouth at his stern glare. She yelped at the next spanking, but her desire superseded the discomfort. Three. That was all it took for her to be addicted to the erotic pain.

Doc rubbed her cheeks one at a time, warming the imprints from his hand before he gently pulled her up and into his lap. His erection pressed against his jeans and to the front of her red panties. Images of feeling him with nothing in between filtered through her hazy mind.

"I think you enjoyed that as much as I did." She nodded and he chuckled. "Every time I catch you rolling those stunning gray eyes, expect a repeat of this."

She licked her lips at the thought, and he palmed her ass. "Doc, I want you—"

"Not yet," he interrupted, shaking his head.

"Why not?"

After kissing the tip of her nose, he pulled her against his chest. "You're not ready."

"Is it because I'm inexperienced—" she started, but he kissed her into silence.

When he finally pulled away, he tucked her hair behind her ears. "You're special, Isa, and you deserve to be treated like a princess. I'd never let any woman's first time with a man be in a clubhouse full of horny bikers." He nipped her top lip. "I want you all to myself. No one else deserves to hear you come."

Goose bumps scattered along her skin, his words only sealing their fate. "When are we moving to the lodge?"

Doc hugged her tight and kissed the top of her head. "Soon enough, princess. Then you're all mine."

15

———

ISA

TIPPING BACK THE TUMBLER OF WHISKEY, ISA LEANED back and eyed Dolly and the nymphs. They'd invited her for a little midday fun while the men were at church. Seeing how friends were limited, she'd agreed. It was better than waiting for the hunky biker who she couldn't get off her mind.

Now, an hour later, she was sipping on something strong while she watched the door.

Ever since their lips met, she desired him. Even if only to touch his muscular arms or trace his elaborate tattoos. She may have been under Macha protection, but she wanted to be *under* Doc more.

A blush crossed her face, and she took a large gulp of the alcohol.

"Oh, looks like somebody's thinking about our Doc," Dolly teased, hopping up on the bar top.

The move from the clubhouse to the bar came after

Brewer asked for help organizing the recent deliveries to the bar that pulled him out of church early. Naturally, the nymphs wanted no part of that manual labor, but they were fond of the man himself, so they'd kept themselves busy while two prospects helped Brewer.

Dolly swung her legs like a pendulum over the side. Her short black skirt was hiked to her upper thigh, showing off plenty of skin. It hit her then that she'd never seen Dolly with any of the members. *I wonder if she's gay.* When the tattoo-covered woman leaned over and kissed a prospect full on the mouth, Isa disregarded her previous thought. Of course, it didn't matter what orientation Dolly was. She was as close to a friend as Isa would get in Colorado.

Isa finished her drink and brought the empty glass to the bar. "Perhaps, but don't tell him." She smirked and leaned her elbows on the bar top. "He'll get a big head."

"Girl, please, he already has a big head." Dolly snorted. "Don't believe me, ask any of my nymphs."

Turning around, Isa studied the array of Macha nymphs. They were all shapes and sizes, but none as tall as her. It didn't happen too often in her experience.

"He's been with all of them?"

Dolly jumped off the bar and patted Isa's shoulder. "Aw, sweetie, that's what the nymphs are for. They keep the bikers sated." She jutted her chin toward the redheaded nymph practicing a dance routine on an empty table. "At least until they find an old lady. Even then, some Macha members have open relationships."

The mere mention made Isa's pulse skyrocket. *I have a*

lot to learn about Macha. The television shows about bikers weren't based on this club. Most people preferred the rough bikers like the ones she'd heard of in Ireland.

Isa shook her head. Not her. She'd much rather learn about Macha. From her short time with them, the MC showed her that all bikers weren't scoundrels.

"'Old lady' sounds so derogative," Isa said, handing the glass to Brewer. He eyed her, then refilled it before returning to his duties.

"Oh, but it's not." Dolly pulled her away from the bar and toward a booth. "Being an old lady means your man values you above any other girl." She grinned. "It means you're in a committed relationship."

"So, then it's the same as being married?"

"Not always, but sometimes. Macha promotes marriage but doesn't tie her members to the tradition unless both parties want it. My parents weren't married, but that didn't stop them from being fully committed to each other until death."

Isa sipped on the whiskey, letting the liquid burn her throat. Already two tumblers in, she was feeling the effects of day drinking.

Dolly kept chattering about Macha's take on marriage and relationships, but she wasn't listening anymore. *I wonder if Doc wants an open relationship or if he'd be satisfied with just one woman.*

She chewed her bottom lip and watched a prospect turn on the jukebox in the corner. A rock and roll song filled the bar, and two nymphs hopped on a tabletop and started grinding on each other. The two prospects stopped what they were doing and watched the girls dance. Brewer smacked them on the back of their heads when he caught them gawking, and the two scrambled to busy themselves.

Isa smirked at Brewer, and he offered her a wink. Out of all the bikers, he was the least intimidating. With a full head of red hair, he didn't have the typical biker look. *Well, at least here.* She'd seen plenty of redheaded bikers on the isle. She watched him hurry behind the bar. He was the sweetest too. Never talked down to anyone. That she saw, anyway.

"He went to jail, you know," Dolly said, cutting into Isa's thoughts.

She turned toward her. "Brewer?"

"Yep."

"When? Why?"

"When we were teenagers, Brewer used to sneak out at night and race motorcycles." Dolly smiled, her memories clearly flooding her mind. "Sometimes, I'd go too just to egg him on and check out the competition."

"Sounds innocent enough. What happened?" Isa finished off her drink and squinted at the new glass full of whiskey waiting for her. *A prospect must've dropped it off.* She shrugged and took a drink.

"He and another guy got into it. Brewer said he cheated on the last lap, and with no one to doubt him, they started scuffling. The cops showed up and tossed him in jail for the night." Dolly gathered her hair into a ponytail. "The next morning, our dad whooped his ass so bad he couldn't sit for a week. It was kinda funny."

"Who was the other guy?" She held her breath, somehow already knowing the answer.

"Doc."

"Lovely." Isa threw back the shot of whiskey. "Can't say I'm surprised. He seems like the type to get into fights."

"Only when it matters." She waved at a prospect, and he brought a bottle of whiskey to the table.

"I shouldn't," Isa protested when the glass was filled to the top.

"But you will." Dolly tossed back the drink and wiped her mouth with the back of her hand. "Drink, then we'll dance. I think I can teach you a few things that'd help you snare your Macha man."

THE DIM LIGHTS OF THE BAR SEEMED BRIGHTER AFTER two more shots. Locals started pouring into the room, and lively music drowned out her better sense. Dolly tried and failed to teach her about dirty dancing. Evidently, the old movie wasn't so *dirty* by today's standards, which meant she was royally flushed.

"Hey, beautiful, what're you up to?"

His voice washed down her back, his chest against her hair. A shiver shot straight to the spot between her legs, and she slowly craned her neck to meet Doc's stunning blue eyes. They were even more glorious after a few drinks.

"Taking a breather after Dolly gave me a dancing lesson." She cocked her head. "How was church?"

Doc rested his left hand on the bar and positioned his body between her and the next barstool. "Same shit. I should be grateful. Better than new shit." He nodded his thanks to Brewer when he set a beer in front of him. "So dancing, huh?" he asked after taking a drink of the dark Guinness. "Didn't you get enough of that the other week?"

Isa thought back to her second night in Colorado. She'd managed to slip away from Queenie and down several very needed drinks. "That was to let off steam." She stood and grabbed his hand. "But this was for fun. Want to see my new moves?"

He glanced around the bar, uncertainty painted on his face. "Princess, you nearly caused a riot the last time you shook your ass." He pointed to her jeans. "And in those, you just might tonight."

"The only riot I want is with you," she said under her breath. Doc's gaze snapped to her and she giggled, pulling him toward the dance floor. If he'd heard, he didn't let on.

Her anxiety momentarily subsided. She wasn't a flirt. At least not a good one.

A popular country tune blared through the speakers, and she wasted no time summoning her eighties-themed moves. Swaying her hips to the tempo, she rested her arms on his shoulders. Doc's eyes darted to their audience, and she gritted her teeth. He was more concerned for her safety. She should have been glad he was so attentive. Instead, all she craved was his attention to her body.

Looping her arms around his neck, Isa forced his eyes to return to her. "Don't you dance, Doc?"

"Not if I can help it."

She turned around and grinded her arse against his jeans. Already, she felt his cock come alive beneath the denim. A shot of desire ran up her spine, and she locked her hands behind his head, deepening the connection.

"You sure that's a good idea, princess?" he said gruffly. He gripped her hips, trying to stop her suggestive moves, but she only tried harder to tempt him.

She spun around and rolled her eyes. His reaction was well worth the act. "Aye, very sure."

His blue eyes darkened. "Isa, I'm warning you."

She leaned forward to kiss him, but Doc stepped back before they could connect. "We can't. Not here," he said quietly.

Pouting, Isa clenched her jaw and moved farther into the throng of nearby dancers. "Well, I'm not done yet, so I guess you can wait."

"You know I don't like to wait."

"And you know I like to dally."

She spotted a single man dancing and moved in his direction. Tossing a glance over her shoulder, she swallowed a giggle at the expression on her biker's face. It was borderline murderous. The man, slightly taller than her, didn't waste any time. He grabbed her hips and pulled her flush to him, gyrating his hips along with her arse. Never had she felt naughtier or more empowered.

"Isa."

She heard Doc's rumbled warning but ignored it.

The song changed to up-tempo rock, and she grinned at her unnamed dance partner. It didn't matter who she danced with. Doc would be watching, and if he was too ashamed to kiss her or dance with her in front of his brothers, then she'd make him suffer a little.

The man smelling of cheese and ale slid his hands down her hips and to her arse. She didn't have a chance to correct him before Doc's large body came into view. With one swift move, he swung her over his shoulder and swatted her left arse cheek.

"What the feck!" She yelped, but it was drowned out by manly laughter. She narrowed her gaze to the table full of club members and opened her mouth to curse them.

Doc walked out of the bar before she could spew one word. She gasped at the unusually cool rain pelting her exposed back.

"That's bloody cold, you wanker."

A low growl emitted from Doc, and she swallowed hard. He set her on the gravel, and she shoved at his attempt to grab her again.

"You can't disregard my words." His brows furrowed together, frustration evident on his face. "The men in that bar...." He shook his head. "They don't care if you're Macha royalty. You're not a member's old lady either. No patch is on your shirt, so all they see is a tight ass, perky boobs, and plump, dick-sucking lips."

His brash words startled her, sending her a step backward. She pushed her rain-plastered hair out of her face. "I'm fair game unless you're going to claim me."

A vein in his neck bulged. "I can't do that, Isa."

She closed the distance between them and poked his chest. "Why not?"

"It's complicated."

"Bullshit. You don't want to—" His lips overwhelmed hers in response. A surprised gasp escaped her, and he picked her up off the ground, this time gently. She looped her arms around his neck and kissed him back, rain splashing on them but neither caring. His tongue invaded her mouth, and Isa matched his frantic act with her own, relishing the tangling of their lips.

"Not here," he rasped, pulling away. His eyes looked nearly midnight, lust rimming the blue. He didn't bother to wait for a response, merely carried her to the clubhouse and to her room. Once the door closed, he pushed her back against it, fingers working beneath her shirt.

Not wasting any time, Isa yanked on his shirt and shivered at the delicious muscles her fingers traced. "Holy shit, you're ripped."

He grinned and tossed his tee to the floor. She stood in adoring silence, taking in the sheer mass of the man in front of her. He was handsome, sure, but his body screamed dedication to a workout routine. The lines that went from his hips underneath his jeans made her flare with heat. *Feck a Greek Adonis. An Irish Doc's better.*

She swallowed the fear his muscles ignited in her. He could snap her neck so easily. *But he won't.* That realization summoned her forward. Her lips hovered at his, their heights ideal for kissing. No other man could make her tall stature appear small.

Doc's hands easily stripped her shirt off and tossed it to the floor. His breathing hitched at her green bra. His knuckles slowly traced the swells of her breasts, her heart pounding beneath his touch.

"Your skin's so soft. I'm afraid I'll hurt you."

Covering his hand over her breast, she met his gaze. "You can't hurt me, Doc. I'm not a porcelain doll. I won't break."

He offered a slight smile. "Isa, you should know I'm not exactly the 'sweet and tender lover' type. I like to get rough, as you already experienced."

"How rough?" A tinge of fear trickled back to her. Never being with a man suddenly sent her nerves into a nosedive.

Doc tilted her chin up with his index finger. "Not as rough as I'm sure you're imagining, but more than you should have for your first time."

Her heart sank. "I was hoping you wouldn't figure that out."

"Babe, give me a little credit." He smirked. "I want you, Isa. I want you so fucking bad it physically hurts."

"But—"

"But I want you to be ready. One hundred and ten percent ready." He searched her eyes. "Because once I have you, princess, I'll want you every chance I get. I don't think you're ready for that. Are you?"

Isa worried her lips together and lowered her gaze. Her body told her she was ready, but her heart disagreed. "Maybe not." She sighed. "But I want to be."

Gently tugging on her bra strap, he led her to the bed. "Then let's get you ready, yeah?"

She nodded and followed him. "What do you want me to do?"

Doc propped his head up on his hand. "Tell me about yourself, Isa."

"What?" She smiled. "What do you mean?"

"Well, I'd like to learn more about you."

He was content to merely lie on her bed shirtless, displaying his ornate canvas of skin.

Getting to know each other was a good idea. She wasn't sure why they hadn't before.

"All right. I grew up in a very Catholic family."

Doc snapped his fingers. "There it is. That's why you're such a naughty girl."

She rolled her eyes. "Yeah, yeah, smartarse."

He chuckled. "Go on."

"It was Mum and me for the most part. Well, and Niall and Orla."

"Your friends?"

She smiled reminiscently. "They were always there for me. It's odd to be away from them even for a short amount of time."

"I can understand that." He kicked off his boots, clearly ready to stay all night. "Have you always wanted to design clothes?"

"Well, no. There was a time I thought for certain I'd be a model."

"You could definitely pass for one." His eyes dipped over her, and she immediately remembered she was half naked. Somehow, it didn't bother her. The slight chill in the room, on the other hand, did. She rolled off the bed and grabbed a sweatshirt, pulling it on fast.

"Mum and I spent a lot of time outside. She loved to garden. I'm not the best at it, honestly. Sketching and designing I learned quickly." She sat opposite him on the bed. "Once Orla found her niche in candle and soap making, it fell together."

"Where does Niall fit in?"

Isa thought back to her two best friends. "Niall is our finance whiz. His family comes from money, so he set us up with the shop. Orla lived with me in the flat above it until she and Niall got together. Orla had a huge crush on him, but the twat didn't make his move until she was almost in love with someone else."

"Timing is everything."

She met his eyes. "I suppose it is." Silence simmered momentarily. She wasn't sure how much to tell him about her life in Ireland. Even if they had an iota of a chance, she didn't want to scare him off with tales of her secondary school adventures.

"Your friends sound nice. You're lucky to have them."

"I really am, but enough about me. I'm boring." She crossed her legs. "What about you?" she asked, turning the tables. "What's your given first name?"

Sitting up slightly, he lowered his voice. "Tad, though nobody but my mom has ever called me by it."

Her brows shot up on both accounts. "Tad? As in tadpole?"

Doc cursed under his breath, a smile lining his lips. "Something like that. I'm just glad Macha gave me a different club name. I doubt I could pull off Tadpole and make it fierce."

She leaned over and kissed him softly. "I think you could, but I am interested in how you got your MC name."

For the next hour, Isa and Doc exchanged stories about their lives. She finally understood his biker name and commended him for his valiant behavior. *He's more than a biker or paramedic. He's good all the way to his soul.*

A loud ruckus woke her in the middle of the night. Thankfully, Doc heard it too, and they both sat up in bed. The sheets were rumpled but their clothing intact.

"Go back to sleep, princess," Doc said, pulling on his boots. "It's the guys being dumbasses." He stood and walked to the door. "I'll be back. Don't go anywhere."

"I couldn't if I tried."

He smiled in the dark, and Isa settled into the warm comforter once he closed the door behind him. They'd fallen asleep sometime after talking about university. His cologne on the pillow beside her made returning to dreamland impossible. She needed him beside her now. Sleeping by herself felt lonely.

Bugger, I've gone and fallen for him.

16

——

DOC

"Everybody shut it!" Shovelhead roared above the chatter in the large room.

One by one, the MC members clammed up and looked to the head of the table. The VP's beady eyes stared them down until there was complete silence.

Doc sat back in his chair on the opposite end, waiting for the president to speak. The last-minute church session was called due to an emergency from their Belfast location. The thought made him queasy from the moment he heard it. *Can't be good news.*

"All right," Reaper began. "Phantom and the boys are still fending off the Twelve Brothers."

A unison grunt resounded from the members. Shovelhead glared at the group, silencing them immediately. Doc studied the VP warily. Shovelhead never gave him a good vibe, but then again, he barely knew the old biker. Each

Macha member had skeletons. So long as they didn't destroy the future, their past could stay buried.

Reaper stood and flipped on the large television at the front of the room. Phantom sat waiting on the other side. "The situation has elevated exponentially. I'll let Phantom get you boys up to date."

Phantom nodded, eyes weary and grim. "The Twelve Brothers know about my daughter, Isadora." He looked at each member and held up a message. The ink looked like blood.

"Tick tock, Phantom, your crew's weak. We'll have your lass within the week," Reaper read aloud.

"As you can see, they're coming for my daughter."

Doc's heart dropped to his stomach. Every eye fastened on him.

"I trust she's been taken care of." Phantom's tone conveyed a skeptical father.

"Isa is safe and well protected," Reaper advised, not giving Doc the opportunity to confirm it himself.

A weight seemed to momentarily lift from the Irishman's shoulders. He wiped a weathered hand over his face. "Good. I'd come over myself, but...."

"We'll deliver her safe once this is finished," Rubble said. As the sergeant at arms, he'd oversee the fight should the Twelve Brothers truly make the flight for Isa.

Their president nodded in agreement. "Worry not, brother. We'll take care of her." He glanced to Doc. "I have my nephew on her protection detail. He's been very attentive to your girl."

Doc swallowed hard at the high praise. While his uncle meant every word, it also came with a double meaning.

Snoopy shot him a knowing look. The dickhead's old lady probably knew more about his relationship with Isa than Doc cared to admit. It didn't matter in the long run. He was tasked to keep Isa safe, and that was exactly what he was doing.

"We'll be ready for them," Rubble added before Reaper finished the video call.

The members began talking once more, business not pleasure this time. Macha had a job to do, and they wouldn't rest until it was done. It was one of the draws to the MC for Doc. His father had conveyed the same throughout his young life, and he couldn't turn his back on his brothers.

Despite being the newest member, he was quickly roped into Rubble's strategy. The man was always prepared and had a plan drawn up before they finished church. By the end, Doc was confident Macha would keep Isa safe. Every member was about to risk their life for one of their own. It was the Macha way, and one he was proud to be part of now more than ever.

Now to tell Isa.

"WHAT'S GOING ON?" ISA SCOWLED AT HIM FROM HER perch on the bed. Her gray eyes were skeptical, head tilted to the side. In her oversized sweatshirt—*his* sweatshirt—and black leggings, she couldn't look more appealing unless she was stark naked.

"We're moving to the lodge. Prez's orders." He grabbed her suitcase and stuffed clothes into it.

"Ugh, you're doing it wrong." She slapped his hands away and unpacked the suitcase before she started folding the clothes.

Doc took a step back and reviewed the room. There wasn't much to take to the lodge.

His eyes landed on Isa carefully placing her belongings in the bag. If he wasn't in a hurry, he'd take advantage of that long braid of hers. Since tasting her the other night, he'd craved no other delicacy. Staying up half the night merely talking to the Irish beauty only solidified it for him. She wouldn't be anyone else's. Not if he had any say in the matter. She was too special, too pure, too unique to let a stranger change her.

He shook his head. His focus had to be on Rubble's plan. They needed to take Isa to the lodge immediately. According to Phantom, the Twelve Brothers would figure out where Isa was within the week, and then they'd come for her. To Colorado. He didn't like the thought. The sooner Isa was safely behind armored doors, the better.

Once the bags were packed according to her standards, Doc hustled them to one of the MC trucks waiting in the parking lot. He tossed the luggage in the back and started the engine. The bright beams from the pickup lit up the dark sky. Klink and Cueball followed close behind in case

Phantom's intel was incorrect. *Better to have muscle in case of the worst.*

He cranked on the heat when he noticed her shivering in the passenger seat.

"Are you going to tell me why we're leaving the clubhouse this late?" she asked.

He eyed the clock on the dashboard. He hadn't noticed the time. After church, his sole purpose was getting Isa to safety.

"How much do you know about the rival MCs in Ireland?"

She shrugged. "Not much. Phantom mentioned an MC when I arrived. I can't remember much, to be honest. It was all a flurry of information, and then I was on a plane."

Doc gripped the steering wheel a little tighter. "The Twelve Brothers is another MC in Ireland. Macha and them never got along, but once your dad—er, Phantom took over, they started encroaching on our territory."

"And that's bad?"

"When Macha livelihood is put at risk, yes, very bad."

They passed an abandoned gas station and he noticed a sheriff on the side of the road. Boulder made sure to inform the local sheriff and police about the impending fight. Of course, the uniforms couldn't condone any firefight, but they'd help if the time came.

He glanced over to see Isa staring out the window, legs folded beneath her on the seat. "Why do they want me?"

"Because you'd be the perfect chess piece in their

fucked-up play for Northern Ireland." He turned onto the gravel road, their destination closing in.

"I barely know my fath—Phantom."

"Doesn't matter. They think you're his little princess and he would do anything for you."

She brushed her braid behind her back. "He would."

Doc noticed Hawk's chopper up ahead. Klink and Cueball were still right behind him. Snoopy had left a few minutes before them on the off chance anything went awry, but no call rang out over the CB radio in the truck, so they were clear all the way to the lodge.

"Then I guess they're right in targeting you." He met her gaze and cursed himself for speaking so candidly. "But you're safe. Macha will keep you safe." He reached over and squeezed her hand. "I will keep you safe."

The rumble of motorcycles got louder the closer they got to the lodge drive. He paused and rolled down his window. Hawk opened the gate and waved them through. They reached the top of the driveway in time to see Legs greet Snoopy.

"Looks like we won't be alone up here," Isa commented as Doc pulled into one of the garages and parked.

"Nope. We're on lockdown until we know what's going on." He grinned. "But don't worry. There's plenty of places here to get away from everyone else."

She didn't respond, but then again, when he glanced the same direction she was staring, he probably wouldn't either. Most of the members stood outside the lodge alongside their old ladies and families. He'd never seen the like of it before. Obviously they weren't waiting around for them, already unloading their shit for an undetermined length of stay at the mountain fortress.

Doc hustled out of the cab, and then opened her door.

"I'm putting everyone in danger."

Tilting up her chin, he shook his head. "It comes with the lifestyle, princess."

"But—"

"None of that. Macha is a family, and we protect our own." He grabbed her hand and guided her from the truck's warmth. Tucking her under his arm, he nodded to two prospects nearby to get her luggage.

Leading her through a side door, Doc managed to avoid the crowd. Once they were inside, he nodded to Queenie, Dolly, and a couple more women he didn't recognize. They were diligently working in the kitchen. Homemade bread from the smell of it.

Isa held tightly to his arm on the way up the stairs, and he feared she wouldn't be able to handle confinement in the lodge very long. Her past was filled with happiness and no hint of MC involvement. In a short amount of time, she'd learned about her father and the club he ran. If it were him, he'd be wary too.

Doc opened the bedroom door and was grateful to see her bed already made and waiting. "Hang on." He left her by the door and quickly checked the room. Even though he trusted his brothers, he wanted to ensure the room was safe himself. "Okay, all clear."

Isa closed the door behind her and slowly walked over

to him. "I'm scared," she said seconds before pressing her face into his chest. He didn't have to see the tears to understand the wetness on his shirt.

Cradling the back of her head, he rested his chin on her soft hair. "You're gonna be all right. I promise."

"I wish I had a different dad." She sniffled. "Or that he had a different job. I understand why Mum kept me away."

Doc's heart clenched at her words. He didn't know how to respond. His mother had gone along similar lines when his parents split. The difference was he grew up around Macha and knew his father's role in the club. There were no surprises for him. Isa's childhood was sheltered. Knowing her history, everything about her life was kept hidden—for good reason. Even before Phantom took over Belfast, he protected his daughter the only way he knew how.

"I know it seems rough right now, but we'll get through this." He held her at arm's length and searched for her gaze. Once it latched on to his, Doc felt his pulse quicken. Even crying, she was an angel. "It's late. Maybe you should get some sleep." He nodded to the bed. "We'll talk more in the morning."

She glanced at the bed, then back to him. "Will you stay with me?"

"Isa—"

"Please. At least until I fall asleep."

He could say her gray eyes swayed him to agree, but it wasn't true. He wasn't going anywhere if he could help it.

Isa was his responsibility, one he'd gladly take on any day of his life.

17

——

DOC

"Got another live one, Doc!"

Glancing up from the chessboard, Doc caught sight of Snoopy and Brewer heading his direction with a prospect loosely hanging between their shoulders. Blood soaked the prospect's face and dribbled down his shirt.

"Isa, I need to take care of this." He nodded to the board. "I know where my pieces are, so don't even think about cheating."

"Whatever you say, Doc."

That smug little smile on her face almost made him think twice about patching up the incoming man. But he wouldn't.

Standing, he met Snoopy and Brewer at the door. "Who'd our guy lose to?"

"Rubble."

He chuckled and followed the trio down the hallway to the makeshift clinic he'd set up right after arriving in

Snowshoe. There was one at the clubhouse too, but that one was better stocked and held medical equipment. The lodge clinic left much to be desired. He made a mental note to chat with Reaper about supplies. If a firefight made its way up the mountain, the club needed to be fully prepared.

Snoopy rested the prospect, a man in his early twenties, on the table while Brewer tugged the guy's shirt off. The man winced but didn't make a sound. Macha didn't promote fistfights, but the club also didn't discourage them.

"So, you thought it was a good idea to fuck with our sergeant at arms?" He inspected the cuts and purple bruises quickly forming.

The prospect shrugged. "A patch told me to."

Doc lifted his gaze to Snoopy, then Brewer. Either one could've prompted the newbie to start a fight he definitely wouldn't win. It was part of club life. The members often got their rocks off watching prospects earn their patches. He'd watched a time or two but would never pit anyone as scrawny as this prospect against the sheer mass of Rubble.

"How long you been with us?" he asked, threading a needle through the man's left brow. The gash wasn't too deep but would scar if left unattended.

"Three months."

Nodding, he finished the stitch and moved to the next cut on the man's shoulder blade. Typically, the prospects were given six to twelve months to patch. If they didn't, Prez could throw them out for failing to succeed or give them another year. Thankfully, Doc hadn't needed more than six months. *Then again, the years I passed intel count for something.*

He carefully slapped bandages on the stitched areas and patted the prospect's back. "Good luck out there."

The prospect shrugged on his shirt and nodded his thanks. Snoopy and Brewer stayed behind and watched the younger man leave.

"Think he'll survive initiation?" Brewer asked, giving Doc a side-eye.

Doc washed his hands and patted them dry. "Dunno, maybe. How many blows did he get in before Rubble leveled him?"

Snoopy smirked. "Three. Once he drew blood, Rubble was done. You know how he gets. Doesn't like prospects showing him up."

"Let's hope none ever do."

They heard the prospect down the hallway, chatting it up with the other men in his group. There'd be an initiation at the end of summer. Macha hosted them twice a year, so if a prospect didn't pass, he had a second chance later that year.

Snoopy pulled out a cigarette and lit it. "We weren't sure you'd make it, you know. Ten-to-one odds."

Laughing, Brewer nodded. "Good thing I bet on you, unlike this guy."

Snoopy scowled. "Shut it, Brewer."

Thinking back to his initiation, Doc had to admit he wasn't sure either. The trials were easy, or so said every patch member. Walking barefoot over a bed of hot coals hadn't been fun, but he'd prevailed. Letting patch members punch the ever-loving shit out of him wasn't pleasant either.

The mountain climb, though, that'd been the bitch. No oxygen tanks and limited food. Macha abandoned the prospects, him included, at separate summits of nearby mountains via helicopter with no provisions. He was completely alone. Just him, the wilderness, and the spirit of Macha to get him to the bottom. For the next three days, he'd foraged for food and warmth while snow fell around him. Despite freezing his ass off, he made it to the base of the mountain before any other prospect.

A month later, the mandatory Macha tattoo didn't seem so bad. He'd passed the trials and was patched right before Isa arrived.

Doc finished cleaning up his small work area. The clinic hadn't been too busy; with the Twelve Brothers dilemma, Rubble made sure the men didn't harm themselves in juvenile fistfights.

"Any word from Phantom?"

Brewer shook his head. "It's all quiet in Ireland. I've a mind to tell Reaper to send one of our men over there to keep tabs on Phantom and his crew."

"Wouldn't do any good," Snoopy said, flicking ash on the table Doc recently sterilized. He narrowed his gaze but didn't bring attention to it. "Phantom would send the asshole back within a week. He's had a snake in the grass before. Wouldn't let another one in."

"When was that?" Doc asked, suddenly interested in Macha's previous traitor.

Snoopy cleared his throat and closed the door. "We don't speak of traitors once they defile Macha's name." His eyes narrowed. "The man was lucky to be able to walk away from the club with his balls intact. If it were up to me, they'd be smashed."

"Snoop, where you at?" a voice called from the hallway.

"Uh-oh, somebody's old lady is looking for him," Brewer teased, nudging Snoopy's arm.

"Fuck off." He straightened his cut. "At least I have an old lady."

Brewer rolled his eyes. "And a fuck nymph."

Snoopy took a step closer to Brewer and waved his cigarette in the other man's face. "Don't be jealous I can satisfy two women." He nodded to Doc. "He knows how to do it too."

"Not lately."

Doc winced at the slight jab. It was true he hadn't been with a nymph since Isa arrived. He didn't feel the urge.

"Give it a bit. Once the Irish girl leaves, Doc will be back at the nymph lair." Snoopy patted his back. "We'll have to tear him away then."

"Snoopy, I swear to God...."

Brewer and Doc glanced to the shorter man.

"Yeah, yeah, I know." He crushed the cigarette on the table, then opened the door. "*Que pasa, bebe?*"

A string of Spanish words came out of Snoopy's old lady, and neither Doc nor Brewer cared to translate. One thing Doc knew for certain; he was damned glad he didn't know any Gaelic. Surely Isa would curse him out in the ancient dialect if he pissed her off enough.

"Where you off to?" Brewer asked, hanging onto the door.

"Chess with the princess." He let a smile escape. She was horrible at the game, but the way her brows furrowed when she was losing was too cute to give up.

"You really have changed, haven't you?"

He met Brewer's curious eyes. "I think I have."

18

—

ISA

THE LODGE WAS EVERYTHING SHE COULD DREAM OF for a mountain retreat. Waking up to the smell of freshly baked bread didn't hurt either.

Isa glanced over to where Doc had slept all night. He wasn't in bed with her but in the reclining chair instead.

At first, she'd been cross about his choice of location, but she quickly learned that he was looking out for both of them. If an emergency popped up during the night, his MC brothers may not look kindly on Doc spooning her under the covers.

Pulling on a fresh pair of socks, Isa eyed the made bed. Doc was assigned to protect her, she knew that, but her body craved something physical with him despite that fact.

She opened her door and peeked down the hallway before stepping outside. Voices drifted from below, and not-so-subtle moans from the room two doors down made her roll her eyes and hurry to the elaborate staircase. The first time she'd seen it didn't do it justice. The wooden railings curved all the way down to the bottom, one on each side. She ran her hand over the Macha emblem carved on one side.

Following her nose, she kept walking until she reached the kitchen. Her eyes widened at the sheer size. There was a walk-in pantry, rows lined with canned and boxed foods. The appliances were top of the line, and the quartz countertops were spotless. Barstools lined the island, an eat-in table long enough to fit twelve people comfortably next to it. In all, the entire space could hold twenty people, and there was also a formal dining area in the room to the left of the kitchen.

Isa smiled at the counter full of breads and streusel. She'd missed the mass of hungry bikers, but plenty of food was leftover for stragglers such as her.

"Eat as much as you want," Queenie said, stepping out of the pantry, arms full of canned vegetables. "Lunch isn't for a few hours, and I'm sure Doc will make you work up an appetite."

Cheeks burning, Isa grabbed a slice of bread and sat on one of the stools. "I don't know what you're talking about."

Queenie snorted and placed the cans near the stove. "Darlin', you two aren't fooling anyone." She opened the refrigerator and handed Isa the milk carton, then grabbed a glass from the cabinet overhead. "Your connection is obvious to everyone. Hell, I overheard Doc tearing Cueball a new one because the guy commented on your ass."

Isa choked on her bite and quickly filled the glass with ice-cold milk. "He did?"

"Yep. I've known the boy his whole life, and he's never been so protective of anyone before." She grinned. "And before you go sayin' it's his job and all that, Doc doesn't take a shine to many women. At least not longer than an hour or two."

Finishing her piece, Isa snatched another one. She couldn't remember the last time she had homemade bread. Her mother used to make it, but that was years ago.

"I don't have much experience with men," she mumbled around another bite.

Queenie added water to the coffeepot. "They're all so different it wouldn't matter. One man isn't like the rest, and vice versa." She added grounds to the filter and pressed the On button. The scent of coffee started to fill the air. "We're all inexperienced with someone new."

"That's not what I—"

"I know, Isa." She winked and pulled out a ceramic mug. "Don't change what I said."

Isa smiled and took a drink. Queenie immediately made her think of her mum. *It'd be so nice to have someone like a mum around again.*

"There she is." Reaper walked into the kitchen, three patch members plus Doc tailing him. He kissed Queenie's cheek before pouring himself a cup of coffee. "How do you like our little *casa*?"

"Little?" She laughed. "This place is huge. I've only

seen the main level and a bedroom. I can't imagine what the rest of it looks like."

Reaper added cream to his cup and took a sip. "In that case, why don't I give you the grand tour? The boys and I have a few things to do today, but I have time to show you the ropes." He glanced at Doc. "Unless my nephew would rather...."

"Like they'd get anywhere other than the bedroom," Hawk heckled.

Rubble rolled his eyes whereas Brewer merely smirked. When she looked over to Doc, Isa was disappointed to see his brow furrowed while he studied his phone.

"I'm ready when you are." She rinsed her glass and put it in the dishwasher before taking Reaper's offered arm. Only Rubble followed; Hawk, Brewer, and Doc moved toward the backyard.

An hour later, Isa sensed a headache creeping into her skull. Reaper outdid himself on the personal tour. From the tech tower to the three bunkers, Macha was prepared for a zombie apocalypse.

She'd left the club president in the den, where a handful of members were playing pool, and walked toward the front door. Two boys darted out in front of her, and she slammed to a halt. Glancing around, she didn't spot anyone chasing them, so she followed them to another set of stairs that went to a lower level she hadn't toured.

Feminine voices carried along the air, and she curiously followed them. Reaching the bottom step, Isa scanned the basement that seemed to go on forever in both directions. The concrete posts throughout reminded her that this place was a bunker before it was a lavish residence.

Finally, she spied the two preteen boys hovering at the entrance of a new room. When she reached them, she understood why. *So this is where the nymphs are hiding.*

Isa peeked through the small crack in the door and held in a laugh. Dolly and four nymphs were playing cards around a circular table, but they weren't what the boys were drooling over. No, it was the two nymphs on the opposite end of the room who were trying on new lingerie that captured their attention.

As if sensing their presence, Dolly glanced to the door. "Oye! You two little bastards better run. I'll whoop you good this time if I catch you." She stood and started for the door. The two boys backed up and right into Isa. They yelped, then ran toward the stairs.

The door swung open, and Isa gave the madam a shy smile. "Would you believe I followed them down here?"

Dolly smirked and jerked her head. "Come on in so I can close the door. Normally Queenie doesn't mind the youngsters peeking, but with all the shit that's about to hit the fan, the old ladies want their kids within spitting distance."

Isa stepped fully into the room filled with lavish décor. The club wasn't stingy with their motorcycles, and they were equally generous with nymphs. Her eyes widened at the assortment of lingerie hanging on one wall and the tent-like rooms set up side by side. She tripped over her feet when she noticed the sex toys lining another wall.

"I should probably go. This isn't exactly my thing." She looked around sheepishly. She'd never even been in a sex shop, and the easy way the women strutted around naked shocked her.

Hooking her arm through Isa's, Dolly led her to the table and pulled out a chair. "Sure it is. You're probably bored to death up there with the guys and their old ladies." Her blue eyes sparkled. "This is where all the fun happens."

Isa cleared her throat and looked around the room. The nymphs were good-looking but not perfect models. Some had curves while others were skinny. Their hair colors varied from brown to blue and several shades in between. It suddenly made her plain blonde hair seem insufficient for what a rough-and-tumble biker like Doc desired.

"They're wigs," Dolly said, cutting into her thoughts.

"What?"

She pointed to the girls with blue and pink hair. "The guys like them to switch things up sometimes. You know, role play. So the girls have wigs for such occasions."

The two women in question walked out the door.

"Who're they going to?"

Shuffling the cards, the shorter woman eyed her. "You sure you want to ask questions like that?"

"Oh, no. I guess not." Her face heated for more than

one reason. "Has Doc ever...? I mean it's none of my business, but has he...? Oh never mind."

Dolly quickly passed out the cards. She could've been a dealer in another life. "I keep track of where my girls go, how long they're there, and if anything of note happens while they're with a club member." She picked up her pile of cards. "Doc's a frequent name on my list."

"I see." She rubbed her lips together, unsure what to think of the statement.

"Calm down, girl. Eventually every man needs to release pent-up energy." She discarded and gave Isa a pointed look. "Know of any reason our Doc might be sexually frustrated?"

Isa inwardly kicked herself. Of course Doc would seek the comfort of one of the club nymphs. It *was* one of the free perks of the brotherhood.

"But he said—"

"Don't believe what men say. Believe what they do."

One of the nymphs hummed her agreement.

"I've never done relationships. I'm kind of lost," Isa admitted.

"Can't help you there, dollface. Those aren't my specialty." Dolly tossed another card to the middle of the table.

Isa sat in silence for a few minutes. The card game continued, as did the nymphs trying out new outfits. Part of her wanted to run and hide from the thoughts filtering in her mind. Another part of her craved information. She'd known from their first meeting that Doc would be the first man she'd sleep with. She just couldn't convince him to sleep with her.

Ironic.

"How often does Doc...?" She stopped herself. She didn't truly want to know. Instead, she wanted to learn. "Teach me how to seduce a man."

Dolly leaned back in her chair, mild surprise registering on her face. "Now *that* I can help you with."

Isa stared at her reflection. Dolly and her nymphs set her up good. Her hair was curled but tousled to look natural. Smoky makeup lined her eyes, and a smidge of gloss made her lips shine. The rest of her makeup was spot-on and professionally applied.

Her gaze lowered to her clothes. The outfit was the only part she wasn't sure about. Her clothes were usually comfortable over sexy.

Not today.

The V-cut blue blouse brought out the gray in her eyes and also gave plenty attention to her breasts. The lace push-up bra also helped define her "best asset," according to one of the nymphs. The jeans were more her style. The dark denim hugged her curves in the best ways and hid the lacy panties underneath.

Dolly insisted she get the proper nymph treatment, including utilizing the spa and waxing station in the basement. Isa was suddenly very self-conscious of hair missing over her body. She wasn't a prude, but anything having to do with sex was off-limits growing up in a Catholic home.

Blowing out a noisy breath, she turned to the side. Her shirt had a matching V in the back as well. It stopped just above her bra but hinted at what lay beneath it.

She snapped a selfie and sent it to Orla. Doing the time calculations, she figured Niall and Orla were prepping for bed after working in the shop all day. Her phone buzzed with a received message.

Orla: Hot damn! Who you looking so sexy for? That biker of yours?

She giggled and bit her lip before typing a response.

Isa: He's not mine yet.

An email came through and threatened to spoil her evening.

Blocked: We're closing in, Isa. Are you ready for us?

Swallowing the fear the message was meant to bring, she shut down her phone. She was safe within Macha's lodge. They'd walked her through the security herself. Nothing bad would happen while Doc was around. It was the one reassurance she clung to.

The clock on the wall struck six in the evening. It was dinnertime, and she was ready to face Macha's bikers. Her stomach pitched at the thought that she wasn't trying to impress anyone but Doc. His reaction to her would tell her everything she needed to know going forward.

Here goes nothing.

19

———

DOC

After working outside with Brewer and Hawk, Doc was ready to do absolutely nothing the rest of the night. It wouldn't happen, but he could wish for it.

He hurried with a shower once Queenie rang the dinner bell, anxious to see Isa again and find out what she'd done with her day. It killed him not to be around her, but she was safe within the compound. No one could get in or out without a dozen club members seeing it. That offered him a little reassurance.

He took the stairs two at a time until he reached the main level. The aroma of corned beef, steamed potatoes, and blueberry cobbler hit him the instant he crossed the threshold to the dining area. Mouth watering, he grabbed an open seat and sat next to Rubble.

"You think we're ready for the Twelve Brothers?" he asked, snagging a roll from one of the baskets on the table.

Rubble looked away from his phone. A shiver ran down

Doc's spine when the other man's peculiar eyes connected with his. He'd probably never get used to the heterochromia paired with a shaved head covered in tattoos, but somehow it fit the bulky man who he'd heard used to be special ops for the Marines.

"I'm always prepared, Doc. But if not, I have a few tricks up my sleeve. With the lodge and our armory, we can hold them off until reinforcements arrive." Rubble tipped back his bottle of Guinness.

Doc buttered the roll and took a bite. He'd be on edge until this whole kerfuffle was finished.

Rubble answered a call, and Doc couldn't help but notice the man's furrowed brows before he stood and walked out of the room. Brewer took the spot on the other side of Doc and nudged him with a beer.

"I brought an extra. Want it?"

"Definitely." He took a long swig. Irish beer was the only kind the club kept on hand, and he was still getting used to the dark stout.

Brewer slapped his back. "You like our beer yet?"

"You work the bar, right? Can't you get some American shit?"

"I could, but then I'd have to keep more labels in stock at the clubhouse and here." He shook his head. "I like the simple life."

"Yeah, yeah." He took another drink, this time the taste growing on him more than the last. Not having eaten since breakfast didn't hurt either. "Whose kids are those?"

Glancing over at the five children at the smaller table

near the kitchen, Brewer smirked. "Cueball's twin boys, Legs and Snoopy's little girl, and Boulder's grandkids. They haven't been around much lately."

"Snoopy has a daughter?" Doc's eyes bugged at the thought. "And Cueball is a dad?"

Brewer smiled behind his bottle. "Weird to think, isn't it?" He rested his elbows on the table. "They're all actually really good parents."

Doc watched Snoopy swoop down and tickle his daughter, who couldn't have been more than three years old. The little girl giggled and hugged him. It was touching in a way to know even members of a motorcycle club could have children who thrived despite animosity. He sighed, knowing he was proof of that after hanging around bikers as a youngster.

"Hey, isn't that your Irish girl?"

"She's not my...." His words fell flat when he looked in the direction Brewer pointed. "Holy shit."

Isa breezed through the door, shoulders back and a confident smile spread across her face. He gripped the beer bottle harder as his eyes raked over her body. The beautiful minx was outfitted in a shirt that turned every male head. Her jeans accented shapely hips and thighs and led straight to her black boots with a small heel. In his opinion, she didn't need a lick of the makeup on her eyes and face. He had to admit, though, she looked striking all done up.

He shoved Brewer's arm when he saw the other man ogling. It was selfish to want all of her to himself, but he couldn't help it.

"What? She's not taken, right?" Brewer chuckled and patted down his red hair with his fingers. "Think she'd be interested in a second-generation Irishman?"

"Don't you have a girl?"

Finishing his beer, Brewer stood. "Nymphs don't count, Doc."

Isa reached them before he could say a word. "Hello."

Her Irish accent washed over him, the silky tone giving him goose bumps.

"Hey, yourself," Brewer replied, smiling enough that his dimples popped into view. "You look like someone special I know." He tapped his lips as if trying to remember. Snapping his fingers, he pulled out a chair for her. "That's right, my future old lady."

Doc stood abruptly, chair screeching on the hardwood floor. He glowered at his brother, but the other man merely gave him a shit-eating grin. *Brewer is fucking with me.* He felt several curious eyes turn to them. *And it's working.*

She sat in the offered chair and started chatting with Brewer once he joined her.

Pounding the rest of the beer, Doc wiped off his mouth as Queenie and the nymphs brought dinner to the table.

The food looked delicious. Reaper said an old Gaelic blessing, and everyone dug into the platters heaping with potatoes and meat.

Doc barely ate a bite. Between hearing Isa's laughter two seats down and the way Brewer was flirting with her, he couldn't stomach the notion that perhaps she didn't want him specifically, just one of the club members.

When dessert came around, Brewer rested his tattooed arm around Isa's shoulders, and Doc's hands automatically formed fists. He didn't even realize he was leering until Dolly poked his side.

"What?" he growled, turning to his right.

She didn't shrink at his tone. Instead, she took another bite of blueberry cobbler and stared at him. "You'll combust if you keep holding that in." She nodded to one of the nymphs across the table. "Misty will gladly work all the frustration right out of you. Last I checked, you like it rough and so does she."

He flicked his eyes to the brunette nursing a beer. "No, thanks. The guys are playing poker tonight. I think I'll join them."

"Oh, you mean the poker night my nymphs are putting on downstairs?" Her eyes shimmered with mischief. "I'll be sure they give you extra attention."

"I don't want a nymph," he said under his breath.

"No, but you might need one." Dolly winked. "At least until your Irish lass decides to give you the time of day."

Thinking over his options, he couldn't disagree with her. He was in desperate need of an outlet. They obviously wanted each other, but now he wasn't sure she wanted anything more than that.

He swore under his breath. *When did my mind change?* He shook his head. He'd been so set on leaving Isa alone that the opposite happened for him. A casual hookup wasn't what he yearned for when it came to her.

Well, fuck me sideways.

Isa and Brewer stood, and after thanking Queenie for the meal, the duo linked arms and started toward the back patio. Rage filtered through Doc, but he had to stop himself. He had zero reason to be jealous. They'd shared kisses and plenty of conversations, but he had no permanent claim on Isa.

Not yet.

20

———

ISA

"I'm curious. When are you going to tell Mr. Jealous over there that we're related?" Brewer asked, dishing cobbler on their plates.

Isa snuck a glance over to the man in question. Sure enough, he was all but fuming smoke from his ears. She tried not to laugh but couldn't help herself. Doc's blue eyes flashed to her, and she quickly looked away.

"Soon, but I think he deserves to suffer a wee bit." She took a spoonful of the cobbler and moaned. "Plus, this is too good to not finish every bite."

Brewer dug into his dessert. "Queenie knows her way around the kitchen." He waved his spoon. "The nymphs too. Honestly, they're the ones who make the best food. Lara over there makes a fantastic crème brûlée." He nodded to a redhead. "And Alyssa, well, her omelets are to die for."

"You're a foodie, then," she stated rather than asked.

"One hundred percent. Our mother owned a bakery in Snowshoe." He glanced over to Dolly. "Sis and I would bounce between Macha and the bakery every day after school. It was the best childhood."

"Being around bikers all the time?" She shook her head. "I think I'd rather hang out at the bakery."

Brewer scraped the last bit of cobbler from his plate. "I don't have anything else to compare it to, but I think the Macha kids turned out pretty well." He gently nudged her arm. "Doc is among them, you know."

Isa watched the bikers finish their meal. Not one frown could be seen. *Well, except for Doc.* From Reaper to Snoopy's daughter, everyone seemed to be enjoying themselves. It warmed her heart to see such a large group of people getting along. She'd never been huge on crowds, and her mother's side of the family was limited to one other member who never had children. Isa grew up alone save for Orla and Niall.

"It's such a small world," Brewer commented, pushing his chair back. "Who would've thought your dad and my uncle were related."

"It's funny how the universe connects us." She noticed Doc chatting with Dolly. "Have any plans for the rest of the night?"

Brewer glanced to Doc and then back. "I was going to take stock of the liquor downstairs, then head to the poker game, but I'm open to suggestion."

"I'll help you with the liquor." She stood and linked her arm with his. That got an immediate reaction from Doc, but she merely walked toward the exit. When they cleared the door, she breathed a sigh of relief.

"He's an idiot, by the way," Brewer said, leading them toward the patio.

"Why's that?"

"Isa, if you and I weren't related, and if you were even remotely interested in me, I wouldn't sit idly by and let some other guy drool all over you." He winked at her. "But hey, we're only like third cousins...."

She rolled her eyes. "Ha ha. Not happening, sorry."

"Damn. Had to try." He opened the patio door. "Reaper built the liquor cellar away from the beer one because, well, Macha men like to drink, and it's better to keep them separated."

Two hours later, Isa emerged from the cellar with more knowledge of Irish whiskey and how the Belfast chapter ran a distillery there.

Brewer locked the door behind them. "I think I'll check out that poker game now. Will you be okay by yourself?"

"Poker, huh?"

"Yeah, plus a bit of a strip show." He rubbed his hands together maniacally. "The nymphs like to treat us every so often."

Alarm flashed through Isa's mind. Doc was undoubtedly in the nymph lair, enjoying the view. Suddenly, flaunting herself around at dinner seemed like a horrible idea.

"Can I come?"

Brewer stuffed his hands in his baggy jeans pockets. "Erm, it might not be a scene you want to see. The guys tend to get raunchy after a few rounds."

"I've seen stuff at the bar."

"Okay," he said slowly. "But if Reaper asks, you snuck down by yourself."

"Deal."

THE NYMPH LAIR LOOKED ENTIRELY DIFFERENT THAN it had earlier in the day. Isa stumbled in the darkness, but thankfully, Brewer caught her arm. Rock music blared over the giant speakers in the room's four corners. Stripper poles abounded throughout the room, scantily dressed nymphs dancing seductively around each one.

Her mouth dropped open at the sight before her. She'd never been in a strip club before, but she guaranteed they weren't as posh as Macha's pop-up one. A multicolored strobe spread dim light around the room.

On the far edge was a table, six bikers sitting around it with cards in hand. They didn't seem to be engrossed in the game. Then again, the three nymphs dancing around their table stole most of the attention.

"You sure you want to be here?"

Isa met Brewer's worried eyes. "Of course. Go have fun."

He didn't need to be told twice. The redheaded man disappeared into a throng of nymphs before she could inhale.

Bracing herself for the worst, she searched the room for Doc's notable stature. Unfortunately for her, the place was filled with bikers of all shapes and sizes. Plenty who fit his height.

She stepped away from the wall and strode toward the first set of men in leather cuts. None were familiar to her, and a whole new set of panic set in. She hurried away, focused on finding Doc and setting him straight.

A group of prospects directed her toward a nearby poker table.

"He was here five minutes ago," one of the men stated, drinking from a tumbler.

Well, he's not here now. She frowned, searching the card players. None were Doc. *Where is he?*

She turned to take in the entire room, her heart drooping lower the longer she watched the nymphs grind on the bikers. One member was in the corner fucking a redhead against a wall while another was getting a blow job from a brunette.

It's a man's paradise down here.

A new song blared over the speakers, and she whipped her head to the left to see a busty blonde leading a familiar hand to the bedroom portion of the room. Following quickly, her heart rate doubled when Doc's profile came into view. He yelled something to Hawk, then disappeared in one of the curtained-off areas.

Feck, what do I do? She bit her thumbnail. *What would Dolly do?* She shook her head. She didn't want to know what Dolly would do.

Acting instead of thinking, she pulled back the red curtain and ducked inside. Sure enough, her missing biker was suddenly found.

"Who the hell are you?" the nymph asked, hands under Doc's shirt.

"The person who will send you to hell if you don't get your grimy fingers off him," Isa replied, stalking over and yanking on the blonde's hair.

"Hey, watch it, bitch!" the nymph shrieked, but Isa didn't give a damn.

She shoved the blonde to the floor. "If I catch you anywhere near Doc O'Brien, I'll show you exactly how much of a bitch I can be."

The nymph cowered slightly, then crawled out of sight. Shock suddenly hit her at what she'd just done. She'd never been in a catfight—or any fight, for that matter—but she'd managed to get herself into one tonight.

Turning on her toes, she met Doc's eyes, which were alight with humor. He stood and gazed down at her. "What was that?"

Shame washed over her. "Damn, I should apologize to her. I was such a—"

"Jealous woman?" he finished for her, tilting her chin up.

"Yeah, that. I don't know what came over me."

His gaze flicked to her lips, then back to her eyes. "Why'd you come downstairs? Didn't Brewer warn you about what you'd find?"

"Aye, but I had to find you."

"Why?"

"Brewer's my third cousin. Actually, I'm not sure that's even right, but we're related."

He dropped his hold. "So?"

"So, I'm not interested in him. Like at all."

"I know."

"And even if we weren't related—" She stopped, his words finally registering. "What do you mean, you know?"

He straightened his cut. "You were trying to make me jealous, weren't you?"

"Not intentionally. It kind of happened."

"You accidentally wore a shirt that showed off your gorgeous tits and jeans that make your ass squeezable?"

She noticed his small grin despite the dim lighting. "No. That was on purpose."

He took a step closer as the thump of the rock song echoed in her ears. "And why would you wear something so sexy to dinner?"

"So you'd want me."

Doc let out a strangled sigh. "Isa, I want you. You already know that. I've done everything possible to stop wanting you, but it always comes back to you. Hell, you could wear a donkey costume and I'd still want that ass."

She rolled her eyes at his attempt at a joke. "Seriously?"

He pulled her against his chest. "What did I tell you about rolling your eyes?"

Her gaze locked with his, the pounding of her heart louder than the bass in the song surrounding them. "That you'd punish me."

"But only if you want me to."

"I want more than that."

"Isa—"

"You say I'm not ready, but I am, Doc." She locked her arms around his neck. "I want you in every way possible."

His lips were on her before the beat dropped, their mouths colliding in a frantic fury. He grabbed her arse and pulled her against his hard groin. She moaned at the feeling of what she did to him. She couldn't get enough of his lips and never wanted to try.

"Not here," he rasped, pulling back. He set her feet on the floor and shoved his hands through his hair.

Isa traced her lips, swollen from their passionate kiss. "Come back to my room."

She watched him wrestle between wanting her and wanting to be a gentleman. She'd never guessed a biker would act in such a way, but it was endearing in all the right ways. "You won't break me."

"You say that now."

She took his hand. "And I'll say it later."

Finally, he nodded. "Let's get out of here before I change my mind and take you on every surface I can find."

21

———

DOC

IF DOC THOUGHT FOR ONE SECOND THAT ISA WASN'T ready, he'd never have followed her up to the bedroom. His cock screamed at him for even considering turning her down for another hot session in the shower.

They managed to leave the nymph lair without anyone stopping them. That alone was a miracle in his book. Once they made it to the main level, he could properly see her full ass shaking back and forth in those blue jeans. It did things to his body he couldn't explain and didn't want to. The slight tremble in her hand reminded him to be gentle.

Isa didn't let go of his hand once until they reached her bedroom. The lock slid in place behind him too easily. A glow from her bedside lamp cast her in a perfect light. She stood beside the bed, looking everywhere but his face. He couldn't blame her. He'd been a bumbling idiot his first time.

"I won't hurt you."

She looked up then, and he saw the fear behind her gray eyes. It sliced straight to his soul. "I know."

Fuck, I'm gonna have to go really slow.

He kicked off his black boots and motioned for her to get on the bed. When she flat-out sprawled over it, he held in a chuckle. "Come here."

She moved to the edge of the bed, and he could almost see the pulse in her neck. Carefully, he unlaced her boots one at a time and tossed them next to his.

Kneeling in front of her, he cupped her face in his calloused hands. "If at any time you're not comfortable or want to stop, tell me."

She nodded.

"Words, Isa. I need words."

"Y-Yes."

He smiled and stood. Taking off his cut, he laid it on the dresser before pulling his shirt away. Her sharp inhale reminded him she'd never been with anyone. Deciding against stripping completely, he moved back to the bed and knelt beside it.

Isa's eyes followed every movement, lust overtaking her gorgeous body already. Slowly, he caught her lips beneath his. She tasted so damned sweet. It was enough to make him swear off all sugar except her saccharine lips.

She kissed back tentatively but eagerly. He'd have such fun with this girl. Going slow meant his stiff cock would have to wait. Isa deserved the best, and that was exactly what he'd provide.

Moving from her lips, he kissed down her neck. Her

breathing hitched, and when she moaned, he realized he'd found a sensitive spot. Flicking his tongue over the area, he waited until he heard another wispy sigh to kiss the other side of her neck.

His lips traveled down her chest. Even her skin tasted sinful. He paused when he neared the V in her shirt. Moving too quickly might scare her, so he eased back to kiss her lips. She greedily kissed him back.

Doc's hands slowly made their way to her breasts. He kneaded them softly through her shirt and bra. Already he felt her nipples harden beneath the cotton. He wanted more of those sounds she made, so he slipped his hand under her shirt. She immediately reacted, arching her back into him.

Using this to his advantage, he pulled away enough to slip her shirt over her head. The delicate bra covering her breasts wasn't long for this world. He met her gaze and smoothly unlatched her bra. The dainty thing fell down her shoulders, exposing rosy nipples against her creamy skin.

"Damn, Isa," he murmured, lightly kissing above each breast. Her fingers threaded in his long hair, nails running along his scalp and sending a chill down his spine. His lips hovered at her nipples. Keeping her gaze, he licked the right one. Her eyes lit up before they rolled into her head. Sucking the nipple into his mouth, Doc traced her left breast with his fingertips. After properly turning her nipple to a peak, he gave the other one equal attention.

By the time he finished with her breasts, his cock demanded an audience. Ignoring his selfish body part, he helped her out of the tight jeans. He climbed on the bed, kissing her again.

The musky scent of her arousal tempted him too much. He moved down her body, lips touching everywhere his fingers weren't. When he reached her hips, he traced the curve above the lace panties. They matched her black bra, and he couldn't wait to see them on the floor too.

Nestling between her legs, he looked up. Her gray eyes were hazy and curious at the same time. "How far have you gone with a man before?"

"Some stuff."

He nuzzled her apex and she jumped.

Evidently not a lot of stuff.

"Tell me."

A stunning blush started at her cheeks and spread over her face. "Second base."

He reached up and grabbed her breasts. "This?"

She nodded and he rolled her nipples between his fingers. The way she pushed toward him enticed him to kiss above her panties. A tremble shook her body and he froze.

"Isa, are you all right?"

"Aye, don't stop." She grabbed his hands and placed them on her breasts again.

Chuckling, he tempted her for another few seconds before slipping one hand beneath the lace that separated her from him. Her eyes locked on him and her breathing staggered. He groaned at her recently manicured womanhood. He didn't give a shit so long as it was tidy, and she was most definitely tidy.

"I see our resident madam has been whispering in your ear," he teased, finding her slit and tracing down it. Her legs clenched.

"I didn't want to disappoint you."

"Princess, you could never do that." His finger reached her core and found it wet. He couldn't stop the groan from escaping his lips. "Fuck, you're drenched."

"Is that bad?"

He licked his finger clean. "No, baby, but you're about to get so much wetter."

Another blush raced down her body, enticing him further. Doc brushed her panties down her thighs and chucked them out of sight. Isa lay before him, the tastiest feast he'd ever seen in his life.

And she was his. All his.

Positioning her against his mouth, he met her eyes and slowly started licking her clit. Isa's eyes bulged but she didn't recoil. Instead, as his tongue made contact, her hips rose to welcome him deeper.

"Damn, you taste so good." He plunged his tongue into her tight hole and gently rubbed her clit. Already he sensed the buzz in her body. He'd make her come undone at least three times before he released.

Switching his tongue and finger, he slid the digit in and out of her. Her muscles clenched him tight. He added a second finger. When he added a third, she mewed. His girl liked big. Well, that was good, because he wasn't anywhere close to small.

Rubbing her clit with his thumb, he felt her thighs against his head. He continued to eat her pussy while she neared her climax. He looked up and caught the sight of her thrashing her head into the pillow, loud moans filling the air. She was nearly there.

He increased the pressure on her clit and his beautiful Irish princess came undone. He eagerly lapped up her pleasure, the taste sweeter than fresh honey. Her hips shook and she cried out his name, clenching his head between her legs. If he died then and there, his only regret would be not loving Isa sooner.

"That's it, baby," he murmured, lapping up the last of her passion. Isa lay back, trying to catch her breath, her cheeks flush with her recent release. Moving to her lips, he caught her mouth and let her taste for herself. Instead of shying away, she tangled her tongue with his, further turning him on.

He released the kiss and shook his head approvingly. "I think you liked that."

She tangled her fingers in his hair. "I did." She looked to his jeans still in place. "When are you going to let me see what you're hiding beneath those?"

"Anytime you want."

She sat up, hands rushing to unbuckle his belt. He pushed her hair out of her face and watched her nimble movements to free his cock. She paused when his belt was off and the zipper down. Seeing her surprise at his girth, Doc stood and shoved his pants and boxers to the floor. He grabbed a condom from his pocket and held it behind his back, not wanting to rush her.

"Holy damn." Her eyes widened as she took in the sight.

He stayed perfectly still while she examined his cock first with her eyes, then with her soft hands. It took every ounce of self-control to remain rooted to his spot. She needed to be comfortable with this, and that meant keeping his balls blue as long as it took.

"I don't think it'll fit." She turned concerned eyes to him.

"Trust me, he'll fit." He kissed her forehead. "And you'll enjoy it too."

Isa crawled to the middle of the bed. "Will it be painful?"

"Only for a moment," he promised, slowly joining her. He'd never forgive himself if it hurt longer than that.

"I'm ready."

He scanned her body, his cock begging to sink into her virginal flesh. She was ready. He'd made sure of that. Tearing the condom open with his teeth, he kept her gaze as he slipped it over his hard length. "Tell me—"

"Fuck me, Doc," she groaned, kissing his neck. "I want to feel you inside me."

That was all the incentive he needed.

Tugging her beneath him, he positioned himself at her entrance. "The first time, I'm taking you like this." He kissed her deeply. "But next time, I want you to ride me so I can watch your perfect tits bounce."

She moaned as he kissed her again, and he chose that moment to plunge into her wetness. Her breath hitched and he paused, letting her adjust to his girth. Stalling had never pained him worse. Her tight core gripped him like a vice. Isa started kissing him again, letting him know it was time.

Ever so slowly, he moved backward and then forward. Her passage was slick and hot. Exactly what he needed. He carefully pushed all the way in, filling her to the brim.

"You feel so good," she whispered against his lips.

"You're sure?"

She nodded and kissed his jaw. "Don't hold back, please. I can take it."

She couldn't, but he'd give her more. Rocking his hips, he jutted into her. When she started moving her hips in unison to his thrusts, he had to remind himself to hold out. He couldn't come this fast. Not when she deserved so much more. Even if she felt like silken heaven.

Isa wrapped her legs around his waist and gasped when it drew him deeper. "Oh my God."

He paused and met her gaze. "Are you all right?"

She rolled her eyes. "Aye."

"You sure, because—"

"Doc, I swear to God, you better start fucking me again or I'll—"

"You'll what?" He nipped her throat and grabbed her wrists, pinning them above her head. Her eyes widened, but she didn't resist. "You'll scream my name when I make you come?"

Before she could answer, he plunged his cock harder into her virginal pussy. Isa's mouth dropped open, but no sound escaped. She nodded and he repeated the act. This time, her moan sent tingles straight to his cock.

"Just like that," she prompted, moving her hips again.

"Greedy lass, aren't you?" he teased, then quickly regretted it when she leaned up and licked his nipple. Goose bumps littered his skin at her unexpected touch. It spurred him forward. She was a virgin no longer. A vixen took her place.

"Somebody likes that," she purred, moving to the other one.

Doc let his body take over from there. He couldn't deny his dick any longer. Lifting her legs to his shoulders, he thrust faster. Isa's screams of pleasure filled the room. He'd have to insulate the walls if he didn't want his brothers to hear the sounds she made.

Kissing her, he momentarily silenced her until another orgasm ripped through her body. She clenched his shoulders and pulled against him, muting her moans against his flesh. Sweat slid from his forehead to her chest, but he didn't stop. Her pussy tightened around him, milking his orgasm. No longer able to resist, Doc groaned her name and shot his sticky load into the condom.

His hips slowed, and he carefully slid her shaky legs to the bed. Hovering above her, he scanned her beautiful features. Every inch of her glowed from their lovemaking. It was the one and only time he cared to look at a woman after coming.

Capturing her head between his palms, he gently kissed her forehead, then the tip of her nose, and finally the point of her chin. Sweat lined her brow, but she'd never looked better. She had a new look about her. A maiden no longer. She was his woman. He'd be damned if he let another man ever touch her the way he did.

"So, that's sex, huh?" she asked, finger snaking down his chest.

He nodded, no words coming to his aid. His brain was a muddled mess after fucking her once. He couldn't imagine what a lifetime would do to him.

"Hmm." She pursed her lips as if in thought, then met his gaze. "Is it always that good?"

"Only with me, baby."

She rolled her eyes and shoved at his chest. Easing out of her, he tossed the condom in the garbage can near the door, then slid under the covers, tucking her safely against him.

"I like it," she finally said, sleep evident in her voice.

"Me too, princess." He kissed the back of her head, never wanting to be anywhere but here. He'd managed to fall for a girl and made her a woman. *My woman.* Life couldn't throw any better curveball.

22

———

ISA

A crick in Isa's neck woke her the next morning. No sunlight streamed through the curtained window as thunder rumbled above the lodge. She slowly opened her eyes, uncertain whether last night had been a dream or perhaps wishful thinking on her part. Doc's disheveled hair met her gaze, and a little part of her heart squeezed. *I wasn't dreaming.*

Taking in the man beside her, she swallowed back the memories flashing through her mind. His left arm was sprawled haphazardly across her pillow, his right hand resting on his naked torso. Her eyes dipped to the sheet covering them both. Nothing lay between them, and it was exactly what she wanted from that moment forward.

Doc snored lightly, the act too cute to be manly. Propping up on her elbow, she pulled back the sheet to review the artwork across his chest. Tattoos lay on top of his muscles, their sizes and shapes varying along with the colors. She recognized a few she'd seen before. The coiled green snake led to an orange Irish trinity cross, the colors interwoven to appear as if they were one unit instead of two separate tattoos. The pectoral muscles on his right side looked as though someone peeled back the skin to reveal a machine in place of his muscles. His left was mostly bare, save for one small tattoo. She peered at the calligraphy, smiling at the familiar language. *Gaelic.*

A flash of lightning momentarily lit the room, and Isa held her breath. When he didn't wake, she continued her perusal. Sleeves covered both his arms. His left was a tribute to the goddess Macha. Whoever the tattoo artist was deserved a huge tip. The goddess looked almost real, half her face human, the other half a ghostly skull. The rest displayed Macha's spirit raven as well as an old-fashioned pocket watch set to midnight.

His right arm portrayed the MC half of his Irish dedication. Nothing cheesy like she'd seen on a few other members. This arm held an atlas with the Irish isle on his triceps and a compass leading north. A road curved down the rest of his arm, a shadow of a motorcycle rolling down the side.

Isa smiled in the darkness. He'd slept near her before, but actually having him under the sheets was surreal. Somehow, he'd managed to make her first time feel like she'd been doing it her entire adult life. Other than the minimal pain at first, she couldn't complain. He'd more than made up for it during the night.

She remembered the way Doc gently kissed her before

they fell asleep, her face on his chest and his arm around her shoulders. The heart within the rough biker exterior was sweet, protective, and thoughtful. No other man could duplicate the feelings coursing through her veins. He was it.

A loud boom of thunder sent Doc sitting up fast, hand toward her protectively. His chest heaved, and she saw the muscle in his neck bulge. Isa gasped when she noticed the handgun in his other hand. *Where the hell did he hide that?*

He scanned the room, then cast his eyes to her. Realization registered on his face, and he slowly placed the gun on the bedside table.

"Bad dream?"

He pushed back his hair. "Something like that."

"Anything I can do to help?"

His eyes lowered to her state of undress and a grin covered his lips. "You're the only remedy I need."

He fluidly swept her to him and kissed her softly. Isa couldn't stop the sigh from escaping. Even after making love three times throughout the night, her body craved more. His hands caressed her back, bringing her completely on top of him, his solid muscles beneath her only encouraging her to kiss him longer. Her stomach, on the other hand, had other ideas.

Sitting up, she laughed at the growling sounds her belly made. "Guess I worked up an appetite."

He leaned over and kissed her belly button. "That you did. Come on. It's early, but I'll bet Queenie has something out."

She moved off him, suddenly very aware of their nakedness. Under the moonlight was one thing, but in the light of a new day... she wasn't so certain.

"Don't overthink it," Doc commented, hoisting his jeans up. He walked over to the bed and kissed her forehead. "It's nothing to be ashamed of. You're a gorgeous woman." He ran his thumb along her bottom lip. "My woman."

A flurry of nerves filled her gut at his words. In one night, Doc claimed her as his own and didn't seem ready to ever relinquish that statement. She loved the thought, but it also scared her.

He zipped his jeans and pulled on a T-shirt. "How're you feeling?"

"A little sore." Moving to the dresser, she grabbed a fresh set of clothes. Her reflection shone back in the mirror, and she did a double take. Her usually straight hair was mussed and curled at the bottom from their combined sweat. Her lips were bruised but in the best way. Small marks lined her neck and chest, a few darker at her breasts. Heat crept from her toes to her cheeks. All of these were firsts for her.

"After breakfast, I'll draw you a bath." He stood behind her.

Seeing them in the mirror, she had to admit they made quite the striking couple. Him completely tatted and muscled, and her pale skin covered in his love marks.

They could both use a bath. The scent of sex lingered in the air, tempting her with every breath.

Turning around, she looped her arms around his neck and closed the minimal distance to his lips. He immediately responded, overwhelming her mouth. She slipped her tongue past his lips and he ravaged her. Flashes from their time last night surfaced and she moaned.

"Isa." Her name came out shaky and filled with warning.

She kissed his neck, then took a step backward. "I wanted to make sure you were real."

Doc offered her a boyish grin. "I'm very real, princess. Your entire body should know that by now."

Giggling at the way he wiggled his brows up and down, she hurriedly threw on her clothes. *If we don't leave the room this instant, we never will.*

23

———

DOC

Everything felt better. The coffee tasted like the beans were grown and ground in the backyard. The sun seemed brighter. The air smelled crisp. *Everything is better.*

Doc grinned at his motorcycle. He and Cueball delegated the washing of bikes to the prospects, but when it came to make them shine, it was every man for himself. He'd never trust another man with his baby.

Just like I won't trust anyone else with Isa.

He licked his lips, the taste of her on the tip of his tongue since earlier that morning. All he could think about was Isa and when he could have her again.

Fuck, stop it.

He stood and adjusted his dick. The damn thing never softened when he thought of her.

Seeing his cycle gleam in the sunlight, he checked his cell phone. A message from Hawk stared back at him.

Hawk: Get your ass up here. Church is starting.

"Shit, we're late." He whistled to Cueball, and they jogged to the room off the main lodge. It was impenetrable and exactly what Macha needed for a mountainside hideaway. They hurried inside and took the last open seats around the large wood table with the Macha emblem carved in the middle.

"Glad you could join us, boys," Shovelhead said lowly.

Reaper pounded the gavel and the room silenced. "It's not good news. The Twelve Brothers crew killed three of our own in Ireland."

The room erupted with angry voices, calling for vengeance.

"Don't worry," Reaper called above the roar. "Our brothers handled it. They've taken three hostages. Until the fighting ends, they'll remain alive."

"Why? Kill them all!" one of the prospects piped up from his spot alongside the wall. Only members earned the right to sit during church. Something Doc was glad he'd gotten sooner rather than later.

Boulder shot the wiry man a glare. "Are you daft? Our club doesn't kill to soothe our pain. If killing is necessary, it happens, but to keep the peace, we must try to stay above the law."

The prospect didn't retort, and everyone seemed glad to get back to the matter at hand. Dealing with a mouthy prospect was Boulder's favorite thing to do. No doubt, the man would teach the prospect a lesson once church dismissed.

"The lad's not wrong." Every eye in the room turned to Shovelhead. The VP shrugged. "We've earned a bit of bloodshed after the way the Twelve Brothers attacked us and threatened our pawn."

"Isa is a lot more than a pawn," Rubble said, brows furrowed. "And this is much more than a game of chess."

Shovelhead stroked his beard. "Perhaps, but she could be of use to our club if Phantom got in line."

Doc's gut churned at the VP's words. From looking around at his brothers, they were torn between wanting to agree and wanting to have a throwdown.

Reaper stood and paced. "Enough. We're rescuing Isa." He stared at Shovelhead. "End of story. Now, I sent two men to Denver. They've informed me that a private airstrip was used last night. The plane came from Belfast."

This time the murmur in the room was a concerned one. The last firefight the club had was with the Greenback Cutthroats, and they were due for a bit of a scuffle. Since then, the need to protect their claim in Colorado was limited.

"What's the plan?" Doc asked, sitting up a little straighter.

Rubble nodded to him. "We have men lining the highways and back roads. Once the Twelve Brothers members go through the pass, we'll put the club on complete lockdown."

"Aren't we already there?" Hawk asked.

Reaper shook his head. "No. We didn't think it'd come to this, but it has." He stopped pacing and rested his hands on the back of his chair. "The Twelve are out for blood. I don't want to see one damn drop, but we must protect our own." He met Doc's gaze. "No matter what."

A chorus of "Hell yes" echoed in the room.

For the next thirty minutes, the club members went over the intricate details of a complete lockdown. Each man had his role and was prepared to utilize Macha's might to ensure their survival.

By the end, Doc's adrenaline was pumping steadily through his blood. He was ready to take Isa to their secondary safe house should the need arise. Rubble assured him it wouldn't come to that, but the expression on their president's face told him differently.

The crew left church solemn yet prepared. His only concern was Isa. He needed to bring her up to speed on the danger.

He bounded up the steps to her room but found it empty. Panic initially flooded his system, but he tamped it down. She was safe within these walls. He just didn't know where the hell she was.

When he found her, he'd lay down new rules. She wasn't to leave his side until this was over.

24

———

ISA

"How's Colorado life?" Orla asked from her perch on the store counter.

Isa rolled to her stomach, the summer breeze pushing her hair out of her face. Sunbathing hadn't seemed like a good idea until she stepped outside. The sun was close enough to warm her skin, but plenty of cloud coverage and sunscreen kept her from burning.

"It's far from boring."

"Ooh, do tell!"

For a moment, she wasn't sure how much to tell her best friend. She'd been there for every step of Niall and Orla's romance, but this felt different. Private somehow. But she couldn't not tell Orla either.

"You remember me telling you about Doc?" Orla nodded, her eyes eager for more. Isa glanced around, and once she saw no one else was around, she continued. "We slept together."

"Like, 'there was lots of snoring' slept together?"

"More like there was barely any sleeping going on at all."

Orla's mouth dropped open, and she teetered from her spot on the edge of the counter. Thankfully, Niall arrived in time to keep her from toppling entirely. "Holy shite!"

She took a sip of water. "That's what I've been saying ever since."

Niall whistled and was promptly smacked on the arm by his wife. "What? I can't help but hear. The two of you aren't quiet, love."

"Out of here before the futon becomes your new wife," Orla said sternly.

Isa watched Niall throw up his hands in defeat, the door closing in the background.

"Oh my God, Isa, you had sex!" Orla squealed like a schoolgirl with a crush. "How was it? Was he gentle? Did you ride him? Was it awkward? Did you, ahem, topple that peak?"

"Jesus, Orla!" She stared off at the mountains in the distance as her friend kept peppering her with questions. "He made me feel so many things. I always thought sex would be amazing, but, wow, Doc made it mind-blowing."

"Aw, darling, I'm happy for you." Tears filled Orla's brown eyes. "When did this all happen?"

"Last night. Well, and this morning, I suppose."

"Then where is this sex god? He should be spoiling you rotten."

Rolling to her back again, Isa caught sight of a club

member on the upper deck. That didn't bother her. The automatic rifle slung across his shoulders did.

Her stomach soured. *Where is Doc?*

"He had club business."

Her friend's face scrunched disapprovingly. "That's rubbish. Go find him and lock him in a room."

"I will later. At present, I'm basking in the afterglow of sex." She dramatically lifted the back of her hand to her forehead, making Orla laugh on the other end.

"You're in for a world of fun. Be sure to rest. Don't want you waddling about afterward."

"I'm going to sketch a bit while I'm outside. It's gorgeous here." She glanced around and noticed two cameras on the garage roof. She hadn't noticed them before. If she were a betting woman, there were more around the compound too. It eased her worry for the time being. After all, she wasn't aware of dire danger. Doc would tell her if there was any.

"Good for you. Maybe you'll have some new ideas to add to the shop when you get back."

She chewed on the straw in her glass of water. "Yeah, hopefully."

"Right, well, I better get back to it. Somebody has to maintain the business while you're off sexing it up." Orla blew her a kiss. "Be safe, love."

"Always."

Isa put the phone away and picked up her sketchpad. Normally her designs were based on Ireland. It was where her inspiration came from back home. *But I'm not there, am I?*

She tapped the pencil against the blank sheet of paper. Images of Doc filled her mind. The suave way he made love. *Well, at least I think it's suave. I've no one to compare it to.* She laughed at herself. Being with the Macha doctor opened her eyes to what love could be.

Whoa, girl, you're getting ahead of yourself.

Putting the pad down, she stood and walked over to the pool's edge. The water was clear and inviting under the warm sun. Dipping her toe in, she was pleasantly surprised at the warmth. Doc's mention of it being a hot spring came to mind. *Might as well enjoy it while it lasts.*

She stepped off the side and closed her eyes, the water enveloping her. Slowly, she sank to the bottom and opened her eyes. The entire pool was pristine. After a few moments, she swam to the surface and lay on her back. Puffs of white clouds rolled by, their destinations unknown.

The sun peeked out behind the clouds every so often, and she closed her eyes against its rays. It was so quiet in the mountains. No rushing cars, beeping horns, or yelling neighbors like at the clubhouse.

This is more my style.

"Isa."

Hearing her name through the water, she sat up and glanced in the direction of the voice. Doc stood at the edge of the pool, thumbs hooked in the belt loops of his jeans. The tattoos on his arms and hands stood out against the black T-shirt but only enhanced his handsomeness. His long blond hair was parted to the right, some of the strands covering his dark-tinted sunglasses.

"Want to join me?" She swam closer and rested her elbows on the side.

He crouched and pulled his shades down his nose enough to fully review the red bikini top, then return to her face. "Tempting. Very tempting." His index finger slid beneath the strap. "Where'd you get this?"

"Queenie found it. Had the tags on and fit perfect." She lifted her arm to compare their tones. "And with my light skin, I could use some rays."

"You really should be inside." He leaned back on his heels and replaced his sunglasses. "You're safer there."

She rolled her eyes and swam backward away from him. "You're no fun."

"That's not what you said last night."

"Well, if you're interested in that kind of fun...." She blushed. "We'd absolutely need to move inside."

He didn't answer, simply retrieved a beach towel from a chair and held it up.

Taking the hint, Isa only pulled herself up the stepladder after she swam the pool length twice. She took the offered towel and wrapped it around her hips before returning to her chair.

"I'm not going anywhere," she said, plopping into the cushion and sipping her water.

The tall biker shifted his weight, and she swore she heard him growl. "Princess, you don't have a choice. You're under my protection, and I tell you where to go and when."

She grabbed her pencil and blank pad. Suddenly, she had an idea for a swimsuit cover that was a mix of risqué and modest. She lightly drew a model and the flowing cover.

"Isa, I'm talking to you."

"Hang on, I'm almost done." She finished sketching the bottom hem, her periphery catching Doc moving her direction.

"Now, Isa."

She waved her pencil at him, not wanting to stop while the inspiration overwhelmed her. By the time she finished, her model was perfectly presentable in the slightly sheer cover that'd be ideal for swimmers on any continent.

"There. Orla's going to love it." She signed the sketch, then placed the book on the side table. Sighing happily, she glanced over at him. He stood inches away, gaze focused on their surroundings. Every few moments, his head swiveled but never drifted to her.

Feck, I think I pissed him off. She reached for him, but he took a step away. Crossing her legs, she stared at him. His jaw was tightly clenched, the sparrow tattoo on his neck popping slightly. If he weren't so mad, she'd find him irresistible.

Isa stood and quickly gathered her towel around her waist. She'd only taken two steps before he lightly gripped her arm. It wasn't painful but held enough force for her to know she'd stepped over a line.

Swallowing hard, she lifted her gaze and met his face.

He pulled off his shades, and the air in her lungs deflated at the cold expression in his usually cheerful eyes.

"Your safety is my number one priority, Isadora." His voice was low, a hint of frustration prevalent in the husky tone. His eyes bored into hers. "If I tell you to do something, it's not because I get my rocks off bossing you around. It's to keep you alive."

She lifted her chin slightly. This behavior wasn't familiar. She'd never worried about her safety in Ireland. Until her father's occupation came to light. Being raised by a single mother, the male figures in her life were minimal. Such an upbringing seemed to cause her to rebel whenever Doc tried to keep her in line. She'd reluctantly obeyed her father, but being micromanaged more with each passing day annoyed her.

"I can take care of myself, Doc." She pulled her arm away and was shocked when he let go so easily. She'd expected more of a fight. This was a club member, after all. Society taught her they were domineering and womanizing.

She pushed back her wet hair. *But not this MC. Not this man.*

He inhaled, his shoulders moving up slowly, as if digesting the force behind her words. He looked behind him, then closed the distance between them. His left hand came up and cupped the side of her face. "I know you can, princess, but I want to take care of you." He gently kissed her, the sharp bite of chlorine on her lips from her recent swim.

Closing her eyes, she returned the kiss, looping her arms around his neck, not giving a damn where they were or who might see them. Her biker lover didn't disappoint. His tongue dipped between her lips, tangling intimately with hers. Pressing her body against him, she shivered at his solid muscle. She barely had time to appreciate it, but now all she craved was to run her fingers along every inch of him until he begged for her.

His hands slid down her back, lightly caressing her spine and sending goose bumps to her toes. He cupped her arse, and she moaned into his mouth. Every touch was new and exciting. Doc didn't compare to any other man, and she wouldn't disgrace him by even thinking such thoughts.

Isa felt the telltale sign of his arousal against her stomach, sending flutters there. When he picked her up off the ground, she wrapped her legs around his waist. The concrete at her back stunned her, and she was glad for the towel between her skin and the rough material. She hadn't even sensed him moving, but now she was pressed up against the side of the house, their acts only hidden by shadows. Her body hung precariously in the air, his keeping her secure and upright. The dangerous position and act spurred her to reach down and cup him through his jeans. Doc immediately stopped kissing her and jerked his attention to her face.

"Don't touch unless you want me to take you here and now."

Taking the bait, she carefully unbuckled his belt, eyes latched on his. She didn't give a feck where they were anymore. All she cared about was having him deep inside her. He slid off her swimsuit top and locked his lips over her nipple. Heat flooded Isa's core, and she ran her fingers through his hair, urging him closer to her breasts. He dutifully caressed each one, pulling them to points with his teeth. She ground her hips into him, adoring the hardness she found there. It was nearly enough to unravel her.

Doc's fingers massaged her left breast before he gripped her hip, forcing her eyes to meet his. A new form of excitement trickled through her veins.

"If you want to stop, you gotta say the words."

Isa let out a slow breath. Never had a man been so rapt for her words. He wouldn't move a millimeter if she didn't allow it.

She reached up and pushed his hair out of his face. He was a complete alpha male, but one who wouldn't make a move without her permission.

"I don't want to stop." She kissed the side of his neck. "I want you right here." She unbuttoned his jeans. "Right now."

The clang of his belt urged him forward, and his fingers slid beneath her tiny swimsuit bottom. She gasped at the sudden intrusion.

"Damn, baby, you're always soaking for me," he murmured, inserting another finger and pumping it in and out.

She arched her back at his fluid movements as she kissed him harder, her breathing staggered the closer she came to release. When he removed his fingers, she let out an annoyed groan. "What're you—"

His lips cut off the rest of her protest. Her eyes rolled back once more, and she suddenly didn't care about his interruption. The sound of foil tearing met her ears, and he pulled away from her lips in time for her to watch him sheath his long cock. She licked her lips at the tantalizing sight. He was the most beautiful man she'd ever laid eyes on.

"You ready for me?" he asked, his voice a sexy combination of husky and commanding.

She nodded enthusiastically, hair catching on the wall. "Please."

Doc entered her as soon as she breathed the last syllable. For a long moment, she couldn't move. He slowly pulled out and slammed back into her. She tightened her legs around him, his cock hitting her just right.

He leaned down and kissed her, hips increasing their rhythm. Isa tried to counter his movements, but the concrete wall behind her made it increasingly difficult. Even with the towel, she couldn't move. She was completely pinned, his hands cupping her arse, bringing her up and down his hard cock. He filled her so full that she wasn't sure she could handle the delightful agony. With each long stroke, her body hummed against him. She squirmed closer until his movements struck her clit, the bundle of nerves pushing her closer to release.

A tickle of wind grazed her exposed nipples, and the sound of the sliding door at the back of the house opening caught her attention. She shuddered but couldn't resist the pulse of their lovemaking. The shy Irish girl was long gone. She didn't give a damn if someone caught them. The sliding door shut again, and she nipped his collarbone. He growled in response, encouraging her to do it again. Goose bumps lined his skin the more she bit his neck, his hips slamming into her harder.

Doc hissed out a curse and grabbed her chin, forcing her to face him. The lust-rimmed blue eyes were too much for her to handle. His tongue intertwined with hers, the connection sending her head into the clouds. He kissed as though it were the last time, and she yearned for more. His thrusts picked up, the sound of his balls slapping against her arse echoing in the courtyard. A strangled moan escaped her mouth, but Doc was there to drown out the sound.

"You keep making those noises and my brothers will come watch," he teased, kissing her again. She could barely hear above the rush of blood in her ears but sensed they weren't alone. The idea of someone watching them didn't bother her. At least not in the moment. All she cared about was Doc and the expert way he pounded into her.

Finally, warmth spread up her toes and to her head. The familiar tingling sensation of an orgasm rushed her body faster than the last time. She opened her mouth to cry out, but only a whisper of his name came through.

His tempo increased as she drifted from the mountaintop of her ecstasy. His cock swelled once more, and he moaned into her neck through his own release. The fervor of his lips slowly decreased, but he remained cuddled against her body.

Isa's breathing evened out, the residual effects of Doc's touch filtering through her. The first night had been incredible, but this? This was pure ecstasy.

She grinned against his leather cut. *And out in the open. You little slut.*

He cupped her face and kissed her gently. No words were needed. Their bodies said plenty. They both felt the connection.

"Isa, you have a call," a deep voice said, cutting into the silence.

She yelped and tried to right her swimsuit. The top half was easier than the bottom since Doc was presently inside her. Her eyes met his, and a proud glint crossed his blue gaze. "Don't get used to taking me anywhere you want," she teased in his ear.

He disposed of the condom, tucked himself back into his jeans, and then helped her fix her swimsuit. "I'll fuck you anytime I want, princess." He winked. "If you let me, that is."

She blushed and bit her bottom lip. He didn't have to ask, but he would.

Taking a step, she cursed when her legs wobbled. She took another and stifled a giggle when her knees knocked together. Tossing a glance over her shoulder, she noticed the smugly satisfied grin on Doc's handsome face. He was damn proud of himself for fucking her legs right out from under her.

Straightening her shoulders, she moved from the shadows and walked around the corner. Brewer stood with a sheepish look on his freckled face.

"Who is it?" she asked, hoping she didn't sound as breathless as she felt. If she didn't find a chair soon, she'd simply topple right over.

"Phantom."

She nodded and lifted her hands to her head. The hair there was in complete disarray. She tried to smooth it down, but it was useless. Until she found a brush, Isadora Walsh would simply have to walk around with *just got fucked* hair. Surprisingly, she didn't mind one smidgen.

25

DOC

Doc sank into the leather couch and exhaled. Isa was off with Brewer and Reaper, chatting with her dad. He would've gone with her if he had the chance, but apparently Brewer was sufficient protection for the walk to the phone.

Doc needed a drink anyhow. After fucking her outside by the pool, his body hummed with adrenaline. He guzzled the rest of his beer and grabbed a fresh one from the side table. Normally, getting his dick wet once or twice would suffice for a while. *Not with Isa.* He wanted her. Needed her, even. It was the best bad news he could imagine.

Klink and Hawk entered the open living room. Each one gave him a knowing look. They'd been on rooftop security and no doubt heard and saw a few things. That fact riled him more than he thought. He'd screwed nymphs in front of his brothers before and didn't give a shit. But with

Isa, he didn't want anyone else to see what they did. It was more than fucking.

"I couldn't help but notice a porno outside earlier," Klink began, plopping into the seat next to him. "It was a bit amateur for my taste, though."

Hawk pulled up a chair and rested his feet on the coffee table between them. He didn't speak, merely watched.

"Fuck off, Klink," Doc said, tilting back the beer bottle.

"Aw, come on, Doc. Brewer said it was even better up close." Klink wiggled his brows. "Care to share the lass?"

He lunged toward Klink and pinned him into the leather. His bottle crashed onto the floor, beer spilling on the hardwood. "If you even think about touching her, I'll cut your dick off and shove it up your ass."

Klink's face turned beet red, and Doc slowly decreased the pressure on his neck. "All right, all right."

Sitting back, Doc crossed his arms over his chest and glared at Hawk. "You got something smartass to say too?"

Hawk scratched his lightly bearded face. "Nah, just wondering when you got pussy whipped."

"Who's pussy whipped?" Cueball asked, entering the room.

"Doc."

Cueball sat on the arm of the couch and laughed. "I would be too if that li'l beauty was under my protection 24-7."

Doc ignored the insinuation. It was just like his

brothers to talk shit. So long as he kept his cool, they'd eventually peter out the teasing.

"Who're we talking about?" Rubble asked, coming into the room.

Getting up, Doc grabbed two handfuls of bottles and returned to the couch. He'd need more booze if he was to sustain these jabs.

"Doc and his Irish lover." Cueball nudged his shoulder when he sat down on the couch again.

Rubble stroked his massive beard, eyes alight with mischief. "Ah, yeah. I heard some very sensual sounds coming from her room last night." He grinned. "Or maybe she was going solo."

"You should've heard her today," Klink chimed in, neck still red from Doc's earlier warning. Evidently he hadn't pressed hard enough. "The high-pitched moans and mewling.... Damn, almost made me nut then and there."

"Have you seen that ass?" Rubble nodded. "It's scrumptious."

"Since when do you have a vocabulary?" Cueball teased.

"Since forever." He shoved Cueball. "Fuck you. I'm sophisticated."

"Yeah, okay, Rubble." Cueball rolled his eyes. "Now, Isa, on the other hand, that girl is sophisticated. Can't you see her sipping tea with her pinky out?"

"I'd like to do something else with that little pinky," Hawk suggested.

Doc bit the inside of his cheek as his brothers tossed around innuendos and suggestive remarks about his girl.

My girl.

He let that sink in and cracked open another beer. He'd known her less than a month, but in that short amount of time, Isa became his. Not just his job or responsibility, but *his*.

Shovelhead stepped into the room, an odd expression on his weathered face. He'd never really cared for the old man, but as a VP, Shovelhead wasn't always well liked. He nodded at the group, then walked through the room and into the kitchen.

Doc followed him with his eyes, an unsettling feeling filling his gut. Something was off about the man, but he couldn't put his finger on what.

Before he had a chance to investigate, Hawk nudged his knee.

"Yo, you heard anything we've been saying?"

He glanced around the circle of his brothers. "Not really."

"His thoughts are too filled with Isa to listen to us," Brewer teased, coming into the room.

He let that one slide off his back. The next one, though, he couldn't.

"More like how her virgin pussy feels. I'll bet it's good too. All tight and innocent. I know I'd like to taste some of it."

Silence fell in the room. Each man looked to the instigator, and Hawk swore under his breath. Talking shit was one thing, but that comment went over the line. They all understood who Isa was to the MC and to Doc. She was off-limits.

With a calm face, Doc stood and finished his beer. He tossed the empty bottle to Hawk, then locked eyes with Klink. The shit-eating grin was no longer on his face. Panic and regret were scribbled across it now.

In one quick movement, he pulled Klink off the couch and pounded his fist into the other man's face, blood spraying when it connected with his nose. Klink fought back, jabbing Doc's side and stunning him enough to crawl out from under him. Doc grabbed Klink's leg and punched the man's kidney. Klink cried out in pain, but the sound was drowned out by the brothers watching on. Bets were called by Snoopy, who suddenly appeared alongside Boulder.

Focusing on the fight, Doc fielded a left kick but missed the punch. He reeled back in pain and wiped blood from his mouth. The fucker had another thing coming if he thought he could talk shit about his woman and not get stomped.

Klink crawled over and put him in a headlock. Using his minimal wrestling skills, Doc managed to escape the hold and pin the other man once more. He threw three more punches before the big man kneed him in the gut. He folded over but wouldn't relent.

Doc jumped to his feet, Klink following with blood dripping from his broken nose. *Serves him right.* He punched Klink in the ribs, and the other man's swing connected with his face. Blood sprayed from Doc's mouth, and he wiped it on his shirt. They circled each other, their brothers surrounding them in a tight ring. More brothers gathered, and the decibel level increased.

Klink threw a left that smashed into Doc's stomach. He gritted his teeth and fought through the pain. He couldn't let this asshole beat him. Doc threw one last punch, sending Klink off-kilter. The older man staggered and dropped hard, lights out. The cheers and yells from his brothers suddenly stopped.

"What the bloody hell is going on?" Reaper roared, his Irish accent thicker with his rage.

Doc stumbled backward, and Hawk caught him before he tripped over the coffee table. Blood and sweat mingled together and raced down Doc's face. He met the prez's fierce gaze, chest heaving from the recent altercation.

"Klink disrespected my—" He paused when he noticed Isa come into the room, eyes wide and mouth gaping by the sight. "A woman. He disrespected a woman under my protection and needed to be set straight."

Reaper glowered at him, the bushy white eyebrows furrowed together. "Is this true?" he boomed.

"Aye," the brothers said in unison.

Only after Reaper eyed each one of them did he nod once. "Get yourselves cleaned up. We have work to do." He stomped out of the room, Isa at his heels. Doc couldn't see her face and swore softly. Acting like a Neanderthal never felt worse.

A sigh reverberated through his entire being. His

muscles screamed at him, but not as much as the recent wounds.

"Come on. I'll help ya," Hawk offered, looping Doc's arm around his shoulders. "Pretty sure your lady didn't appreciate all the blood," he teased.

Doc tried to smirk, but the act threatened to open his bloodied lip. "Yeah, yeah. Shut up and get me patched up."

Boulder checked on Klink—who was still out—and then he and Rubble took the man back to his room.

Snoopy patted him on the back. "You did good, Doc. Hell, if Rubble wasn't our longstanding champion, I'd wager on you."

He cracked a smile this time and winced. *Worth it.*

"Grab some ice," Hawk called. One of the prospects hurried to do his bidding.

They made it to the stairs before Hawk paused. Facing him, he asked, "She worth all this?"

"And more," Doc replied without thinking twice.

26

—

ISA

Doc didn't come to bed that night. After his fight with Klink, his brothers set him up in his room. Isa didn't bother to check on him right away, waiting until after Hawk and Snoopy cleared out and Doc was asleep to sneak into the room. It wasn't as big as hers, the décor purely masculine. The mocha-colored paneling and drawn curtains gave the room a dark vibe.

She ran her fingers along the wooden railing at the foot of the king-sized bed. Doc's steady breathing along with the slight rise and fall of his chest and subtle snore told her he was sleeping.

When she'd walked into the living room earlier to Doc battered and bloodied, she didn't know what to think. After she saw Klink on the floor, her temper flared. *Men and their idiotic fights.* Doc's explanation didn't help matters either, but Queenie's translation did.

"Klink said some shit about your, um, virginity, and

Doc, well, he defended your honor," Queenie said hours earlier. "Macha doesn't condone such behavior, especially when you're under our protection. How Doc feels about you may also have something to do with it."

Isa softly sat on the mattress and brushed her fingers along Doc's face. The cuts were minimal, but the purple bruises made her insides jumble. He'd purposefully put himself in danger for her. *What kind of man does that?*

Doc shifted on the bed, and she held her breath. He didn't wake, so she continued her visual perusal of his injuries. With his shirt off, she could see bruising on his left ribs and his right shoulder. *And to think, an hour before his fight, I was admiring his strength.* She shivered at the power he had over her.

She lightly traced the bruises with her fingertips, then with her lips. He'd more than earned her respect after the day's events.

She thought back to the conversation with her father when Doc was roughhousing. Phantom warned her of the Twelve Brothers in Colorado and urged her to stay close to her protector. Isa's eyes dipped over the light sheet on his waist. She'd stay by his side until the very end if it came to that.

Lying beside him, she traced his nose. Thankfully, that part of him hadn't seen any punches. "You're a beautiful dolt, you know that?"

"I do, actually."

Isa gasped and her stomach flipped when Doc's blue

eyes locked her in place. "Bugger, I thought you were asleep."

He tried to turn on his side, then thought better of it. "I can't sleep with your hands on me." A small smile crossed his face. "Or with your scent filling my room."

She slipped her hand in his and cozied closer to him, mindful of his injuries. "I heard what you did for me."

Doc cleared his throat. "Wasn't a big deal. Klink gets on my nerves anyways."

Isa sat up slightly to look into his eyes. "It's a big deal to me. I've never had anyone defend my honor." She smirked. "Even if it came from the same man who screwed me against a wall."

He reached up and traced her lips. "I'd do anything for you, Isa."

"I know." She studied the back of his hand and the scabs on his knuckles. "Is this real, Doc? You and me? I don't have much relationship experience and don't know if you're merely protecting me because it's your job or...." She realized she was rambling and stopped.

He sat up and motioned for her to come closer. Once she was securely in his arms, he looked down into her eyes and caressed her cheek. "I protect you because I want to, Isa. It may be my job, but I've never been happier than when I'm with you."

She snuggled into his wide chest and closed her eyes. Even if only for the time being, she'd be content with their relationship—or lack thereof. If it was all he could offer, her heart would make do.

27

———

DOC

Damage control was something Doc was used to from working as a paramedic. He'd come across many scenes on the road where blood and guts were sprawled out for everyone to see. That part of the job was far from fun but wasn't hard to clean up. A little bleach or tarp would do the job and avoid residual catastrophe.

But the damage control when it came to his fight with Klink was another matter. Isa slept by his side all night. It was sweet in a torturous sort of way. His body craved her touch, but his injuries told him otherwise. He wouldn't apologize to Klink. No, that was his brother's job to do. The fucker hadn't yet, so Doc woke at the crack of dawn to get Isa off his mind.

Now he was doing what he'd done as a kid when he fucked up: he baked. Every Macha brother gave him shit for it too. Especially this morning. Waking up and starting in on his famous cinnamon twists made even Rubble crack a joke about Doc's baking.

"I'll take mine with an orange glaze, sweetheart," Snoopy teased, taking a seat at the kitchen table.

Ignoring him, Doc sprinkled a handful of cinnamon into the mixing bowl and kneaded the dough. He'd had to glove his hands this morning, a fact that only irritated him more as the dough stuck to them.

"And don't forget extra cinnamon on mine," Brewer said, grabbing a cup of coffee.

Doc looked up in time to see Brewer wink and add cream to the cup. "Extra cinnamon is a must."

"Well, then good. I won't be disappointed." Brewer walked back to the table and sat beside Rubble and Hawk. They chatted nonchalantly, the early morning wake-up understandable given the ongoing threat. Normally his brothers didn't wake before ten, but they could all feel the chill of the Twelve Brothers in the mountain air.

Covering the dough, Doc let it rest and washed his dishes. When the dough rose once more, he'd start making the twists.

He looked at the clock on the microwave, then glanced down at his clothes. The Macha tee was a smidge too small, and his jeans were ripped on the back pockets. It'd been early and he'd just grabbed clothes and hightailed it from the room before Isa woke. He couldn't face her perfection after yesterday's brawl.

He poured a cup of coffee and sat next to Brewer.

"If we move Isa to the high mountain cabin, it'd be better for us all," Snoopy was saying.

Rubble shook his head and sipped his black coffee. "Not happening, Snoop. I already laid out the plans." He narrowed his gaze. "Unless you think you'd like to challenge my sergeant at arms status."

Snoopy held up both tattooed hands in surrender. "Nah, Rubble, I'd never do that." He looked over his shoulder and lowered his voice. "I just wanna make sure my old lady and kid are safe."

"We'll send the women and children to the other safe house," Rubble stated, setting his cup on the table. "Will that satisfy you?"

"Yeah, brother, it would. Thank you." Snoopy stood and hurried off toward the bedrooms.

Doc could only imagine why. He was worried about Isa too. If he had the chance to spirit her somewhere safer, he'd jump at it.

"Really wish Kevlar was here," Rubble mumbled. "He never talked back."

Brewer chuckled. "Yeah right. Kevlar talks shit more than Snoopy."

"True, but he knows when to shut the hell up."

Doc blew on his coffee. "Kevlar die?"

"Nah, he was deployed." Brewer snatched a piece of banana bread from the platter on the table. There was always something sweet in case of midnight snacks or early risers. "He's special ops in the Army. Been gone two years."

"He's one of the best," Rubble added. "He and I met

overseas, and he convinced me to join Macha. I trust no one more than Kevlar."

"Sounds like a good dude." Doc took a drink and listened to the cabin coming alive with the morning light. Somebody was getting fucked, that much he could tell from the sounds. A baby cried for her mother, and the stomping of feet could only mean Macha's bikers were awake.

"He'll be back soon."

Doc glanced at Brewer. "How do you know?"

Brewer bit into the bread. "He touched base with Rubble. His deployment is done. Not sure if he's re-upping, but he'll be home within the week."

"Good. We can use all the help we can get."

Rubble's eyes flicked between the two men across from him. "That we can."

***

OVER THE NEXT HOUR, MORE PEOPLE WEAVED IN AND out of the kitchen, grabbing breakfast and trying to hurry Doc's cinnamon twists along so they could taste them.

He was rolling out the dough when Isa's silhouette caught the corner of his eye. He looked up in time to see her smile at Brewer. *Thank God they're related.* His redheaded brother was a subtle charmer and wouldn't think twice if she was interested.

"What're you doing?"

Doc stamped down his excitement when she touched the small of his back. It felt so innocent, yet he knew precisely what she could do with that hand. "Making cinnamon twists."

"You bake?" Her brows rose.

"Yeah, so?"

She chuckled. "I never imagined you covered in flour."

He lowered his eyes and swore. His black shirt was nearly white from the flour.

"I like a man who knows his way around the kitchen." She kissed his cheek. "Anything I can do to help?"

"Actually, yes." He grabbed the bowl of cinnamon and sugar. "I'll paint the dough if you add the cinnamon sugar."

She quirked her brow. "Paint?"

He held up a bowl of melted butter. "Yep, paint."

Shrugging, she agreed, and they quickly started an assembly line, Doc using a small brush to apply the butter and Isa smothering the dough with cinnamon sugar. By the end, every countertop was covered in dough.

"Now what?" she asked, rinsing the bowl in the sink.

"We cut and twist." He unsheathed a knife and started cutting long lines in the dough. Next, he took two slices of dough and twisted them together. Isa came up beside him, watching his swift movements.

"Wow, you're really good at this." She grinned. "I never would've pinned you for a cinnamon twist kind of biker."

He quickly finished the dough in his hands. "My mom loved to bake, and I picked up a thing or two." He glanced at her. "Just don't ask me to cook. I'm shit at that. Takeout is my specialty." He motioned for her to come closer. "Try it out. You'll catch on real fast."

Isa moved in front of him, her hair tickling his chin. She smelled better than the cinnamon twists, a rarity for his love of the spice. Her hands moved swiftly, her technique not the best but improved by the next twist.

"This is kind of fun." She started in on her third one, and he had to commend her. She was brilliant in the kitchen. He brushed her hair off her shoulder. Of course, it wasn't a surprise. She was brilliant everywhere.

"Told ya you'd catch on." He tore himself away from her sweet body to preheat the oven and prepare the baking sheets. If he had his way, they'd sneak into the pantry and rattle the shelves in between baking.

Isa beamed at him. "I like learning new stuff. Helps me feel well rounded." She laughed. "Oddly enough, my mum never liked to bake. She could cook one hell of an Irish stew, though."

Doc put the first round of twists in the oven. "I'd love to try it sometime."

"Maybe you'll get lucky."

He leaned against the oven door and watched her finish putting the twists on her tray. When she reached down to grab another sheet, her hair swung to the left, uncovering her braless state. He swallowed the urge to fuck her right there on the countertop, sweet treats be damned. Instead, he ignored his hard-on and started putting dishes in the dishwasher. Anything to get his brain off the way Isa sent his blood pumping.

"All done." She set the last tray on the counter beside

the oven. "Any particular reason you chose today to make these?"

He turned around and met her teasing gray eyes. "Nope."

Her brows shot up. "Really?" She walked closer, arms resting on both sides of the sink, trapping him against it. Her eyes slowly drifted up his body until she met his gaze. "You sure it had nothing to do with the brawl yesterday?"

Doc kept his soapy hands at bay. "Maybe." He shrugged, and Isa pushed her long hair behind her shoulders, giving him an ideal view of her white T-shirt. He couldn't resist placing his wet hands on her breasts.

Isa's jaw dropped and she squealed as the water transferred over her shirt. She swatted at his hands, but Doc merely squeezed her breasts, adoring the way they felt against him.

"Happy with yourself?" she finally asked after he'd soaked the entire front of her T-shirt.

Doc lowered his head and brushed his lips against hers. "Very."

When she didn't immediately kiss him back, he slipped his arms around her neck and tilted her chin up. Gorgeous gray eyes met his, and he lost his breath. He didn't deserve even a smile from this stunning woman, but she graced him with one anyway.

"Doc?"

"Yeah, baby?"

Her eyes searched his. "Kiss me."

He didn't need to be told twice. Lowering his lips, he

fused his mouth to Isa's within moments. She hopped off the floor, wrapping her legs around his waist, lips never leaving his. Doc held her steady, walking them to the pantry. He'd always wanted to screw a girl there and wasn't about to miss the opportunity.

He flung the door open and shut it again once they were inside. Soft moans left Isa as he kissed down the side of her neck. Her pussy ground against his cock, and he groaned at the clothes between them.

"Won't someone catch us?"

"I don't give a shit." He pushed up her shirt and pulled her nipple between his teeth. She gasped and arched her back. There was no better sensation than to feel his girl come alive beneath his touch.

Her dainty fingers slipped under his shirt, slowly tracing his back. It was pure heaven. She was heaven.

"Have you done this with many nymphs?"

He paused his attentions and pulled away from her breast. "What?"

She bit her bottom lip, eyes darting from him to the canned tomatoes on the shelf. "Fucked in the pantry. Have you done it with a lot of the nymphs?"

Doc carefully set her feet on the floor. "No, Isa, I haven't done this with any nymph." He searched her eyes. His reputation clearly preceded him, and his beautiful Irish princess was skeptical. He couldn't blame her.

"What do they call you?"

"Who?"

She gave him an exasperated huff. "The nymphs."

"Oh, erm, just Doc. Or Doc O for, um, obvious reasons."

"And the women before me?"

He ran his hands through his hair. *This woman will be the death of me.*

"O'Brien, usually."

Rubbing her lips together, Isa walked to the other end of the pantry. "I want to call you something different." She met his gaze. "Please."

He leaned against the wall and crossed his arms over his chest. "All right, princess, what's your poison? Macha man? Doctor Sexy? Hot biker? Those are all available."

She closed the distance between them and lightly nipped his bottom lip. "When I come, I want to call you Doc T."

For a moment, Doc wasn't sure he'd heard her right. No woman had ever called him any variation of Tad during sex. His teasing smile slipped from his face. "What?"

"Please?"

"Why would you want to?"

Isa cupped his jaw. "Has anyone ever called you that?"

"No."

She pressed her lips to his again. "That's why. I want to be the first and only."

His head spun at the notion. Somehow, she had figured out his kryptonite: his name. No one ever called him by it. Especially during sex. He'd always gone by one nickname or another. She was so perfect for him it hurt.

He wrapped his arms around her waist before he could stop himself. "All right, princess."

She grinned and pulled him down to her mouth. He overwhelmed her lips in the next moment, never getting enough of her candy taste. He'd be damned if anyone else ever called him Doc T. He was Isa's now, and he didn't want to let go of the sensations she caused in his body and heart.

Not giving a damn, he yanked at her tight leggings and spun her around. His cock was sheathed and inside her sweet pussy before her throaty moan reached his ears. Isa gripped the shelf in front of her to steady herself. Cans toppled over, hitting the ground and rolling.

Thrusting in and out of her harder, he relished the first, second, and third time his princess screamed his name for the whole damn house to hear.

28

———

ISA

"THIS PLACE IS INCREDIBLE." ISA GRAZED HER FINGERS along the railing that led to the tattoo parlor attached to the bar. She'd only seen the place once, during her tour, and heaven knew she wasn't paying attention to anything other than Doc.

"Legs and Snoopy run the shop most of the time, but Hawk is the best artist here." He nodded toward the man currently bent over a male client, tattoo gun in hand.

Hawk jutted up his chin and grinned. "Fuck yeah. And they know it too."

Isa perused the wall behind Hawk. It was covered with Polaroids of his clientele and their new tattoos. She had to admit, they were pure art. "You're amazing."

Hawk wiped the tattoo he was working on and met her gaze. "That's what all the women say."

Doc cleared his throat behind her, but Hawk didn't seem to take that as a threat.

"You got any tats, princess?"

"Actually, I have one." She lifted her shirt, displaying a small clover on her rib. "Got it in memory of my mum after she passed. She was as religious as they come but always believed in the power of a four-leaf clover."

"Why haven't I seen this before?" Doc asked, his calloused fingers tracing the small tattoo.

"Probably because you were more interested in her other assets," Hawk heckled good-naturedly.

He didn't answer and she giggled. "I'm sure you subconsciously saw it." She patted Doc's cheek affectionately.

"I'll pay extra attention tonight, then, to make up for it," he said lowly.

A delightful shiver shot up Isa's body. Meeting his blue eyes, she recognized the familiar hue of lust.

"I'll be done in an hour if you guys want to meet up at the bar." Hawk put the finishing touches on the tattoo and covered it before sending the man on his way.

"Actually, I was hoping you'd tattoo me." She glanced between the two men. Both had amused expressions on their handsome faces.

Standing, Hawk held out his hand. "Anything for our Macha princess."

After getting comfortable in the chair, she pulled out a small drawing from her pocket. "Think you can do it?"

Hawk studied the drawing and his smile broadened. "You drew this?"

"Aye."

"Damn, girl, you should've been a tattoo artist." He patted her thigh. "Better yet, I could use you for the people who have no clue what they want. You could sketch something up."

Isa shook her head. "Thanks for the offer, but I think I'll stick to designing clothes."

"All right, don't say I didn't try to cut you in on a sweet deal." He nodded to her body. "Where we doing this?"

She held out her hand. "My wrist."

"Isa, that'll hurt like hell."

"I know." She smiled at Doc. *Always trying to protect me.* "But I've wanted one here for years. Hawk will make it painless." She winked. "Right?"

Hawk chuckled. "I'll do my best."

An hour later, Isa stared into the mirror. She couldn't wipe the smile from her face if she used steel wool. The intricate vine of ivy traced her own rendition of the goddess Macha. Green, blue, black, and red wound together perfectly. It wasn't a small piece, but one she'd spent hours designing specifically for herself.

"You won't be forgetting Macha anytime soon," Hawk said, covering it with a bandage. "Try to keep it dry for a few days, and be sure to use this spray to ward off infection." He handed her a small bag full of treats.

"Do you give these to all your clients?"

"Nah, only the pretty ones." He grabbed her hand and helped her out of the chair. "Be gentle now, Doc."

"Always am with this one." He took her goody bag and led her to the saloon doors. "First round's on me."

Hawk laughed. "All the rounds are on you, Doc."

Isa followed Doc into the bar, the steady stream of customers filling the space. Thankfully, a small clump of tables in the back of the bar were reserved for Macha members. They plopped into one of the booths, and Doc waved to Brewer.

"What did Hawk mean?"

"About what?"

She shifted on the red seat. "About you being gentle."

"Oh, that."

When he didn't expand, she cocked her eyebrow. "You told me you were too rough for a girl like me. From what I can tell, you're not as rough as I expected."

Doc waited until one of the nymphs dropped off their drinks to answer. He leaned forward over the table. "That's because I'm holding back."

"What? Why? I told you not to."

He took a long draw of beer. "Baby, if I showed you the beast in me, you'd shatter."

"Then shatter me." She locked eyes with him. "I want to see and feel it all."

"No can do, baby doll." Doc turned his gaze to the bar, and hers reluctantly followed. The slow country song had tempted couples out to the dance floor, and plenty of groping abounded. He nodded every now and then at fellow Macha members.

"Why?"

He shifted on the seat. Letting out a heavy sigh, he finished off his drink. "Because you can't handle it."

"And the nymphs can?"

His brows rose. "That's not what I said."

"So then what's it like, Doc?" She folded her arms across her chest. "You gently shag me, then ravage one of the club sluts to let it all out?"

Doc's eyes narrowed, and the gorgeous depths of blue turned stormy once more. Just like when she'd first met him.

There it is. That simmering danger she wanted to exploit.

"I haven't had sex with a nymph since you arrived."

"Bullshit. You can't honestly expect me to believe that." She pounded her whiskey. "Not after you admitted to taking it easy on me because I can't handle your *beast*."

He slid across the booth, pinning her to the back with nowhere to go. "I hold myself back because I don't want to hurt you."

She leaned closer, her nose touching his briefly. "That's not healthy, Doc."

"I never said I was good at taking prescribed medicine."

She tilted her head to the left. "Then maybe you should try one dose of me at a time."

"Isa, let it go." He laid his large hand over hers. "Please. We're just starting something here. I can't lose you because of my selfish needs."

Shoving at him, she wiggled out enough to climb over the table. "If you haven't noticed, I'm not the scared little virgin you met." She straightened her shoulders and gave him a defiant glare. "I'm the daughter of Macha, and I'll kick your arse if you don't treat me as such."

Doc's stern face slightly broke into a small grin, but he quickly smothered it. Isa didn't give him the opportunity to respond. She stalked outside and fished his bike keys from her pocket. He hadn't even felt her lift them.

She'd get it through his thick skull eventually. *I'm not easily broken. Macha's made sure of that.*

29

—

ISA

"Well, how's it going with your sexy biker?" Dolly asked. She plopped onto the couch next to Isa and got as close as humanly possible without touching.

Isa looked away from the television show. Aside from the night before, when Doc promptly shut her down, she couldn't hide how she truly felt about the stubborn arse. "I don't even have words to describe it." She chuckled. "Not like I have anything to base it on."

"Girl, try. I'm dying over here." Dolly bopped her nose to Isa's. "Tell me."

Doc's shadow fell across the doorway, and Isa glanced over to see him talking with Cueball and Rubble. He caught her gaze for an instant but then returned to his conversation. They'd yet to discuss their disagreement the night before. *Seeing how I stole his motorcycle, I doubt he wants to chat.*

"Is he always so stubborn?

"Uh-huh." Dolly grinned.

Isa chuckled. "Thanks for being honest, I guess."

Dolly sat back and crossed her legs. "Girl, you're not in a relationship with him."

"Well, I know that, but—"

"No buts. I'll give it to you straight." She faced Isa on the couch. "Sometimes, women fall for the first guy they sleep with. It's totally normal, but you need to prepare yourself."

Frowning, she crossed her arms over her chest. "It's not like that. Doc and I have a connection. We had one before sleeping together." She instantly hated how naïve she sounded.

"Sure, sweetie."

"I'm serious."

"So am I. Look, sex is my job. I'm trying to warn you." Dolly tightened her ponytail. "You're under Macha protection. Doc's protection. Of course he's going to do everything in his power to keep you as close to him as possible. It's not unusual for Macha men."

Blood drained from Isa's face. Suddenly the ham sandwich she ate an hour ago didn't settle so well. "You're saying he slept with me only because he wants to keep me safe?"

Dolly shrugged and pulled out her cell phone, checking the messaging app. "I'm saying don't get emotionally invested. Once a playboy, always a playboy."

Isa clenched her jaw. Surely the madam was wrong.

She tried to focus on the reality show on the big screen,

but her mind wouldn't let her home in on it. Their interactions filtered across her memory. She'd instigated their kisses and hours filled with sex. Not Doc. He didn't want to hurt her; he'd said so last night. He'd purposefully restrained himself during sex. The whispers around the clubhouse reminded her that was abnormal. Doc wasn't a soft, gentle lover.

Brewer popped his head in the room and called his sister away. Isa didn't even hear them leave, just felt the empty loneliness fill the space.

Maybe I read too much into Doc's words and actions. She tucked her feet under her and whined. *You've done it this time, Isa.* She had to accept Doc was doing his job. He said he'd do whatever it took to keep her safe, and evidently he meant it.

Bloody fool.

THE DISTINCT SCENT OF ROAST CHICKEN WAFTED UP the stairs and to Isa's room. She'd wanted to skip the big family dinner tonight, but her grumbling belly had other ideas. Putting down the book on Macha history written by one of the founding members, she slipped a button-up shirt over her pink tank top. The bedazzled shirt usually made her giddy, but not today. Not since she spoke with the club's madam.

Heading down the hall, she watched the club from her perch at the top of the catwalk. Hawk was chasing a youngster around the living area, rubber snake in his hands, while the child laughed happily. Snoopy was chewing out a prospect about cleaning his roadster incorrectly. Brewer had a nymph on the line, the brunette an easy mark. And of course, there was Doc sitting on a leather recliner nearby, a nymph on each arm of the overstuffed chair.

Isa held her head a smidge higher and started down the stairs. Only once she made the bottom did she look anywhere but Doc's handsome face. He hadn't spotted her yet, which was fine with her. If Dolly was right, she'd accept the fact that she'd been a fool with Macha's doctor.

Getting over him will be a whole different problem.

"You look comfy," a low voice complimented.

Looking to her left, she smiled at Rubble. The big man didn't normally socialize with her, but tonight, she was grateful for the distraction.

"Thanks. I am." She looked down at her sweatpants. "Didn't feel like dressing up for a meal."

Rubble chuckled, the sound cheerful yet low and rumbling. He was the one biker she was wary of due to the sheer mass of the man. He was all muscle and beard.

"What do you look like without the beard?" she asked before she could stop herself.

Shifting his weight to his left leg, Rubble subconsciously stroked the long black beard. It was trimmed but wild enough to look the biker part. That paired with a perfectly shaved head and mismatched eyes made him appear unapproachable.

"Young." He winked his blue eye, and she felt a blush creep up her neck.

They walked toward the dining room, Doc long forgotten in her mind. "I'd guess as much. But honestly, doesn't it get hot with all that hair?"

Rubble shrugged. "Can't really remember a time I didn't have one form of scruff or another. In the Marines, I had to be clean cut. At least until we were deployed. Nobody gave a shit about that when we were knee deep in sand."

Isa watched his smile droop. "Do you miss the action?"

"No." He pulled out a chair for her. "I've found a brotherhood with the club like I had in the Marines. More so even. Macha was there when I returned. They didn't give me grief for not having any professional skills. They accepted me as I am. I can't say many other jobs would."

"I've never thought of that. It must've been hard adjusting to civilian life again." She took a sip of water, ensuring her eyes never left his face. The club's sergeant at arms was much more than mere muscle.

"It was. Still is, depending on where I go."

"I'm sure it also affected your relationships. Have you ever been in one?"

Rubble met her curious gaze. "Why the sudden interest, Isa?" He jutted his chin toward the living room. "Doc here not giving you proper attention?"

The blood drained from her face. "Oh no, that's not what I meant. I, um, well, I really just—"

"Calm down. I was teasing." He patted her hand. "To

answer your question, not too many women approach me. Evidently I give off a tough vibe." He outstretched his large hands. "I wonder what it is."

She opened her mouth to respond, but he waved her off.

"I don't do relationships. Never had much luck in them. It's part of the reason I joined the Marines. My parents were shitty, and I was bounced around foster homes until I aged out of the system." He took a breath. "I've never been good with women. No offense, but y'all are hard to read. Battle plans, though. Those are natural to me."

"I admit, we women can be difficult." She offered him a small smile. "But you can't avoid women because you don't understand us."

He took a sip of beer. "Watch me."

Isa rolled her eyes. It was like talking to a brick wall. She'd heard a prospect mention Rubble's previous stint in MMA, where he'd earned his nickname. That was a story she'd like to hear, but for tonight, she was content merely gaining a new friend, albeit not a close one.

Dinner was served, and she couldn't help but notice Doc stayed at the other end of the table. Boulder sat to her left, and she instantly felt small between the two men. *In between a rock and a hard place.* She giggled to herself.

She did her damnedest to not look Doc's direction. It would've been easier if the slutty nymphs didn't chortle every two minutes at something witty the lout said. The flirting was one thing. Ignoring her was what set her off.

"He's a dick sometimes," Rubble said under his breath.

Isa looked over to Doc, and for a split second, their eyes connected. "Yeah, definitely an eejit." She focused on her apple crisp. "Do club members always utilize the nymphs when it suits them or just him?"

Rubble's eyes grazed over her. "The goddess Macha was a warrior. Legend tells she was also very sensual. The club tends to merge these two when it comes to the nymphs. Before you arrived, Doc was rarely without a nymph or two at his side."

"Lovely." She picked at the apples in the bowl. No matter what transpired between her and Doc, he'd always return to his playboy ways. *Any sort of future with him will be the same.* Tears sprang to her eyes, and she stood abruptly. Suddenly, not even cinnamon apples could settle her nerves.

She hurried from the room, grateful no one tried to stop her. Reaching the dual staircase, she took the steps two at a time until she made the top. She promptly sat on the step and massaged her head. "This would be so much easier if I didn't sleep with him."

"Ah, now don't go back on your own advice."

Isa whipped her head up to see Rubble standing a few stairs down. "What?"

He easily ate the distance with his long legs and plopped next to her. "You can't avoid Doc because you don't understand him."

She let out a disgruntled huff. "There's nothing to

understand. He prefers a different woman every night. Seems rather cut-and-dried."

Rubble sighed and laced his fingers together over his knees. "He's scared too. You're a first for him."

"First what? Irish lass?"

"Nah, I'm sure—er, that's not what I meant." He gave her a sheepish grin. "You're the first woman to give him a hard time. You don't fall at his feet and beg him to kiss you."

"In my dreams I do," she mumbled.

"Huh?"

"Nothing." Isa straightened her back and took a cleansing breath. "But you're right. I need to take my own advice."

"Good, glad that's settled."

"I didn't say I would start with Doc, though." She heard him sigh but didn't respond, merely stood and made her way back to the haven of her room.

Doc could be solved another day.

If ever.

"So, tell me everything. I'm dying to hear something other than what Ms. McKellen had for breakfast every morning."

Isa stared at her best friend's face on the phone. She'd once thought they'd end up old maids together. That was until Niall finally gave up pretending he wasn't head over heels in love with Orla.

"It's a mess," she admitted. "I've never been good with men."

Orla pursed her lips. "You don't say?"

"Shut it. I can't help if Mum kept me chaste." She crossed one leg over the other and stared at the bedroom door. Doc wouldn't barge through it anytime soon. She'd heard him in the hall earlier before heading to church. "But I don't want to talk about it. I want to hear all the town gossip."

For the next ten minutes, Orla dished on the locals and

the new couples who'd emerged since Isa's departure. The shop managed to make rent, pay bills, and earn a bit in excess. The weather was rainy, but a bit of sun was out today. How she desired an Irish breeze through her long hair!

"But I told Niall I wasn't about to up and move in with his parents. Could you imagine? Me sipping tea every morning with his mum? Not happening. Ever."

"At least you have someone to sip a cuppa with. No one here can brew a good one." She stood and started wandering the halls. "And they call themselves Irish."

"Love, they're Americanized."

Isa reached the main floor and made her way to the kitchen. The scent of cinnamon twists still clung in the air. They instantly pulled her back to the previous morning she'd spent with Doc. Blinking back tears, she opened the fridge and grabbed a bottle of water before slipping out of the room. Suddenly, kitchens were her enemy.

Isa pushed open the door to the back patio and plopped into a chair by the pool. A warm breeze tickled her arms and legs, the sun beating down on her alabaster skin. Her Colorado vacation had given her a tinge of a tan but nothing to call home about.

Focusing back on the conversation, she heard Niall in the background. The door shut and she noticed Orla roll her eyes. *Doc would have a heyday with her.* The thought chilled her. The only person she wanted Doc to play with was her.

The sound of the shop bell clanged, and Orla hopped

off the counter and set the phone down. "Damn man forgot to lock the door again. Oy, we're closed."

Isa narrowed her gaze when no answer came back. "What's going on? Who's there?"

A scuffle of feet and the sound of a vase crashing to the floor brought Isa to her feet. The muffled scream sent her stomach into a nosedive. "Orla! What's happening? Are you all right?"

Heavy boots clomped toward the phone. A man wearing a ski mask filled the frame, and Isa stood frozen. She made out a leather cut on the man's body. "Sorry, lass, your chums won't be opening tomorrow or the next day." He chuckled and grabbed the phone. "Tell Macha we're coming for you next."

The video call went dead, black staring back at her. The man was clearly from the Twelve Brothers MC. Reality crept in, and she raced toward the lodge.

Flinging open the door, she cried, "They have Orla and Niall!"

Heads popped up from every direction to look at her. Boots clambered on the stairs, and before she made it to the kitchen, the entire Macha crew stood before her.

"What happened?" Doc asked, trying to meet her eyes. She wouldn't let him. She could barely see anything other than the image of the man in black.

"I was talking to Orla, and somebody came into the shop." She managed to fill in the rest of the details. When she was done, every face surrounding her was grim.

"Oh God. They're going to kill them!" she shrieked,

grabbing a fistful of Doc's cut. "This is all Macha's fault. If my father wasn't in your club, none of this would be happening." She hit his chest hard, the impact hurting her fist more than him.

"Get her upstairs," Reaper directed, taking control of the situation. "Rubble, take Hawk and Snoopy down to Snowshoe. Tell our boys there to be ready. We're going into lockdown. Brewer, take Dolly and track down the nymphs in town. Get them up here before nightfall. Cueball, go grab the rest of the kids at school. They're missing a few days."

Bodies rushed this way and that, no one talking directly to her but rather at her. Childish cries and manly hollers overwhelmed her already short circuits. She sank onto the floor, bringing her knees up to her face, and covered her ears with her hands. Tears snaked down her cheeks as her body shook.

"Isa?" Doc crouched down and lifted her chin. "Dammit, baby, I'm sorry." He scooped her into his arms and barked orders at two prospects. She couldn't understand what they were saying. His heat enveloped her, and she buried her face in his chest. Despite being safe for the time being, panic crept in and overtook her weary body.

31
—

DOC

Sitting and not doing anything quickly wore on Doc's patience. Reaper ordered him to stay with Isa, but he felt out of touch with his brothers. They needed him just as much as she did. He stopped pacing the bedroom and sat in the chair near the window. Her steady breathing calmed him momentarily. She'd passed out and slept through dinner. He wasn't sure if he should wake her or let her stay in dreamland. *It's safer there.*

After their fight at the bar, he hadn't wanted to speak with her until he could figure out what the hell he was doing. He'd never wanted something deeper with a woman, but he did with Isa. It scared the living daylights out of him.

He typed a message to Rubble on his phone. The sergeant at arms wouldn't answer; he was too busy making sure their club was ready for an attack. Doc bounced his left leg up and down, eyes fixed on the tree line. The lodge was secure and even offered several tunnels in case of dire emergencies. Still, he couldn't shake the feeling that something was about to change his life.

"What time is it?" Isa asked, sitting up. Her voice was groggy with sleep, and tearstains streaked her cheeks. His gut pitched at the sight. He hadn't been able to protect her from her friends' abduction.

"Just after seven." He laced his fingers together and rested his elbows on his knees. "Are you all right?"

"Bugger. Is there any update?"

"No. I'm sorry." He watched her fight back a new wave of tears. "Hawk and Cueball are keeping tabs on the situation in Belfast. A couple brothers over there are attempting to find where Orla and Niall are being held."

Isa sat up and gathered the blanket to her neck. In that moment, she looked so small and vulnerable. There was more wrong than just the kidnapping. He could sense it in the way she wouldn't keep eye contact.

"We should talk about last night."

"I don't want to."

He let out a frustrated huff. His woman was equally as stubborn as him. More so even. "Baby, look at me."

She flicked her head up and glared. "There? You happy?"

The combination of her Irish accent and her fiery words only reiterated his thoughts. "If it's about what we argued about... I'm in uncharted waters here."

She rolled her eyes, and he fought back pressing that particular nuance of her personality. Pushing her too far too fast would only cause more pain.

"Princess, I'm not used to this."

"Why don't you just leave me alone?" she snapped. "You did your job. Congratulations, you fucked the woman you were tasked to protect. You can officially brag to the boys that you got the Irish virgin." She sniffled. "Do you feel better now that I've completely fallen for you? Bloody wanker."

Doc wasn't sure which part of her rant to focus on first. He went with the obvious misunderstanding. "What do you mean? I don't sleep with any woman under Macha protection."

Her gray eyes might as well have been daggers to his heart. "Of course you do. Dolly told me all about it. I suppose it makes sense. Who better to fuck than a woman who'll leave after the danger's gone?"

He steepled his fingers over his nose. "Jesus Christ, Isa, it's not like that and you know it."

Anger flashed in her eyes. "Oh sure. It makes sense to lure women into your bed and say it's for their protection." She crossed her arms. "How many have there been? Two? Five? Twenty?"

Laughter erupted from him before he could stop it. He shook his head and let the situation play out in his mind. Isa glowered at him, and he wished he could show her how adorable she looked all flustered. His Irish princess was one hell of a jealous woman. Her sentiment warmed him. Half the time, his one-night stands didn't give a fuck about him. That all changed with her.

"What're you cackling about? This isn't funny."

He held up his hands. "It's not to you, but to me, it really is."

"Sure, laugh about how I caught you in your stupid little trick for all naïve women. Laugh it up, twat."

"Baby, I don't sleep with any women Macha protects. They're off-limits." He licked his bottom lip. "Swear on my mother's grave. Crossing that line is unprofessional, and Macha could kick my ass out for doing it."

Her rage slowly tapered. "Then Dolly was wrong?"

Searching her face, Doc saw her uncertainty. "Yes, Dolly was wrong." He quickly stood and walked to the side of the bed. Leaning down, he gripped her chin, forcing her eyes to stay latched on him. "You are the one and only woman I've ever crossed that line with, princess. I don't regret it, either."

"Oh."

The magnitude of her wariness urged him to not stop until she was wholly compliant. "You're in my blood, Isa. You're in my very heart. The thought of anyone else by my side makes me want to lie down in front of my bike going full speed on the highway."

"But—"

He kissed her roughly and only pulled away when she grasped the front of his cut. "I love you, Isadora Walsh. I've loved you from the first moment I heard you talking to yourself in the terminal."

Tears sprang to her eyes, but they weren't sad ones this time. "Really?"

"Really."

"Dolly was wrong about a lot of things."

He frowned and made a mental note to chew out the madam later. At present, all he wanted to do was show Isa how much she meant to him. "Don't listen to her about shit." He sat on the bed and cuddled her to his chest. "I'm the only one you need to talk to about us. If you have questions, worries, rants, whatever, I'm here for you, and I'm not going anywhere."

"Bloody hell, you're good." She leaned forward and rested her forehead against his. "For a moment, I thought maybe it was chemical for you."

"It's a lot more than that." He nipped her top lip. "I'm also very attached to the sounds you make when you come."

Her blush was well worth the cheesy line. Being a player was in his past. He only had eyes for Isa as long as she wanted him.

Her fingers danced along his jaw, the overgrowth of hair reminding him of the vast change his life took. Instead of a clean-cut EMT, he was a long-haired biker. *Life's funny like that.*

"I've missed you," she whispered, kissing his cheek.

"I didn't go anywhere."

"In my mind you did." Her lips drifted down his neck. "Don't ever leave me."

"I swear I won't."

"What about holding back? I don't want you to." She kissed his jaw. "I want all of you, Doc T. Not the edited version."

Cupping her face, he nuzzled her nose. "Okay, babe. You'll get all of me, but we gotta go slow. I can't bear to hurt you."

"Neither can I." Her hands dipped under his shirt, and he closed his eyes. *I don't deserve this woman.*

"Doc, we got a situation," Hawk yelled, banging on the bedroom door.

Cursing under his breath, Doc hurried to the door and pulled it open. "What's wrong?"

"The Twelve Brothers crew is in Snowshoe, but it gets worse," he shared, green eyes alight with worry. "Cueball and Snoopy were on their way back when it started to rain. They wiped out on the side of the mountain. They have kids with them."

"Shit." He glanced to Isa, her face scrunched in worry. "I gotta go. Stay with Queenie." After grabbing his gun and kissing her fast, he followed Hawk down the stairs and out into the darkening night. With the storm overhead and the Twelve Brothers gaining ground, he hoped he lived long enough to see the dawn.

32

ISA

Stretching to her toes, Isa listened to the classical music through her earbuds, the storm raging outside. It'd come over the mountains quickly, and she was glad to have remembered to grab a pair of earbuds. A crack of lightning illuminated the sky. She glanced to the window and worried her bottom lip. Somewhere, her biker was out in the elements, helping his fellow brothers out of a sticky wicket.

She slowly stood and rolled her shoulders. Queenie kept her busy for the first hour, preparing the croissants for breakfast. It kept her mind occupied, but her thoughts were never far from Doc or her kidnapped friends in Ireland. *If only I could see them to know they're okay.*

Following her baking venture, she'd sought out Reaper and begged for an update. Sadly, he had none. They video chatted with her father, but the search was ongoing for Niall and Orla.

Dolly and her nymphs made an appearance for dessert. The cherry tartlets made with club-grown cherries didn't tempt Isa's palate. No food did.

She ignored the nymphs and their madam and explored the labyrinth of the lodge instead. History oozed out of every plank and sturdy wall. She could only imagine how many lives had been affected by this biker club within these walls over the years.

Isa lifted her leg onto the sofa arm and leaned over until her head nearly reached her ankle, stretching her hamstring. This was as close to graceful as she got. Her mother insisted on ballet lessons until she was a teenager. With her tall stature, she'd failed more than succeeded in the ornate art. The one thing she took away from the classes was stretching. She did it every night before bed. *When I remember*. It soothed her mind and allowed her to focus on something other than herself. Normally. Tonight, her thoughts raced with the possible outcomes for Doc and her friends.

He loves me. His words had rotated in her mind all afternoon. She smiled absently. He'd said it so easily, almost as if he was always meant to say those three words to her.

And I didn't bloody tell him I love him back. Isa cracked her neck and cursed silently. The words would've flowed if Hawk hadn't interrupted them. It was the reason she couldn't fall asleep without seeing Doc. She needed to tell him.

"I'm heading upstairs," Queenie said above the hum of Mozart.

Tilting her head, she paused her music and smiled at the MC mother. Queenie's brown hair was pulled back in a messy bun on top of her head, a tattoo poking out from her sleeve. "Okay. Have you heard anything?"

Queenie shook her head. "Sorry, sweetie. I'm sure Doc and the crew will be fine. They'd call if they ran into any trouble. That boy knows his way around an injury."

Isa smiled and stretched her left leg next. "He does. I'm still amazed he never finished medical school after his mum died."

"Sometimes life has a way of showing you what's important. For Doc, family became his number one priority. It's why he came to Colorado and joined the club."

"I thought Reaper asked him."

"In a way, yes, but it was Doc's decision." Queenie gave her a hug. "One he made after weighing all the options. I think you've known him long enough to realize my nephew doesn't jump into something without thinking."

"No. I guess he's special in that way."

Queenie chuckled. "Hell, I'm glad you came around when you did. Doc's not the same man who patched."

"Thank God."

They both laughed, and then Queenie looked at the large clock on the wall. "You going to be all right down here by yourself?" Isa nodded. "All right. Rubble and a few prospects are over in the tech tower, but they'll check in on ya. Night."

She waved goodnight before returning to her stretches and turning her music to a local pop station. Normally she'd go to bed, but with Doc gone, she couldn't close her eyelids until he was safely in her arms.

After another ten minutes of limbering her limbs, Isa made her way to the kitchen. With a catchy Maroon 5 song blaring in her ears, she flicked on the light switch and frowned when nothing happened. She tried it again with the same result. Immediately, she wondered if the storm cut out the power.

Pulling out one earbud, she listened to her surroundings. A creak of wood sent her heart pumping.

"Hello?" She poked her nose out of the kitchen and glanced around the lodge. "Anyone there?" Several other lights shone in the darkness, but no response came. *Odd.* When no other sounds met her, she chalked it up to faulty wiring and her overactive imagination.

Grabbing a bottle of water from the fridge, she opened it and turned. A scream caught in her throat at the sight of three bulky men towering around her. She dropped the bottle, water splashing up and hitting her leg.

"If it isn't the Macha princess herself," one of the men said, his Irish accent prevalent.

Before she could react, a beefy hand clapped over her mouth. Another face came into view, and her eyes bugged. He was so familiar, but she couldn't place him. That man hoisted her off the ground. She struggled at the sudden restraints on her wrists and bit her captor's palm to no avail.

Oh God. This is how I'll die!

She couldn't remember leaving the lodge, but the

distinct smell of blood stayed with her long after she passed out.

33

———

DOC

It wasn't good. The rain completely washed out the right shoulder of the mountain highway and sent Cueball and Snoopy off the road. By the time they arrived, Cueball had pushed his motorcycle back up on the main highway and a red flare sat next to him. He stood with his hands on his hips, his body completely coated in mud.

Judging from the matching bike, Cueball was lucky, laying his bike down just before he tipped over the edge.

"You okay?" Doc asked, hopping out of the pickup, medical bag in hand. Hawk clambered out of the driver side and went to the truck bed for supplies.

Rain steadily fell as his brother reached him. "Yeah. Got cut up, but I'll be fine."

Doc cautiously touched Cueball's head. A large gash above his left eyebrow needed stitches, but otherwise he didn't look half bad, given the circumstances. "Could've been worse," he finally said. "I'll patch you up when we get to the lodge."

They moved closer to the edge, and Hawk whistled low. "Shit, looks like the truck rolled a few times. The windshield's shattered."

Peering through the rain, Doc caught sight of the truck bashed against a fallen tree. One wrong move and both would fall down the side of the mountain to a rocky fate below.

Hawk hooked up the winch to the truck, then tied the rope around his waist. "I'll check on Snoop and the kids."

"We got your back, brother," he said, grateful Cueball took over manning the winch. It freed him up to help Hawk with the kids.

Hawk carefully slid down the embankment, mud clinging to him by the time he reached the red truck. He spoke with Snoopy, their words drowned out by the storm overhead. Doc stood patiently at the top, ready to move when he was called. He'd packed extra medical supplies in his bag, always prepared for the worst. The local ambulance was on its way but wouldn't get there in time if someone needed immediate assistance.

Finally, Hawk opened the passenger door, and a small body scurried out before the door closed again. He whistled and tugged on the rope. Slowly the winch started to wind, Hawk carefully walking up the side of the slippery slope.

When he was closer, Doc saw the issue. The child nestled against Hawk's chest wasn't moving. Doc grabbed the rope and met Hawk halfway.

"Snoop said he ate one of the granola bars in the truck and started blowing up like a balloon. I think it's an allergic reaction," Hawk relayed, handing off the boy no older than three.

Working fast, Doc checked for a pulse and hurried back up the muddy incline while Hawk stayed behind. Reaching the top, he settled the boy on the ground and immediately grabbed an EpiPen.

"C'mon, little guy," he urged, jabbing the pen in the boy's leg. Rain dripped down his face, blurring his vision.

Finally the boy gasped a lungful of air, and Doc sighed with relief.

"Hey, buddy," he said softly. "You're gonna be all right. Let's get you in the truck, okay?"

The child's bright blue eyes shone back at him with a mixture of panic and uncertainty. He didn't utter a word, merely nodded his understanding.

Once Doc stabilized the youngster in the truck, he returned to the real issue at hand. Mud slid down the hill at rapid speed now, and Snoopy's truck creaked with movement. Jumping into the middle of the problem, he raced down to the truck and helped Hawk secure the winch.

"Hit it!" Hawk called amid a thunderclap.

The winch groaned at the heavy load, and he started to panic when Snoopy's truck barely moved. "Try the engine again."

Snoopy cranked the key, but only sputtering echoed among the raindrops. "Shit!"

Doc exchanged a worried glance with Hawk. If they

couldn't get the truck back on the road soon, the mudslide would take it down the mountain instead. Snoopy kept trying, but the only sound that came from the truck was the biker's cursing.

Waving to Hawk, he waited until the other man neared. "We gotta evacuate them or they're not making it to breakfast."

Hawk's eyes snapped between the truck and the steep incline. "We can't unhitch the truck or it'll slip."

"Then we need Cueball to keep the winch on and we'll take the kids up one at a time."

"All right, let's do it." Thunder boomed overhead, and Hawk wiped rain from his brow. "And fast. I don't like how this night's going. I've got a bad feeling."

"Same, brother, same." Doc took the first child and scaled the slope, keeping a steady grip on the winch's rope. Once he safely handed off the little girl to Cueball, he met Hawk halfway up with a boy in his arms.

Ten minutes later, Hawk was on the last run, and Doc patted the truck hood. "You're up, Snoop." He frowned when the man didn't respond. Rounding the truck, he checked for a pulse and gritted his teeth when a weak one met him. He opened the door and immediately saw the issue. After the truck rolled, a piece of the dash broke, and a shard stuck in Snoopy's leg. Blood dripped down the chair and pooled on the rubber mats below.

"Fuck." Doc reached over and grabbed a towel from the passenger side, then followed the blood to its origin wound. He swore again at the recognizable femoral artery. Medical training surged in his mind. Untreated femoral injuries could lead to death, and he wasn't about ready to let that happen on his watch.

He rummaged through the glovebox and found a box of bullets. *This'll work.* Fixing it wouldn't happen then and there, but he could plug the bleeding until the ambulance arrived. Moving fast, he whipped out his knife and cut the jeans around the wound. The plastic sticking in Snoopy's leg was plugging the artery and limiting blood loss, but it needed to be removed in order to get him out of the truck.

He broke open the bullets and poured them in the empty box. Recalling his emergency training, he searched the cab for a lighter. "Of all days to forget your light," he muttered, checking Snoopy's pockets only to come up empty.

Stepping away from the truck, he whistled and waved at Hawk to help him. Within a few minutes, the two were ready for the cauterization.

"And you're sure this'll work?" Hawk asked, hands ready to pry the shard out of Snoopy's leg.

He flicked on the lighter. "It's the best shot he has."

Hawk paused, then nodded. "All right. Here goes nothing."

In one swift movement, Hawk yanked the plastic out of Snoopy's leg, causing the man to jerk to consciousness. Doc moved fast and poured a thin layer of gunpowder on the wound, then held the lighter over the powder. Hawk held Snoopy down when he started to thrash against the pain.

Once the powder sealed, Doc quickly placed a damp rag over the wound to put out the flame.

Snoopy's body went slack, and they carefully pulled him out of the truck. The wind picked up, and Doc held tight to the winch rope as Hawk slowly carried Snoopy up the slope on his back.

Once they were at the top, he waited for a signal from Cueball to unhook the truck. After trying for five minutes, he cursed at the tight rope. It wouldn't budge. Rain slicked his hands and he shook his head. The winch wouldn't come loose.

"Doc, the mud's getting faster," Hawk yelled from the ledge.

His eyes flicked to the hill and he gritted his teeth. The mudslide was quickly picking up speed. If he didn't high-tail it to the road, he may never make it.

Abandoning the truck, he grabbed the winch and trudged through the mud. He lost his footing a few times but managed to crest the hill. Cueball and Hawk grabbed his hands and pulled him the rest of the way.

The truck on the road groaned at the winch, and Cueball hurried over to it. Grabbing an axe from the bed, he swung hard, and the thick rope flung out noisily.

The three peered over the edge and watched the fallen tree give way. The truck slipped next, slowly moving toward the edge. The loud crash of metal echoed alongside the thunder, and a strike of lightning flashed as the truck came to a stop at the bottom and burst into flames.

"Shit, that was a close one," Hawk stated, clapping his back.

The flashing lights of the ambulance reached them, and they all sighed at the sight. "Let's get back to the lodge," Cueball said, smiling for the first time that night. "I think we've earned a drink."

Doc grinned, and after filling in the paramedics on Snoopy and the small boy, he jumped in the truck and they started the trip back to their haven. He'd cheated death once more.

The night can't get worse.

He buckled his seat belt and smiled. Isa's pretty face was the only one he wanted to see the rest of the night.

34

———

DOC

The storm tapered off slightly by the time they reached the lodge. Walking up the driveway, distant rumbles told Doc the night hadn't seen its last flash of lightning. Cueball and Hawk joshed with each other, the mood light. After the near-death experiences earlier, he was all for a good vibe. One of the nymphs collected the children and hurried them in the side door, promising chocolate ice cream after baths.

As he neared the front door, the light above it flickered. His gut dropped at the sight. He'd helped Rubble replace all the bulbs last week, and they had two backup generators. There was no reason for the flashing unless something happened. He eyed the rest of the lodge but didn't spy any other flickers.

The front door swung open, catching the trio off guard. Reaper filled the doorway, brows furrowed and gun drawn. He eyed his men and lowered the gun.

"She's gone," he shouted, his loud voice booming across the open air.

For a moment, Doc's brain didn't compute the words.

"Who?" Hawk asked, his gun in his hand.

Cueball glanced around the darkness. "What happened?"

Reaper bounded down the outside steps and placed both hands on Doc's shoulders. "The Twelve Brothers have Isa."

A wave of nausea pounded Doc, and his dinner threatened a reappearance. He swallowed it and tightly clenched his jaw. "No. She was safe here. We made sure," he said through his teeth. He wouldn't believe his MC failed to protect someone.

Patches and prospect alike poured out of the house from all exits. Rubble looked ready to kill someone, blood streaming down the side of his head. Evidently, Doc wasn't the only one who wanted to commit murder in that moment.

"What the fuck happened?" he barked, breaking out of Reaper's grip. He stalked over to Rubble and swung hard. His fist connected with the bigger man, and he cursed at the pain.

Brewer and Boulder pulled him away before another punch could be handed out.

"Calm down, Doc," Brewer said, fighting to keep him from the sergeant at arms.

Rubble wiped blood from his mouth, his eyes fierce. "They jumped us in the tower. Two prospects are still out.

I fought them, but they had more muscle than we did." He shook his head. "I'm sorry, Doc. This is my fault."

"How did they get in?" Reaper asked.

By now the entire Macha crew stood in the driveway, rain spitting on them. They exchanged glances, no one uttering a word. The fact that another MC infiltrated their haven unsettled every last one of them.

Finally, Klink piped up. "Where's Shovelhead?"

Each member perused the group, but their VP was nowhere to be found.

"Is he with a nymph?" Hawk asked.

Dolly shook her head. "The girls and I searched the house with Queenie. He wasn't there."

Reaper let out a low growl and pulled out his gun again. "That's how the Twelve got in so easily. They had an inside man."

Adrenaline coursed through Doc's body, but he tampered the urge to body-slam someone. He couldn't lose control.

"The Twelve Brothers won't kill her," Rubble stated, stepping into the middle of the group. "She's too important."

He nodded, no words forming to fit the situation. Losing Isa would destroy him. He wouldn't let it come to that. "What do we do?"

Reaper exchanged a glance with his sergeant. "They'll contact us soon with their demands," the president stated. "Rubble's right. Isa is too important to harm."

"Klink, Cueball, search the lodge and make sure it's

airtight. I don't want another motherfucker sneaking in here ever again," Rubble shouted. "Hawk, check on the kids you brought in and make sure the old ladies are taken through the north tunnel to the safe house on the other side of the mountain. Take a prospect with you to stay there with them until you're relieved."

Reaper pulled Doc aside while Rubble barked orders. When push came to shove, the big man wasn't to be trifled with, and they all knew it.

"Are you okay?"

Doc shot him an incredulous glare. "Am I okay? How the fuck do you think I am? My club failed tonight." He broke away from Reaper and ran his hands through his hair. "Our VP sold us out, and for what? We don't know." He shook his head, face screwed. "And I might lose... Macha might lose their first client ever, and under my watch too. She was mine to protect, and I failed her."

Reaper sighed and laid a fatherly hand on his shoulder. "I know what Isa means to you. Hell, she means a lot to all of us, but we can't let emotions drive us tonight. Isa needs us to figure this out. That won't happen if your heart controls your actions."

Lifting warring eyes, Doc saw the shimmer in the other man's gaze. He wasn't the only one in pain. The betrayal of a brother cut the deepest.

"I'm sorry. It won't happen again."

"Yes it will, but for now, keep it together." Reaper offered a small smile. "You'll get Isa back, and Macha will get revenge."

Doc watched his brothers disperse to ready themselves.

The Twelve Brothers brought their battle from Ireland to the States. Macha would end the war. He'd make sure of it.

35

—

ISA

A BRIGHT BEAM OF LIGHT WOKE ISA. LIFTING HER hand to stop the intrusion, she slowly opened her eyes. Head pounding, she struggled to sit up. It hurt more than her binge weekend after graduating university. "What the bloody hell happened?"

Eyes finally open, she looked around the small room. It held a twin-sized bed, the four walls cement. The only sound was the rush of blood through her veins. In an instant, her memory flooded back to her. The power outage. The spilled water bottle. The clammy hands over her mouth. The familiar face. She quickly stood and winced at the pain.

"Well, you took your sweet-ass time waking up," a rough voice stated from the door.

Isa whirled around and gasped when she read the name on his leather cut. "Shovelhead?"

The short man stepped fully into the room and

crossed his tattooed arms over his chest. He hadn't even had the decency to remove his Macha vest. "The one and only."

"It was you." She shook her head and backed up against the wall, finally placing the man from her abduction. The cool slab did nothing to alleviate the heat coursing through her at the blatant disregard of Macha. "But you're VP. Why would you do this?"

"Money." He leaned against the door and studied her. "The Twelve Brothers offered quite a bit of money to get the upper hand against Phantom. No one even knew you existed until your mother died. They reached out when they couldn't find you, and I filled them in on your whereabouts."

Bile rose in Isa's throat. Her mother was right to keep her away from the MC life, though a small part of her didn't agree. There'd be no danger if her father had been a mechanic instead of MC man. "What do they want with me? My—Phantom barely knows me."

"You know the details already. The Twelve want to expand in Ireland, and that includes Macha territory. Phantom refused the monetary kickbacks, so the Twelve Brothers had to get inventive."

"Why wouldn't Phantom work with you?"

Shovelhead smiled coldly. "The Twelve Brothers MC isn't like Macha, sweet thing. They're violent, they run drugs, and they don't give a shit about what happens afterward."

Isa crossed her arms over her breasts, a sudden chill

tickling her spine. "Then why would you want to go into business with them?"

"I've been VP for fifteen years. Reaper won't choose me as successor. I'm too old and there's too much new blood. The Twelve Brothers offered me my own chapter. It's a win-win."

"They'll probably kill you the instant they get what they want."

He narrowed his dark eyes. "You can't talk me out of this, Isadora, so don't try."

"I don't give a toss about talking you out of anything. I just want out of here." Her head pounded, and she reached up and felt her own sticky blood in her hair. She couldn't force her way out, and she didn't know him well enough to try another tactic.

"Where are Niall and Orla?" she asked, recalling her friends and their similar abduction.

"In Ireland with the Twelve Brothers, where they'll stay until this is resolved."

His phone rang, and he pulled it out of the back pocket of his jeans. They were covered in mud, immediately making her wonder if he had anything to do with the accident Doc left to assist with.

"How long have I been asleep?"

"You passed out last night," Shovelhead replied, not looking up. "It's almost noon."

Isa racked her brain, trying to remember anything after being taken from the kitchen. It was all a hazy blob of black. If she knew how long they'd traveled, she could guess where they were keeping her hostage. Given the cement box, she assumed the outskirts of Snowshoe.

"Have they contacted the club yet?"

"No."

Her mind went to Doc. He'd been assigned to protect her. *And he left thinking I was safe.* She resisted the urge to curl into a ball and cry. No doubt he'd beat himself up for the night before. She could get through this. Somehow. But none of her university studies would help. Using her wits was the only way out of this mess.

"When, then?"

"Don't know, don't care."

Stomping over to him, she smacked his phone out of his hand. The older man cast deadly eyes on her. "Find out how long I'll be in this shithole with no food, water, or loo." She kept her gaze stoic. "Now."

Shovelhead dropped their connection and retrieved his phone. "You've definitely earned the name of Macha princess, haven't you?"

"Damn straight. Now move your arse."

He paused, body language showing his uncertainty.

"Just because Phantom isn't here to whoop you doesn't mean I can't." She kept her eyes locked on his and hoped to God he believed her farce. Dolly taught her a thing or two, but nothing that would overpower a hardened biker.

Chuckling darkly, Shovelhead opened the door. "You've come a long way since you arrived. Phantom would be proud of you. The Twelve Brothers, not so much." He lowered his voice. "Keep your smart mouth shut or they just might pass you around their MC, sweetheart. Your precious Doc won't want you after that."

Panic flooded Isa's veins, but she didn't waver. Showing her fear wouldn't help. The Twelve Brothers were probably watching her at that very moment. "Hurry the hell up. It smells horrid in here."

Macha's Judas left, slamming the door shut on his way out. Isa slowly walked around the cube and searched for a hidden camera. After she came up empty, she flopped on the bed and muted her sobs in the pillow. She'd never relied on a man before coming to Colorado. Her mum made sure of it. Now, she understood why.

She couldn't blame Doc. He'd done nothing wrong in her eyes.

But if she knew Doc—and she did—he'd tear down every door necessary to find her and protect her. And she'd figure out a way to help him. *Somehow.*

36

———

DOC

Doc did his damnedest to listen to Rubble speak to the room full of bikers. So far, it was a lost cause. The Twelve Brothers hadn't made contact yet. His nerves were shot despite members coming out of retirement to aid the MC during this time of need. Reaper seemed to appreciate the extra bodies, but Doc wasn't sure the aged-out men and women would be any help.

Ten minutes after the meeting began, a new man came into the room. Rubble seemed glad to see him, as did the rest of the members. Doc didn't recognize the tall man with military tattoos peeking out from his shirt, but the name Kevlar on his leather cut rang a bell.

Rubble and Brewer sang the man's praises. Evidently the rumor was right, and Kevlar was back from deployment. From what he'd heard, the tall man was special ops.

Good, maybe he can do something.

"Prez, there's a call for you," one of the prospects said, coming into the room.

Reaper's bushy eyebrows rose. He snatched the phone from the prospect and put it on speaker for all to hear. "Speak."

"You know, I always find it funny when MCs have some dumb schmuck answer their phones," the accented voice on the other end started. Every Macha member balled their hands into fists, hatred simmering below the quiet surface.

Macha's president leaned his fists on the table. "Viper, is that you?"

"Aye, old man."

"You took something of ours."

"Is this wee lass yours? I don't see a Macha patch on her clothes." Viper chuckled. "It's too bad. She'd make a grand old lady. Hell, even some of my men are tempted to taste her."

Doc clenched his jaw until he was sure it'd shatter. He'd put his motherfucking boot up this Viper guy's ass if he hurt one hair on Isa's head.

Brewer nudged his side and offered a silent warning. Doc glanced at the redhead, then around the room. Each club member had the same look of distain scribbled on their face. No one fucked with Macha and lived to tell the tale without a broken body part or two.

"What do you want?" Reaper asked, steering the conversation back to the goal in mind.

Viper clucked his tongue. "Northern Ireland."

"That's not happening, and you know it."

"Hmm, all right. Then I suppose I'll let my newest president of my Dublin chapter escort Phantom's daughter to the bullpen. It's funny how easily men are purchased, Reaper. Take your Shovelhead character. Hell, it barely took fifty thousand before he jumped at the chance to break Macha."

Lacing his fingers together, Reaper stared at the cell phone. "I don't know a Shovelhead. Our club doesn't have a man by that name."

Viper laughed. "Of course not."

"Get down to the details. I'm sure you've already contacted Phantom."

"Aye. He told me to pound sand. I'm shocked since I have his precious daughter. Isn't Macha supposed to idolize women?"

Rubble stood, his phone to his ear, and walked to the door. He snapped his fingers, and Hawk and Kevlar immediately followed. Only once they exited did Reaper respond. "I can offer you a new territory. You saw how quickly Macha took over Colorado. We only have one competitor."

"So?"

"So, think about The Twelve Brothers taking over another US state. The MCs here are weak compared to Ireland's. You could wipe out any competition within months, and the entire territory would be yours. In fact, the MC in Nevada is in between presidents right now. You could take their men and territory in one swoop. Plenty of casinos and strip clubs in that state."

Reaper kept his eyes fixed on the door. *He's trying to keep Viper on the line for a trace.* Doc cursed himself for thinking even for a minute that their president wouldn't do everything to get Isa back to safety. It hit him square in the gut.

"That is tempting. I see why you've earned your president status." Viper hummed on the other end. "But what happens if we stray into Colorado?"

"You won't. Colorado is Macha's."

Hawk entered the room and nodded. A collective sigh echoed silently in the room.

Picking up the phone, Reaper stood. "The choice is yours, Viper. Either take the win or prepare for a bloody loss."

"I could, or I could say *fuck you* and keep this little princess for the Twelve Brothers." A shuffling of feet, then a woman's cry filled the air. "Isadora would make very pretty babies with my brothers. Perhaps we should come to a truce between our MCs. A marriage would work for me."

"Touch her and I'll make your death one no MC will ever forget," Doc seethed before he could stop himself.

Every Macha member looked to him, but he didn't apologize. The Irish fucker who held Isa hostage would feel his wrath. *The bastard might as well know it's coming.*

"Typical Irish temper." Viper chuckled. "What do you say, old man?"

Reaper walked to the window and opened the blinds. "Macha doesn't trade in women and children, Viper."

"Right, I guess your crew really does worship women instead of the other way around." Viper cleared his throat. "If you'd like Phantom's daughter alive, be on the county road outside Snowshoe Lodge seven tonight."

The line went dead, and Doc's heart thudded against his rib cage. He didn't dare look up. He simply stood, walked out the door, and headed into Snowshoe on his bike faster than any lawman would condone. He couldn't handle the possibility that Isa would never be the same after this fiasco was through.

37

———

ISA

"Oh well. I tried to keep you as our own, lovey." Viper walked back into the room and passed his phone to the man next to him, then hunched down in front of her. "I guess you won't be our wife after all."

Isa struggled at the restraints on her wrists. Viper's right-hand man had put the duct tape back over her mouth after she cried out when she heard Reaper's voice on the phone call. If it wasn't in place now, she'd spit on Viper and his goon. After that, her captor had left the room for the duration of the call, not that she minded much. The greasy-looking man gave her the creeps. His beady, snakelike eyes didn't help matters either. *Probably how he got his club name.*

"Right, I forgot you're mute at the moment." Viper traced her face with his fingertips, and she reared back in disgust. He laughed but didn't stop his fingers from dipping over her exposed skin. "I prefer women this way. Except in the bedroom, of course." He kissed the side of her neck. "Want to give me a little sample of the sounds you can make, princess?"

Isa held back the vomit rising in her throat. His touch combined with the putrid scent of raw fish from the kitchen they were currently hiding in made it more difficult by the moment. The Twelve Brothers' president purposefully moved her from the cement box to a nearby restaurant so Macha couldn't trace their headquarters.

A chef walked back to the freezer and eyed her warily before grabbing a filleted trout and then retracing his steps. The cold air had her teeth chattering for the past hour. Only after the call began did Viper allow his younger brother to pull her out of the freezer and into the kitchen. Viper left her alone in the kitchen with his brother fifteen minutes ago, but her body hadn't recovered yet, though from the arctic temperatures or the looming threat, she wasn't sure which contributed more.

Viper sat back on his heels and studied her. "It's a pity. I think you'd like my brothers. We could have a reverse harem if you say the word."

Isa bit at the tape over her mouth, but it didn't do any good. She had more than one thing to tell the pompous arsehole.

"Eh, no matter. Once we get Reaper and his men here, I don't care what happens to you." He released her chin and stood. "Let's get out of here before Macha arrives."

The younger biker roughly grabbed her arm and pulled her out of the straight-backed chair. He marched her through the kitchen and out the back door. A black SUV with dark-tinted windows sat running. The biker paused to chat with the driver while Viper made a phone call. Isa saw her opportunity and steeled herself for the next set of events.

Acting fast, she kneed the biker in the groin and smacked Viper with her fisted hands. Both men grunted at the pain, and she sprinted down the alleyway. Shouts filled the space behind her, and she held back her panic when she came to a street. Looking left, then right, she swore. Nothing was familiar. She couldn't even guarantee she was in Snowshoe anymore. After spending most of her time with Doc at the clubhouse or lodge—*or bedroom*—her surroundings were as strange as when she'd first arrived.

"Get back here, bitch!" Viper yelled.

Isa veered right toward the convenience store up the road. If she could make it there, she was safe. *I hope.* She crossed traffic without stopping, cars honking at her jaywalking venture. She peeked behind her shoulder and saw five bikers headed her way. *Shite! I need to hurry.*

She pushed her body faster, her legs somehow obeying her despite not seeing such activity in years. It was fight or flight, and she was absolute shit at fighting. Sweat poured down her forehead, but she kept running. Cars swerved to miss her, and she yelped when one nearly hit her. If she were smart, she'd stop somewhere and get help.

Heavy footballs behind her steered her away from stopping. She was barely ahead of the bastards. If she paused even for a moment, they'd be on her within seconds.

Lungs burning, she turned right and tried to get the tape off her mouth, knowing breathing would be a lot easier without it. She managed to get part of it off but had to slow down for even that painful inch.

"We're closing in," she heard an accented voice yell. "Cut her off at the next corner."

Isa yelped and kept her gaze ahead. The years spent jogging did her no good. The blocks whizzed by, and she lost track of where she was. She couldn't even tell how long she'd been running. The scenery didn't look familiar, but the Snowshoe name was plastered on nearby billboards.

Just make it until you get help.

She walked for a moment, trying to catch her breath. The sun beat down on her, a drastic change from the freezer they'd kept her in not an hour ago.

"There she is!"

Isa's eyes bugged and she glanced over her shoulder. Her captors seemed to have multiplied. Panic set in once more. She didn't want to think about what they'd do to her once they caught up.

Facing forward again, she suddenly hit a wall. Dazed, she stepped back, and tears filled her eyes.

It wasn't a wall.

"Isa? Oh my God." Doc wrapped his arms around her. She buried her face in his chest for a moment, the scent of him momentarily overtaking her fear.

"Are you hurt?" he whispered, pulling the tape off her mouth. His blue eyes scanned her anxiously. Rubbing her lips together, she held back tears at the agony the tape caused. He carefully untied her wrists and ran his fingers along the indentations. "I'm gonna kill that fucker."

The horde of bikers stopped just shy of their location. "You're outnumbered, Macha," Viper said, a smug smile on his bearded face.

Isa trembled at the sight of ten men with guns pointed toward them. Doc tightened his hold on her.

"And you're a fool to think I came unprepared," he said coolly, drawing his gun.

A large body came into view from around the corner of the convenience store. She immediately recognized the deputy star on the man's tan uniform. Another man appeared behind him, a similar law enforcement emblem on his shirt. Relief coursed through her prematurely, but she didn't care. It was three to ten, but she was hopeful they'd win the standoff.

Viper's gun remained cocked despite the new additions. "I don't care who's in your pocket, Macha. The girl is mine until I get the territory deal your president and I discussed." He used his gun to motion for Isa to walk to him. She shook her head and he sneered. "I have no issue shooting her, then you."

The two law enforcement agents took giant steps forward. "Get out of town and Macha may forgive you for putting this woman at risk. From what we've heard and seen, she was snatched by your MC."

Viper glanced at his men, then back to the deputy. "I don't give a shit about shooting police either." He trained his gun on Doc. "How much do these guards cost? I'll need to get Nevada's in my pocket before we take over the state."

Doc's arm muscles twitched. "There are innocent bystanders, Viper. Don't make this end in gunfire."

Shrugging, Viper pulled the trigger, and all hell broke loose.

Doc shoved her to the ground, firing off rounds toward the offending MC. Isa covered her ears with her hands and watched the scene play out. Four of Viper's men fell right away and lay unmoving on the sidewalk. The two police officers struggled to contain the gunfight to the store parking lot, both calling for backup.

Distant rumbles of motorcycle engines neared, and she held her breath. If they weren't Macha, she may as well pick out a casket.

Crawling over to the building, she stayed low. Doc dodged bullets, and Viper gained on him. Her heart thrummed in her ears the closer the two got to each other.

Viper's bullet made contact with Doc's side, and she screamed. He fell to the ground, hand covering the oozing wound. The Irish biker preened and stalked toward his prey, clicking a new magazine in place.

"This'll teach you not to fuck with the Twelve Brothers again."

Thinking fast, Isa ran over to where a discarded gun lay next to one of Viper's men. Grabbing it, she aimed it toward the hulking biker and pulled the trigger. The blowback stunned her ears, and she took a step backward to steady herself. Viper swiveled his head and glared at her with dark eyes. She'd hit his shoulder, wounding but not felling him.

"Bollocks!" Swallowing hard, she lifted the barrel again. This time, Viper stopped and waited. Keeping her eyes fixed on him, she yelled, "Drop the gun or I swear to God, I'll hit you between the eyes."

Viper's eyes narrowed to slits, and he took a step toward her. "You'll never be safe, princess. My men are every-where. They'll come for you. And if they fail, my eleven brothers will come for you."

Isa responded by shooting his leg.

His face paled. "You bitch!"

She stood her ground, worried about a motionless Doc on the ground but unwilling to let the bastard take her hostage again. She looked over and saw the two police offi-cers arresting the remaining Twelve Brothers crew who were still alive. All it'd take was one wrong move and she was Viper's prized chess piece again.

"We got it, lass," Reaper's voice gently said, coming up from her left. He closed his hand over the gun and slowly took it away from her. "Phantom got Niall and Orla too. They're safe."

Isa staggered on her feet, watching Rubble and Hawk tackle Viper to the pavement, both getting punches in. She couldn't utter a word, the severity of the recent moments hitting her hard.

Doc grunted and rolled to his side.

"Oh God." Running over, she tore off a strip of her tank and pressed it to his side. The wound wasn't gushing, but his once white shirt held a pink tint. "You're some kind of dolt," she muttered, pulling up the hem to examine the wound. She had no idea what she was doing, but she'd seen people do it on the telly. *Can't hurt anything.*

Doc winced, and it was then she noticed the scrapes on his face and arms. How had she missed those before? She roughly examined his side, her head suddenly spinning.

"I'm fine, princess," he said, grabbing her hand and pressing it to his heart. "It's a through and through."

She slowly lifted her eyes to meet his. Sure enough, his gorgeous blue eyes didn't look worried one bit. Tears threatened to spill, but she held them back. "You're sure?"

He leaned his forehead to hers. "No, but I hope it is."

The tears fell steadily, blurring her vision. She was safe. Doc was safe. It was all she cared about.

Isa pulled back long enough to search his face before kissing him hard. Tears mixed with blood met her tongue, and she held him closer. She couldn't get the recent events out of her mind. One wrong move and they all could've died.

Doc eased back and grunted in pain. "Sorry, princess, I gotta wait to finish this until after the doctor patches me up."

Isa looked down in horror. She'd mistakenly agitated his wound. Standing, she watched Brewer and Hawk help him upright.

"Come on, Doc," Hawk said, walking toward the ambulance that had recently arrived on the scene. Paramedics filed out of the vehicle, and she wiped her face of the blood, sweat, and tears.

It's over. Everything's going to be fine.

She swallowed at the underlying realization. Her Macha protection detail would end.

Doc's face creased when the paramedic pulled away the haphazard wound dressing. The Emerald Isle awaited her return. Her friends awaited her.

She watched Doc joke despite his injury. He was perfect. *Can I leave this all behind?*

Her answer scared her more than when The Twelve Brothers kidnapped her. She was safe, but her heart wasn't.

38

DOC

"I'll be fine. Just give me a minute," Doc growled and pushed off the end of the ambulance. The bullet hadn't gone straight through like he'd hoped. *Damn, Viper.* If he had his way, he'd patch himself up once he was home. A sudden rush of adrenaline left his mind foggy, and he cursed the bullet wound in his side. *Maybe not the best idea.* He should've let the paramedics force him in the back of the ambulance. Hell, they'd be halfway to the hospital by now, but he couldn't leave yet. Not until he knew she was all right.

Isa stood on the other end of the parking lot, looking lost yet found at the same time. She chewed on the thumbnail of her left hand, eyes scouring the area. Macha bikers surrounded the convenience store alongside uniformed officers getting their official statements. Evidently, the horde of protectors didn't put her at ease.

He bit his tongue when his footsteps sent new fibers of

agony up his legs and into his side. He gritted his teeth and kept moving toward her. *She's worth the pain of the bullet and more.*

Reaching her, he gently laid a hand on her arm. "Isa."

She turned slowly, and the tears in her eyes sent his heart into a nosedive. For a moment, they merely stared at each other. He wouldn't close the distance. After all she'd been through over the last twenty-four hours, he wasn't sure how she'd react.

"You shouldn't be here," she finally said.

"Why?" He glanced around and shook his head at Kevlar before he got closer. They didn't need more of an audience than they already had. Walking in front of her, he tipped up her chin.

The tears she'd desperately been trying to hold back trickled down her face. "You need to go to hospital. You're shot." She pointed to the dark crimson on his side.

"Just a flesh wound," he joked, but the irony fell short. "All right, I'll go to the hospital."

"You will?"

He chuckled at the befuddled look on her face. "Baby, I can patch myself up really well, but even I will pass the fuck out if I try to dig this bullet from my side."

A small smirk crossed her cheeks, and his heart lightened. "You're an eejit."

"Probably, but I don't care." He carefully pulled her into his embrace, pain be damned. His girl needed him, and he wouldn't let her down. Not again. *Not ever.*

Doc nestled his face in the nape of her neck, remnants

of lavender and vanilla seeping from her skin. She smelled so damned good despite recent events.

"I was terrified I'd never see you again." She laced her fingers behind his neck, burying her face in his shirt.

"You're safe, baby." He looked up in time to see the coroner's van drive away, bodies safely stowed for the drive to the morgue. He'd gladly spit on their graves, but he wouldn't grace the deceased with his presence. They didn't deserve anything but a shallow grave after terrorizing Isa and his club.

"Brother, you need to get to the hospital," Kevlar said gruffly behind him. "You're bleeding on the concrete."

Doc looked down and saw a red trickle all the way to the ground. He hugged Isa once more, doing his best to push down the desire to overwhelm her lips when he felt the slight tremble in her touch. "Hawk can take you back—"

"No." She gripped a handful of his shirt. "I'm not going anywhere without you."

He nodded and swallowed the grin he so badly wanted to give her. There'd be time for that later. Plus, the blood oozing from his side made any other thoughts impossible. His mind was fuzzy the longer he stayed upright.

Kevlar came up beside him and looped his arm over his shoulder, allowing Doc to use him as a crutch. He was never more grateful to be part of this band of brothers. They had each other's backs no matter what happened. He hadn't been sure of the recently returned biker, but the

Army sniper held his own during the firefight. He owed him.

"You better make her your old lady," Kevlar mumbled under his breath. "Or I'll make her mine."

He eyed the other man and noticed the shit-eating grin on Kevlar's face. "I like you and all, but fuck off."

They both chuckled, and Doc instantly regretted the joking when his side warmed with blood. He glanced over his shoulder and noticed Isa close behind. They needed to figure out some shit, but he'd do exactly as Kevlar suggested.

Isa isn't going anywhere but home with me.

39

———

ISA

Sleep eluded her. Sitting next to Doc lying in the clean hospital bed, her body refused to succumb to rest. If they'd come directly to hospital, he wouldn't have had to stay overnight. She rolled her eyes. Her man was one stubborn son of a bitch.

Isa rubbed her lips together, smothering her smile. Her man. *My man.* He wasn't like any of the boys of her past, and there wouldn't be another man like him. Not for her.

Sitting back in the uncomfortable chair, she watched his chest rise and then fall consistently. His wound would heal—that much the doctor said after they brought Doc back from surgery. She was more worried about what came next. The danger was gone. *Then why does it still feel like it's here?* Viper's warning before the police officers dragged him off rang in her mind. *Surely he was merely spewing words.*

She stood and paced in front of the bed. The heart

monitor beeped comfortingly. The room was private, a special service from the hospital since Doc volunteered at their free clinics. Hawk was stationed outside the room, Cueball in the parking lot.

I should feel safe. Isa chewed her bottom lip. *But I don't. Why?*

But she knew why. Macha had found the flight manifest from the Twelve Brothers. One man was unaccounted for between the morgue and police station.

Her phone rang a familiar video chat chime. Answering it quickly, she sighed at the sight of Niall and Orla. "Oh God, you're okay. If I could hug you through the phone, I would. What happened? Who saved you?"

Niall held up his hand. Both looked weary beyond belief. If Reaper hadn't told her they were safe, she'd have gone completely mad.

"We're fine. A bit of a bump on the head for me, but Orla wasn't hurt." Niall tenderly patted the knot on his skull. "Some sleep, meds, and I'll be right as rain."

"Your da came for us," Orla said.

Isa focused on her best friend for the last twenty years. Her hair was darker, most likely damp from a recent shower. "I'm so sorry. I never thought in a million years someone would try to hurt you because of me." She let out a breath to keep from crying. "Once I'm back in Ireland, I'll sort it all out with the club and Phantom."

Orla chuckled and rested her head on Niall's chest. "Love, he's your dad. You can call him that, you know."

"No. He put you in danger. He doesn't deserve to be called anything but his club name."

"Maybe, but not because he wanted to." Orla yawned, and Isa cursed herself. It was long past bedtime in Ireland. "Denying your relationship isn't good for you. Face it head-on. You might be surprised what you find."

"We're not talking about Phantom anymore, are we?"

"No, but it applies to both."

Niall took over the frame. "We'll sign off for tonight." She opened her mouth to reply, and he added, "We're safe at home, Isa. See you soon."

She offered him a small smile. "Sleep well."

Putting away the phone, she opened the curtain and gazed out to the darkness. The city spread out with lights to the left, though the right was pure wilderness. It was hauntingly beautiful.

"You're still here?"

Whirling around, Isa caught her hand over her mouth to silence her gasp. A prospect stood in the doorway, the light behind him hiding his face. The leather cut stood out, but no name was patched on the front yet.

"Um, who're you?" She took a step closer to her slumbering biker, her gut not liking the unexpected intrusion. Hawk told her he'd be at the hospital all night. There wasn't a planned guard shift for another hour.

The stocky man cleared his throat. "Hawk told me to relieve him." He jutted a thumb behind him. "The guy was really tired."

She squinted, the prospect's face still shielded by his overgrown hair and dimly lit room. "No one told me."

The man shrugged, and she caught sight of his dark eyes for the first time. "You're a woman. Why would we?"

His words immediately sent a shiver down her spine. Macha taught their prospects better. *This man is no prospect.* She gulped, doing her best to keep her face straight. *At least not for Macha.*

"Sure. You wouldn't mind if I stayed, would you?" She sank into the chair next to the hospital bed.

"You've had a big day. Cueball is outside waiting to take you home." He turned his face to Doc. "I'll take care of him."

Eerie goose bumps littered her arms. The depravity in those words meant exactly what she thought. Racking her mind, she tried to remember where they put Doc's firearm. *Surely they didn't take it.*

The man took a step closer, and the gun on his hip glimmered in the light. "I said leave, woman."

Isa's eyes widened, and she stood automatically. Doc's bloodied clothes caught her attention on the other side of the bed. His personal effects were there, which meant his gun was too. Rubble made it a point to ensure the hospital security allowed Macha's men to keep their weapons safely hidden and she was damn glad he did. *If I can just make it over there and grab it....*

"Now, princess."

The sound of Doc's nickname for her on the scumbag's lips sent her stomach into a tizzy. On some level, it was ironic. She used to hate the pet name, but now all she wanted was to hear Doc say it once more.

"I need to gather my things."

Standing, she walked around the bed, the man's eyes glued to her every move. She swallowed her anxiety, the brown bag with Doc's clothes mere inches away. *I can do this.* She looked up to see the man studying his phone. Taking her moment, she quickly rifled through the bag, cursing at the loud crinkling.

"Hey, what're you doing?" he barked, phone suddenly gone from his hand.

"Just need to grab one last thing," she replied, faking a smile. Her fingers felt the cool metal, and she wrapped her hand around the handle.

"Hurry up. I have a job to do." He checked over his shoulder.

Acting fast, she pulled out the gun and flicked off the safety. "Leave or I'll blow your head off."

The longhaired biker scoffed at her. "Right, sure you will, princess."

"Don't call me that," she fumed, motioning for him toward the door. "Get out!" The gun shook in her hand, but she kept it focused on the intruder. "I'll pull the trigger."

"Please, you don't even know how to—"

Isa fired off a shot, and it connected with the man's arm.

"Bitch!" He stormed toward her and she screamed, firing off another shot. That one missed but still stunned him.

He pulled out his gun and aimed, and she quickly

dropped to the floor. The bullet hit the window, glass shattering. A shard hit her face, and she winced. Reaching up, she felt the slippery blood. *Just a flesh wound.*

Crawling, she made it to the side of Doc's bed. She had to defend her sleeping biker. He couldn't do it himself, and after all the times he'd saved her arse, it was owed.

No. She shook her head. *It's because I love him. He can't die. I have to tell him.*

A blaring alarm sounded throughout the hospital, the gunshots clearly announcing the peril. She popped off another shot, this time hitting the man's leg. "Feck, feck, feck!"

She stared at the gun, then her hands. They weren't trembling anymore. *Adrenaline. It must be adrenaline. I'm not a coldblooded killer... right?*

"Isa, give me the gun," a raspy voice commanded.

Looking up, she met Doc's blue eyes and mutely handed it over.

He checked the chamber, then sat up and fired the rest of the magazine into the Twelve Brothers prospect. The man's face went blank, and he staggered backward before crumpling into a mass of blood and flesh. Isa held a hand over her mouth at the bullets' precision. One hit him in the stomach, one in the chest, and one in his forehead.

"Are you all right?" Doc asked, standing and shaking her shoulders.

She slowly looked away from the dead man and into Doc's worried eyes. "I'm fine. What about you? He shot at you. Are you okay?"

He pulled her against him, cupping the base of her neck. "Yeah, baby, I'm okay."

A thundering of boots echoed down the hall. The doorway filled with two security guards and three Macha members. Hawk stood with blood trickling down his face, a vicious expression in his eyes. Cueball was behind him, equally pissed and bloodied.

Doc eased her out of his arms enough to give her a quick once-over.

"It was the missing Twelve Brothers member, wasn't it?" she asked, already knowing the answer.

"Yeah, he got the drop on Cue, then me," Hawk filled in. "I came to and heard shots. A car was outside waiting for you, Isa, with a hired hand from the Twelve Brothers. I got that much out of him before I rather nicely punched his lights out." He rubbed his knuckles. "Either of you injured?"

Her eyes dipped to Doc. The recent events reopened his stitches, a crimson circle expanding on his hospital gown. A sheen of sweat lined his brow, and his face was nearly as white as the sheets on the nearby bed. She gasped at the littering of bullet holes where he'd been lying. A few inches to the left and he would've been killed.

"We're good." He nodded to the dead imposter. "Him, not so much."

"He came to take Doc out," Isa explained. "I had no choice but to shoot him." She swallowed. "Twice."

Hawk and Cueball exchanged an impressed glance and stepped fully into the room.

"But I finished him off," Doc said as the security guards covered the dead man with a sheet.

"There'll be an investigation, of course, but with the security camera in the corner, you should be fine," the shorter of the two security guards said. "The police will be here shortly to get statements."

Isa glanced over her shoulder. She hadn't even noticed the small camera positioned in the corner of the room near the ceiling.

"Talk about one hell of a day." Hawk carefully stepped over the body on the floor.

"Prez is on his way," Cueball said, putting away his phone.

"Good, he can take Isa back to the lodge." Doc shifted his weight, pain etched on his brow.

"I can't leave you here." Her head spun, and suddenly she couldn't stop her hands from shaking.

Cueball was there, easing her into one of the chairs before she could fall.

"Whoa, I think you need to sit too." Hawk jumped over and helped Doc into the last open chair, brushing off the glass shards first. "That dress of yours sure shows off the goods," he teased. "Mazel tov, brother."

"Didn't know you were Jewish." Doc chuckled and flipped Hawk off.

"And I didn't know you were packing heat down there." He laughed when Doc gave him both middle fingers. "I'll go grab the doc, Doc."

"This is no place for you, princess." He glanced around the room in disarray. "You need to go home."

Isa glanced to Cueball, who nodded once, then moved to the doorway. He wouldn't leave completely, but she was grateful for the minimal privacy. "I am home."

"Nah, you're in Colorado, where you keep getting shot at." He shook his head. "That's not home, baby. You need to be somewhere safe."

Kneeling in front of him, she cupped his face. Worry and pain overwhelmed his blue depths. "Ireland and Colorado aren't safe. The Twelve Brothers made sure of that."

"Then what?" He frowned. "You want to go somewhere else? Australia maybe? I'll take you where you want."

"You beautiful idiot." She gently kissed his mouth. "I'm only safe when I'm with you."

He didn't immediately reciprocate, and she cursed herself at her lack of sympathy. Pulling back, she examined his injured face. "Bloody hell. Sorry, love."

"Don't you dare apologize for loving me." He tucked her hair behind her ear. "I'm so stupidly in love with you that I couldn't bear it if you left."

"Really?"

"Fuck yes, princess." His thumb traced her bottom lip.

She closed her eyes. Hearing him call her that washed away the bad memories from not yet an hour earlier. Opening her eyes again, she smiled. "I love you."

"Hell yeah you do," Hawk teased from the doorway.

This time, it was Isa who flipped him the bird. "I never told you before you left, and I wish I had."

"I knew, baby." He winked, and she rolled her eyes. "You'll be my old lady, that much I know for certain." A frustrated sound escaped him. "I really want to kiss you."

She chuckled and placed her finger on his lips. "Don't you dare let a day go by when you don't."

"I promise."

She kissed his cheek, the rest of the world melting away. Well, at least until the doctor came in to yell at him for opening his stitches.

Eyes heavy, she watched Doc bullshit the doctor and his club brothers. It was the best dream and one she never wanted to wake from.

40

DOC

A week turned into three before Doc felt halfway decent. His injuries weren't completely healed, but the doctor in him knew it was only a matter of time. Phantom called earlier that day, letting them all know he'd come to a truce with the Twelve Brothers. No one believed it'd last long, but peace even for the time being was preferred. The Twelve Brothers members who attacked Macha and survived were extradited to Ireland.

We definitely haven't seen the last of them.

He sipped the glass of Guinness and watched Isa over the rim. She and Brewer were prepping the bar for the Saturday night crowd. With the upcoming summer festival, the tourists of Snowshoe would abound.

He shifted on the seat, doing his best to not grimace. It was easier when it was just him and his princess. Recovering had its perks, and Nurse Isa was a sight to behold. He'd be damned if any other man tasted the medicine she prescribed. His cock hardened at the thought, but he hadn't been able to yet. Doctor's orders or some bullshit. Sure, he sampled Isa, but his body craved another type of procedure that'd leave them both satisfied.

Country music drifted over the speakers as he finished his beer. Tonight was the night. He'd have Isa all to himself. No volunteering with Queenie or slaving away on her latest designs.

"You ready to go?" Isa asked, coming up to the table. She looked too beautiful to be in this bar. Hell, he was the envy of all his brothers. With her short jean shorts and white lace tank top that showed just enough of her breasts to tease him, she was perfection. She pushed back her long hair with new highlights courtesy of Queenie.

"Always ready for you, princess." He winked and she rolled her eyes. "You sure you wanna do that tonight, baby?" He stood and tugged on the belt loop of her shorts. "No restrictions mean I can punish you."

A knowing smile lit her face. "Maybe that's why I did it." She not so subtly traced his dick with her palm before swaying that gorgeous ass of hers toward the door.

"Oh, you'll be sorry you did that," he growled, catching up to her.

She laughed, the sound music to his ears. He'd have more of that every day if he could manage it.

She swung open the door and held it until he stepped outside. "I doubt it."

His bike sat in the parking lot, and she reached it first. Straddling it, she nodded. "I'll drive."

He clucked his tongue. "Sorry, not tonight."

"Why not?"

"Because you don't know where we're going." He got on the motorcycle and turned her on, the purr only outdone by the sounds Isa made under his touch.

They started off before she could say another word. Her arms hung loosely around his waist, a vast difference from the first time they rode together. The sun slowly made its way across the horizon, the red-orange hue falling over them. Isa hugged him close on curves, her hair tickling the back of his neck.

The drive ended before he liked. He'd gotten used to having Isa on his bike over the past months. Somehow, riding without her felt incomplete. He pulled off the road and killed the engine.

"Where are we?" she asked, setting her helmet on the back of the bike. She took a few steps toward the small cabin overlooking Snowshoe.

"My dad left this place to me when he died." Doc walked to the door and laughed at the rotted wood. "It's not in very good shape. I kind of let it go to waste because I was pissed at him for abandoning my mom and me."

Isa kept her gaze on the city below. "I can understand that."

He shoved his hands in the front pockets of his jeans and joined her. "But then I realized why my dad cut off contact and how it actually helped my life." He laughed. "At least until I grew up. It made sense once I joined Macha, but I couldn't grasp it until I met you."

She stayed silent, his words floating in the air.

"I'd never let anyone hurt you, Isa." He turned to face her. "I think your dad was trying to do the same for you."

"Well, he went about it all wrong."

"Yeah, he did, but when someone threatened you, Phantom stepped up and protected you."

"No, he exiled me to Colorado."

"He sent you to me." Doc searched her eyes. "I'll always be thankful he did, too." He took her hands in his. "Because if he hadn't, I'd never have met you."

"I can't imagine never meeting you."

He smirked. "Never thought you'd say that."

She rolled her stunning gray eyes. "Just can't take a compliment, can you?"

Doc wrapped his arms around her and breathed in her lavender shampoo. The woman always smelled so damned good. His brothers were right. He was lost to this woman and never wanted to be found. "I only desire compliments from you, princess."

They stood in silence, enjoying the cool mountain air, the view, and each other's company. It was the most comfortable he'd been in years. With Isa, he wasn't the doctorate washout or the biker doctor. He was simply Tad O'Brien, a man in love.

"I need to go back to Ireland." She said the words so softly, he wasn't sure he'd heard correctly. "To see Orla and Niall." She cleared her throat. "And Phant—my da. I owe him my thanks."

"You know, phones are pretty handy for that kind of shit."

She playfully swatted his chest. "I live there, smartass. All my clothes, books, everything is there."

"That's true." He ran his right hand over his bearded chin. The thought of Isa leaving even for a week sent a shiver of worry down his spine. *What if she never comes back?* He took a step closer to the run-down log cabin and rested his left forearm on the side.

"Come with me." She looped her arm around his waist and rested her head on his shoulder. "You'll love Ireland."

He glanced down, and a tiny part of his heart leaped at the dreamy look in her eyes. "I love anywhere I'm with you."

"Such a sweet talker." She leaned up and kissed his jaw. "What ever will I do with you?"

Doc cupped the side of her face. "Love me. That's all I want from you."

"Loving you is the easiest thing I've ever done." She lightly nipped his bottom lip. "Most of the time."

He caught her mouth beneath his before she could add another sassy remark. He deserved them all, but the moment was too precious.

He'd make Isa his once and for all. Tonight was supposed to be the night, but now, Ireland sounded like the perfect place to make both their dreams come true.

41

———

ISA

IRELAND. SHE TOOK A DEEP BREATH, LETTING THE island's scents consume her nostrils. Only that didn't happen. A combination of leather and oil overwhelmed the air instead.

She opened her eyes and glanced at Doc. They were overlooking the ocean, her hometown behind them. Niall and Orla weren't in the shop yet, so she'd persuaded him to explore the countryside with her until the little Open sign popped up in the shop window.

"It's gorgeous here." His hair ruffled in the wind, his eyes hidden by dark sunglasses.

"Be glad it's not raining." She laughed and slowly turned in a circle, arms splayed. "But this is home for as long as I can remember. I never left the island much. Mum couldn't bear to have me far."

"Seems like a good place to raise a family." His voice

dropped off as if those words were meant to be a thought instead of verbalized.

She hid a smile. What they had wasn't a passing thing. While she had limited experience with men, she'd seen all the romance movies and read all the raunchy books. A man didn't change. Not unless he truly wanted to for himself. Doc wasn't the same biker she'd met a mere three months ago. Just the same, she wasn't the innocent woman who'd left Ireland either.

"I don't know, I kind of enjoy Colorado." She kept her gaze on the horizon, the sun bouncing off the waves. "It has an eclectic aura."

His black boots shuffled through the green grass until he stood behind her, lacing his arms around her waist and resting his chin on her shoulder. "You think so?"

"I do." She turned her face just enough to see his smile. It'd knock her off her feet if he wasn't holding her upright.

"Isa?"

Whirling around, she nearly hit his nose at her quick movement. "Orla?"

Her best friend let out a whoop and started running toward them. Isa grinned, then broke into a full sprint.

"Oh God, you're finally home," Orla said once they collided in a mass of arms, tears, and laughter. "I've missed you."

Isa pulled back. A faint shadow of a bruise lined her friend's brow. "They did that to you?" Angry tears outweighed the excited ones. She traced the small line. "I'm so sorry. I never meant for any of this to happen." She hugged her friend again, relishing their reconnection.

Orla stepped back and wiped Isa's tears, then her own. "I'm all right, you loon. I told you a hundred times before you arrived." She laughed. "It'll make a great story for the baby someday."

Isa held her out at arm's length, eyes dipping to her friend's stomach. "Wait, you're... you're pregnant?"

A secretive smile crossed Orla's lips. She vigorously nodded. "I found out this morning."

"Oh my God." Isa pulled her in again for a hug, this time the tears ones of joy.

"Love, we're about to open...." Niall's words fell short when his eyes met Isa's. "You're back." He grinned. "About bloody time."

Isa held out her right arm and brought Niall into the group hug. Having her best friends with her once again felt better than she imagined. Tears mingled until she wasn't sure whose were whose. She didn't care. She was home, and her friends were safe.

A slight breeze brought Doc's presence back to her, and she knew she wasn't home anymore. Ireland wasn't home.

She lifted her gaze to her biker. He was her home, and she never wanted to leave him again.

Sprinkles of rain suddenly started falling, and the group hurried into the shop. A torrential downpour happened the moment Doc closed the door, the bell announcing their entry. Isa walked behind the counter and rested her elbows on the wood. It all looked the same. The homemade lotions and soaps were still displayed by the register, the scent of lavender light but poignant. If she left, she'd be thousands of miles away from her dream store.

"You must be Isa's biker," she heard Orla say above the storm. She looked over in time to see a proud smile on Doc's face.

"I am."

Niall's left brow lifted slightly. "I hear you saved our girl more than once."

This time, he glanced her way and winked. "No more than she saved me. She's quite wiry when she wants to be."

Orla chuckled. "Yep, that's our Isa. Feisty and fearless."

Doc walked over to the counter and leaned against it. "Among other qualities I find irresistible."

"So, what're your intentions with our best friend?"

"Niall!" Isa and Orla said simultaneously.

"What?" He shrugged and eyed Doc from head to toe. "I'm not about to let one of my oldest friends get hurt."

Isa shot Niall a glare and then an apologetic glance to Doc. He held up his hand.

"I got this, don't worry," he whispered, then replied to Niall. "I want to be the first person she sees when she wakes up and the last person she sees before she goes to sleep for the rest of her life."

"Aw." Orla placed her left hand across her chest.

"But that's not all." He met Isa's gaze. "I will do everything in my power to make her the happiest woman alive because that's what she does to me."

"She makes you the happiest woman alive?" Niall

asked with a smirk.

A red tint covered Doc's face, and he shook his head. "No."

"Niall, I swear you'll be on diaper duty for a year if you—"

"It's okay," Doc interrupted Orla's scorning. "I fancy myself a lady's man, but since I met Isa, I don't want anyone else. Ever."

He walked behind the counter and locked Isa in place with his hands. His blue eyes sparkled with mischief and adoration. "My intentions aren't pure, but they're lifelong."

"Oh. My. Bloody. Hell."

Isa held in a giggle at Orla placing both hands over her chest this time. Lifting her right hand, she ran her fingers through Doc's wind-tousled blond hair. He wasn't an ordinary man. She could search the world and never find anyone like Doc T O'Brien.

"That's good enough for me," a new voice chimed in from the doorway. The bell clanged loudly, spoiling the moment.

Isa looked behind her and caught sight of her father. "Da." He looked older than when she left Ireland. His beard was a shade whiter, new frown lines on his face.

"Isadora, you're safe." Phantom closed the distance between them, his black leather squeaking from the recent rainfall.

Moving toward him, she paused before he could embrace her. Other than their reunion three months prior, she barely knew the man who sired her. But her time in

Colorado altered her opinion on him. Doc also had something to do with her change of heart.

Phantom reached out his hand, then pulled it back awkwardly. Neither knew how to react. Out of the corner of her eye, Isa noticed Orla and Niall busy themselves restocking the shelves with Doc close by. *One of his more endearing protective qualities.*

"You look so much like your mum." His voice cracked, and he let out a shaky breath. His gray eyes watered, reminding her of her parentage. She may have been her mother's replica, but the eyes were all her father.

"I miss her."

He nodded. "So do I, lass. More than you know."

"You didn't want her to leave, did you?"

He forced a smile. "No. I never did, but it was for your safety." He timidly touched the top of her head, his calloused hands running along her long locks. "Macha wasn't safe back then. By the time it was, it was too late. You were grown, and your mum, well, she'd lost hope. Years apart will do that to a relationship no matter how strong."

Isa looked over her shoulder and met Doc's eyes. She couldn't imagine a time when that would happen for them. "Well, I won't lose you again, Da. That much I can promise you." She closed the minimal distance, wrapping him in a tight hug.

Phantom gradually returned the embrace, and Isa felt his tears against her hair. Reconnecting with her father was never in her plans. Then again, neither was falling in love with a Macha biker.

42

ISA

Isa spent the rest of the day sharing stories with her father, Orla, and Niall. Doc looked on and added some tidbits about their Colorado adventure but mainly stayed quiet. His silence was abnormal, but here he was the outsider. *In Colorado, he's always chatting up the other members and I'm the one listening.*

She brought the last of the dessert dishes to the sink. Being back in her one-bedroom flat above the shop felt different. Phantom left five minutes prior, and Doc was currently chatting with her two best friends in the living room. The sun set hours ago, and she was thankful her friends took the day off work. Staying here long term wouldn't work, and running the shop was impossible to do from Colorado. *Plus, it looks like Orla and Niall took over most of it.*

Rinsing the ceramic cups, she placed them to the side. While she loved Doc, she couldn't give up on her fashion dreams. Queenie suggested she design clothes for Macha's stores and Doc wholeheartedly agreed, but Isa wasn't so certain. *What if we return to Colorado and we don't work out?*

She worried her lips together, staring out the window into the darkness. A lone light shone in the distance from a lighthouse. The view usually calmed her. The beacon of hope in the moody night. Tonight, it did nothing to resolve her tension.

"Niall and Orla left."

Turning, Isa took in the sight of Doc walking into the kitchen. He overwhelmed the small space, his wide shoulders seemingly larger in his green T-shirt. His cut was lying on her bed, but he kept his bike boots on all night. While he hadn't brought his handgun overseas, he didn't need it to protect her. He'd proven that multiple times since they met. His love was all she needed to be safe.

"Thanks for playing host." She grinned. "I'm sure it was difficult at times. Orla and Niall can be a handful."

He kissed her temple. "No more than you."

Hugging his torso, she carefully leaned in to him. Ever since the shoot-out, she'd been terrified to do anything more than light caresses.

He kissed her head and moved to the bedroom. "You coming to bed?"

"Soon." She pointed to the sink. "Dishes don't do themselves."

Doc frowned and grabbed her hands, moving her away from the sink. "I'll take care of those in the morning. Right now, I want to take care of you." He searched out her eyes. "You gonna fight on this, princess?"

She smiled. "It'd be pointless."

"Glad you're finally seeing it my way." He narrowed his eyes and suddenly lifted her off the floor. "Because it's the only way."

She laughed as he walked her into the bedroom and plopped her on the bed.

"Get undressed."

She cocked her brow and almost made a snarky retort until he tore off his shirt. The dim light from her bedside lamp beautifully cast him in a muted glow. His muscles appeared more defined, his tattoos almost shimmering in the cool air. Not remembering to turn on the heater had a few advantages, the main one being that Doc would keep her warm all night long. A scar on his side reminded her of the past months and his bravery. She'd never forget how he'd protected her and how he continued to do it each and every day.

Sitting up, she slowly pulled off her wool sweater and bra. He watched with rapt attention, his eyes darkening with each article of clothing lost. When she had nothing left on, she stood by the end of the bed, long hair covering her peaked nipples. Lust lingered on his face, his eyes darting along her body.

"Are you sure you're up for this?" She crawled on the bed and sprawled out, arm holding her head up. "Because you could always just watch me."

Doc hissed a breath, a muscle in his cheek twitching.

"You sure I was your first?" He kicked off his boots and the rest of his clothes.

"I said I was a virgin, not a nun." She crooked her index finger at him.

Instead of immediately obeying, he leisurely ran his fingertips along her legs. His touch sent goose bumps across her skin, the sensation too good to deny.

"You know why I like your sassy mouth?" he asked, bending over and kissing the inside of her thigh.

Isa's breath hitched as a bundle of nerves shot straight to her apex. She shook her head, thoughts suddenly muddled.

Doc slowly positioned himself between her legs. "Because we both enjoy the punishment."

Before she could reply, he wiggled his brows and flipped her on her stomach. She gasped when his palm connected with her arse once, then twice, the singeing pain only turning her on more.

"Doc!"

"Yes, princess?" He kissed up her spine.

"Do it again."

"Nah, baby, can't spoil you already." He kissed the side of her neck. "I think that's enough for now." He nipped her bottom lip. "I'm going to show you exactly how rough I can be, princess."

"I'm ready."

"I know you are." He flipped her to her back. "I've craved you from the moment we met. And after a month, I'm desperate for you. For the way we fit so perfectly."

Isa wrapped her legs around his waist, urging him closer. "Show me."

As his answer, he slid his cock into her warmth. Her mouth dropped open involuntarily. The sensation of skin on skin was better than how she'd imagined it. "We don't have protection."

He leaned down and kissed her hard. When she came up for air, her mind was blank and vision blurry. Doc paused his hips and cupped her face. "I don't want anything between us ever again."

"But what if—"

"I love you more than life itself. That'll only grow stronger if we have a baby. Unless you don't want one. Then I'll—"

"No. I do." She rubbed her lips together. "I always thought I'd, um, be married." She held her breath, waiting for his reply. They'd never discussed marriage and only just mentioned children moments earlier.

He eased out of her and she instantly felt lonely. He hurried off the bed and rummaged through his carry-on bag. She tilted her head, staring at his firm arse. It was bite-worthy, that much she knew for certain. Scars lined his body where bullets had grazed him. They didn't scare her anymore. They made her love him even more.

He caught her gawking and gave her a cocky smile before walking back to the bed, right arm behind his back. He knelt next to her, his face filled with confidence.

"I love you, Isa. I've known since day one I wanted you as my own. You've shown me what it truly means to be a man. You brighten my life one moment at a time, and I don't want the sun to ever set on our love." He pulled a small box from behind his back and opened it.

Isa's heart thudded against her rib cage. The deep green gem was unlike any other she'd seen before. It wasn't one from a jewelry store the public could easily obtain. It was one of a kind.

"A normal ring isn't you, princess. You're the best kind of unique, and I wanted this to represent your past and our future." He licked his lips. "There's no one but you for me. Will you be my old lady?" He laughed. "My wife. My old lady. Damn, never thought I'd say that out loud."

Isa's eyes welled with tears. She leaned forward and kissed him, wrapping her arms around his neck. "Aye," she managed between kisses. "I'll marry you."

Doc let out a loud whoop and kissed her until her head nestled against the pillow. He slipped the ring on her finger and laid a gentle kiss on it. "You'll always be my old lady, my wife, my Macha princess.

EPILOGUE

DOC

Four months. Damn, has it been that long already?

Doc parked his bike outside the shop and rested his helmet on the handlebars. Summer came and went, as did the turning leaves of autumn. Now, the winter winds blew in from the mountains, and the daily rides on his bike were shorter if not nonexistent.

He followed the sidewalk to the front door and pulled off his shades. The ski shop hadn't changed much except for the addition of Isa's line of clothes. He glanced over to her dedicated portion of the store. It was full of customers—men, women, and children alike—each one finding an item from her line to purchase.

He nodded to Queenie, who was helping a customer, and made his way up to the loft area. Originally, she'd wanted to put a café up there, but Isa quickly changed her mind and the duo made it a workspace. It was mostly for

Isa, but with a comfortable recliner next to the window, Queenie also enjoyed the slice of heaven during the slow hours.

"Baby, where you at?" he called, not seeing Isa at her usual place by the drawing desk, courtesy of Brewer. Evidently, the redhead was a bit of a woodsman at heart.

"The loo. Be out in a moment."

Doc walked over to the recliner by the window and grunted in pleasure at the soft plush. Snowflakes dotted the windowpane, telling him to put the bike away for winter. Snowshoe would be bustling soon enough with holiday shoppers and tourists. Once January hit, the town would be filled with extreme snow seekers thanks to the winter games. It was the club's busiest time of the year and one that set them up for the down season.

"From what I saw, your clothes are flying off the hangers," he said, hearing the bathroom door open and close. "Good thing we found that manufacturer in Denver to keep up with demand." He stared out the window at the town already setting up for the Christmas holiday. "Hell, you'll probably make more money than the club this year."

"Maybe, but I'm afraid I won't have much time for it in a few months."

He glanced over and noticed her pale face. Worry immediately lined his gut, and he walked over to her. He kissed her forehead, checking her temperature. "What's wrong? You don't feel warm. Are you hungry?"

Isa's hand went to her mouth, and she shook her head. "No. God, no."

He stood in front of her and cradled her chin. "Tell me."

Her gray eyes met his and all anxiety slipped away. She wasn't sick, that much he could tell from her expression. "You remember how we got married?"

Doc thought back to their Halloween nuptials. It'd been one hell of a night, complete with a full moon and plenty of drinking. Her best friends and dad even flew over from Ireland to celebrate. "Yeah."

"Well, next year, we'll have a little pumpkin to take trick-or-treating on our anniversary."

For a split second, his brain stopped working. He slowly registered her words, and his eyes widened. He looked down at her flat stomach, then back to her face. "Really?" She nodded, and he placed a palm on her belly. "I'm gonna be a daddy?"

"Aye."

He whooped with joy and picked her up.

"Stop spinning me or I'll hurl again," she warned, patting his back.

Doc gently put her down and knelt in front of her. Lifting her shirt, he kissed her stomach. "You are so loved, little one." He looked up to Isa. "Your mama is the best there is, so don't give her too much grief."

Isa threaded her fingers through his hair. "And your daddy is the best biker doc in Colorado."

He got to his feet and tenderly kissed her. "And we'll raise the baby with both parents. No running. No hiding. Just us against the world."

She kissed him longer this time. "And we'll teach *her* all about Macha."

"Hell yeah." He carefully rubbed her stomach. "And how *he* should treat a woman."

"Or how *she* should be treated."

He chuckled. "All right, all right. Either way, I'm glad to have a miniature of us running around." He lowered his voice. "And maybe even another one after that."

She looped her arms around his neck. "One of each sounds good to me."

"As long as I'm with you, I'm the happiest man alive." Doc leaned his forehead against hers and closed his eyes. He'd never have imagined this life. He fell deeper in love with her with each passing day. She made him better, and he never wanted to return to the life he once knew.

"I guess Cameron was right. Once I found the woman who makes my heart beat, I never want to be without her."

Leaning back, she eyed him warily. "Who's Cameron?"

He smirked. "Just a mobster I knew once upon a time. I used to give him shit for being so in love with his fiancée." He kissed her nose. "But after falling for you, I get it."

"Sounds like a good guy."

"Yeah, he is." Doc grinned. "You'd like him"

She kissed his jaw. "But not as good a man as you."

Lifting her off the floor again, he led them over to the couch and settled her on top of him. "I'm only good because of you. I'm a mess without you, Isadora."

"Did I hear somebody mention a baby?" Queenie's voice drifted to the rafters, and he reluctantly paused his affections. There'd be plenty of time to show his old lady how much he loved her.

Isa swiveled just enough to say, "You already knew, Queenie."

The older woman laughed and, to his surprise, didn't join them in the loft. Isa turned back to face him and captured his lips. "Now, where were we?"

"I love you so damn much."

"I know." She cupped his jaw. "Now kiss me, Doc T, and never let me go."

He closed the distance to her lips. He'd always give in to his princess's demands.

EPILOGUE

ISA

THE SNOWSTORM TOOK OVER THE TOWN BEFORE SHE could prepare for it. After telling Doc the good news, she'd promptly reserved the loo for the remainder of the afternoon. He'd only left after she convinced him that Queenie would take care of her. Plus, he couldn't very well drive her home on the bike today.

Isa turned off the neon sign in the window and made her way to the counter. Only the security lights were on, Queenie having left ten minutes prior. She flipped off the last set of lights for the display wall and grabbed her coat.

Tightening the belt, her hands hovered over her stomach. She pressed her lips together. *A baby.* She didn't try to hide her excitement. *A mini Doc or mini me.*

After their return from Ireland, she was positive they'd be pregnant before they tied the knot. When it didn't happen, she'd worried herself into a tizzy. Sighing, she rested her hand on her belly. *But Doc hadn't.*

"We'll have one when the timing's right, princess." That was what he'd said whenever she doubted. He was right, of course. The entire subject was put on hold during the summer and fall. Between preparations for their nuptials, club business, and her design line, the little time they had together was spent riding his motorcycle through the mountains and enjoying each other's company. She had to admit, she wasn't sure she could handle every rough inch of Doc T, but she was sorely wrong. He was everything she desired and more.

A blush crept up her body recalling the times they snuck off the road to "experience nature," as Doc called it. Being part of Macha felt right. In one summer, Isa gained a family filled with annoying brothers, protective father figures, and doting mothers and aunts. It was the exact lifestyle she wanted their baby to experience.

Isa slipped her scarf around her neck and locked the door behind her. A gust of air littered her hair with snowflakes. Inhaling deeply, she carefully made her way down the sidewalk to Doc's truck outside. Even with her long legs, climbing into the jacked-up Dodge was difficult in heeled boots.

Her phone beeped with a new message from Orla. Checking it, she grinned at the photo. Her best friend's belly looked like she'd swallowed a basketball. Niall, of course, was every bit the proud father next to her. She saved the picture to her phone, making a mental note to visit Ireland before she was too pregnant to fly. While she missed her friends and their little shop, being in Colorado with Doc was home.

She sent a reply to Orla, bursting to tell her the good news but not wanting to spoil the final part of her friend's pregnancy. They deserved all the attention. After the last six months, they'd earned it.

She cranked the diesel engine and quickly merged with traffic. Snowshoe's streets weren't covered with snow yet thanks to the orange plows making their rounds. She easily followed the road, country tune on the radio.

Only after she reached the clubhouse did she check her phone again.

Orla: You know you can tell me anything, right?

Isa: What're you talking about?

She kept the car running, the prospects moving the motorcycles into the shop next door.

Orla: Doc just spoke to Niall.

Shite, that little bastard. She rolled her eyes. Her old man was nothing if not boastful.

Isa: What'd he say?

She tapped on the steering wheel as little bubbles showed Orla's typing.

Orla: That our little girl will have a playmate.

Deciding a call was better suited, she dialed. "I'm sorry. I didn't mean to steal your thunder," she said the moment her friend answered.

Orla laughed. "Please, we're best friends. All of us. I'd

never worry about that. Hell, I'm glad you're pregnant too. We can be belly buddies."

Relief coursed through her and she chuckled. "Seeing how you have two months left and I have more than that, I doubt it very much."

"Hmm, true. You suck."

They both laughed, and she wished Orla was close enough to hug.

"I'm kind of scared, honestly."

"Why?"

"My mum isn't around to talk to about this parenting stuff."

"No, but your da is," Orla reminded. "Even though he wasn't around all the time, I think he'd be ecstatic to give you advice."

"Well, I guess that's true. I bet he'll be excited to hear the news."

"You haven't told him?"

"I just told Doc today." She turned down the radio. "He's so excited."

"Damn right he is," Niall said in the background.

She heard Orla say something under her breath but couldn't make it out.

"Sorry, my husband is quite cheeky lately."

"I can get cheekier," Niall called.

This time, Isa giggled when she heard a manly yet high-pitched squeal.

"There. That ought to keep his bloody mouth shut for a while."

"Did you gag him again?" she teased.

"He wishes." Orla cleared her throat. "But don't worry. I'll manhandle him later."

"Oh, you little minx! Let me out of these cuffs."

Isa stifled her laughter. She'd never guessed her best friends to be kinky of any variety, but then again, she'd thought the same about herself.

Doc came out of the clubhouse, Rubble and Hawk on his tail. Isa unbuckled her seat belt and simply watched him. The trio was nearly inseparable ever since the Twelve Brothers fiasco. Their comradery was endearing. She didn't worry about him so long as he was with his brothers.

"Love, I need to go. Something pressing came up. Talk later." Orla signed off, and Isa shut down the truck and braced herself for the cold.

The moment her boots hit the pavement, Doc's eyes locked on her. He nodded to Rubble and Hawk, then jogged away from the duo. Snow fell on his shaggy blond hair, his Macha cut hugging his hooded sweatshirt.

"Hey, beautiful." He kissed the top of her head and tucked her beside him as they walked toward the clubhouse's warmth. "How're you feeling?"

"A little tired." She yawned and linked her arm in his. "But better now."

"I may have accidentally told a few people about the baby," he said sheepishly. His blue eyes darted to the door, then back to her. "I hope that's okay?"

She smirked. "I haven't even told my da."

"Oh." He scratched his chin. "Yeah, I may have done

that too." He opened the door and a rush of warm air greeted her. "But I'll make it up to you."

"How so?" She stepped inside and the scent of cinnamon drifted to her. Eyes wide, she met his face. "You didn't."

He grinned. "I did."

Isa beamed at him, then rushed down the hallway to the kitchen. Sure enough, his mouthwatering cinnamon concoctions sat fresh from the oven on the countertop. "Oh my God, they're still warm." She grabbed one, icing dripping onto her fingers, and took a bite. "This is better than sex," she moaned around her mouthful.

"I sure fucking hope not or you're doing something wrong, Doc," Rubble teased, walking into the room.

Sitting on one of the barstools, Isa happily munched on the twists of cinnamon. More Macha members filed into the kitchen, their noses bringing their rumbling stomachs toward the goodies. Soon, the noise level attracted Reaper and Queenie. They stood in the doorway, Reaper's arm around Queenie's waist, a proud smile on their faces. They were the pure epitome of Macha.

Doc joked with his brothers and took the baking comments with ease. Every now and then, he'd glance her way. His eyes always held more adoration than she could comprehend. It was something she'd come to love about her biker. No one else would do. She was a Macha princess first, but now she was more than that. She was a Macha old lady, and nothing compared to the pride her new title instilled.

A tall and muscular biker walked into the kitchen, and she eyed him warily. She'd only spoken to Kevlar once. Something suspicious hovered just below the surface with him. There was chatter amongst the nymphs, but none she could pin down. The gossip revolved around Kevlar and a mysterious tattooed woman they'd all seen around Snowshoe over the autumn.

With the Twelve Brothers currently sated, Isa could only imagine the recent discussions at church involved their neighboring MC rival, the Greenback Cutthroats. She'd been too entangled in her love bubble with Doc to really know what—if anything—simmered between the two MCs.

Dolly slipped into the room and smiled at Isa. Thankfully, after her return, the two had cleared the air. Isa was never more grateful to have a sister, even if she was a bit loony at times.

"All right, fuckers, I'm outta here," Doc called, flipping his middle fingers up.

"Good luck, big daddy," Hawk teased.

Isa followed, but only after grabbing another five rolls. The fresh treats wouldn't last till the morning—she'd learned the hard way over the last few months.

"Everything okay with the club?" she asked once they were safely stowed in his truck.

"Not really, but it's nothing to worry about." Doc cranked the heat and turned toward her. His eyes slowly scanned her face, then down her torso. "You, on the other hand, should worry about something else completely."

She recognized the lustful gleam in his blue eyes. "And why is that?"

"Because I'm going to dote on you so fucking much you'll be sick of me by the time this baby's born." He slid across the seat and caught her lips in a heated kiss. Isa couldn't catch her breath, nor did she want to. With Doc, she was the woman she was always meant to be.

"I'll never get sick of you."

He lifted his tattooed hand to her face and gently caressed her cheek with his knuckles. "Good, because I'm not going anywhere."

"Promise, Doc T?"

"Always, princess." His lips brushed against hers once more, and Isa succumbed to his touch like every time before. They'd met under strained circumstances and fell in love despite kidnappings and shoot-outs. If they could survive those, she was positive their future would be filled with passion, suspense, and a few surprises along the way.

ACKNOWLEDGMENTS

First off, thank you to Hot Tree Publishing for encouraging me to pursue a motorcycle club series. I also want to thank my beta readers and editors for making me smile despite the grueling editing process.

To my faithful readers and friends who preorder just because you see my name, thank you from the bottom of my heart.

ABOUT THE AUTHOR

Skye McNeil began writing at the age of seventeen and has been lost in a love affair ever since. During the day, she moonlights as a paralegal at a law firm favoring criminal law.

Skye enjoys writing romantic comedies and cozy mysteries novels that leave readers wanting more and falling in love over and over. She writes contemporary and historical novels ranging from sweet and sassy to steamy and sultry.

Her constant writing companions are two cats and Australian Shepherd. When she's not writing, Skye enjoys spending time with family, photography, volleyball, traveling, and curling up with a cup of coffee and reading.

Website: www.skyemcneil.com

Facebook Readers Group: https://bit.ly/2we93r3

ABOUT THE PUBLISHER

Hot Tree Publishing opened its doors in 2015 with an aspiration to bring quality fiction to the world of readers. With the initial focus on romance and a wide spread of romance subgenres, Hot Tree Publishing has since opened their first imprint, Tangled Tree Publishing, specializing in crime, mystery, suspense, and thriller.

Firmly seated in the industry as a leading editing provider to independent authors and small publishing houses, Hot Tree Publishing is the sister company to Hot Tree Editing, founded in 2012. Having established in-house editing and promotions, plus having a well-respected market presence, Hot Tree Publishing endeavors to be a leader in bringing quality stories to the world of readers.

Interested in discovering more amazing reads brought to you by Hot Tree Publishing? Head over to the website for information:

WWW.HOTTREEPUBLISHING.COM

www.ingramcontent.com/pod-product-compliance
Lightning Source LLC
Chambersburg PA
CBHW061050190726

48286CB00006B/1695